The Birth of *Wuthering Heights*

This book is to be returned on or before
the last date stamped below.

Also by Edward Chitham

A LIFE OF ANNE BRONTË

A LIFE OF EMILY BRONTË

BRONTË FACTS AND BRONTË PROBLEMS (*with Tom Winnifrith*)

CHARLOTTE AND EMILY BRONTË: A Literary Life (*with Tom Winnifrith*)

SELECTED BRONTË POEMS (*co-edited with Tom Winnifrith*)

THE BLACK COUNTRY

THE BRONTËS' IRISH BACKGROUND

THE POEMS OF ANNE BRONTË (*editor*)

THE POEMS OF EMILY BRONTË (*co-edited with Derek Roper*)

The Birth of
Wuthering Heights

Emily Brontë at Work

Edward Chitham

palgrave

First published in hardcover 1998

First published in paperback 2001 by
PALGRAVE
Houndmills, Basingstoke, Hampshire RG21 6XS and
175 Fifth Avenue, New York, N. Y. 10010
Companies and representatives throughout the world

PALGRAVE is the new global academic imprint of
St. Martin's Press LLC Scholarly and Reference Division and
Palgrave Publishers Ltd (formerly Macmillan Press Ltd).

ISBN 0–333–68352–8 hardback (*outside North America*)
ISBN 0–312–21266–6 hardback (*in North America*)
ISBN 0–333–94545–X paperback (*worldwide*)

This book is printed on paper suitable for recycling and made from fully managed and sustained forest sources.

A catalogue record for this book is available from the British Library.

The Library of Congress has cataloged the hardcover edition as follows:
Chitham, Edward.
    The birth of Wuthering Heights : Emily Brontë at work / Edward Chitham.
        p. cm.
    Includes bibliographical references (p.) and index.
    ISBN 0–312–21266–6 (cloth)
        1. Brontë, Emily, 1818–1848. Wuthering Heights—Criticism, Textual.
    2. Brontë, Emily, 1818–1848—Authorship—Chronology. 3. Fiction-
    –Authorship. I. Title.
    PR4172.W73C48 1998
    823'.8—dc21
                                                        97–35324
                                                          CIP

10   9   8   7   6   5   4   3   2   1
10 09 08 07 06 05 04 03 02 01

Printed in Great Britain by Antony Rowe Ltd, Chippenham, Wiltshire

Contents

Preface to paperback edition

It was pleasing that the response to the hardback edition of this book was deeply appreciative. This new paperback edition gives me the opportunity to correct some very minor typographical errors. I also wish to add thanks to members of the Brontë Society for their interest in the book, and for comments by members of an Open University staff seminar in the West Midlands.

Throughout, I have wished to avoid the impression that in trying to peer into the mystery of Emily Brontë's working methods, and in exploring the way she (in her own words) 'toiled in learning's golden mine' I am in any way diminishing her genius. Far from it: her poems and *Wuthering Heights* are superlative monuments to the partnership between conscious and intuitive art which we expect from a really great practitioner. An understanding of how these great works came into existence should enhance our awe concerning them.

Edward Chitham

Acknowledgements

The idea for this book came from Tom Winnifrith's suggestion that *Wuthering Heights* must have been very much expanded in 1846–7. We discussed a possible joint book on the topic, and he read my initial draft, giving it a great deal of encouragement. In the end, the notion of a joint book fell through, and my draft attracted additional material, partly based on research for my doctoral thesis, partly on recent discoveries in the field of Brontë studies. One such discovery was the Latin translations Emily made, brought to prominence by Alexander and Sellars' book, *The Art of the Brontës*. Tom Winnifrith also discussed these with me, pointing out some important considerations. As a result of all this, my book expanded to fill almost twice its original space, and this is very fitting since it echoes what happened to *Wuthering Heights*, its subject.

I have also discussed the content of the book with Derek Roper, with whom I had collaborated in the early stages of *The Poems of Emily Brontë* and whose text, established on principles we had agreed, I shall use for quotations throughout. On a previous occasion when I used a reading from this text, I was told by a reviewer that I had 'misquoted' Emily Brontë. The reader unaccustomed to these restored readings should be aware that Emily's spelling and punctuation are highly eccentric, and that the readings have been checked over and over again by Derek Roper. All my quotations, therefore, reproduce what Emily Brontë wrote. I thank both Tom Winnifrith and Derek Roper for their interest and encouragement.

I have also derived great benefit from the biography of the Brontës by Juliet Barker, though I disagree with some of the arguments and emphases, particularly her comments on Gondal poetry. Nevertheless, her biography is monumental and highly accomplished. The staff of the Brontë Parsonage have been as helpful as always. In particular I must mention Jane Sellars, who has always been ready to help, Kathryn White, whose help was often available and who measured the envelope in which Newby's letter was enclosed, and Ann Dinsdale, who looked out further illustrations of High Sunderland.

Permission to make use of the Latin translations was readily given by the librarian of the Hugh Walpole Library, The King's School, Canterbury, who furnished xeroxes of the manuscripts. Texts of *Wuthering Heights* are based on the early (pre-1850) editions, available now in the texts of Penguin Classics (1965) and Oxford World's Classics series (1981) (the former with modern chapter numbers). As these are the two commonest reputable texts, I shall try to refer to both.

All Brontë scholars owe debts to the pioneers such as Mrs Gaskell and Mrs Chadwick, and to the initiator of the 'new wave' of scholarship, Winifred Gerin. I also need to record thanks to many Brontë Society members with whom I have exchanged ideas, and to the countless contributors to *Brontë Society Transactions* who sharpened my perceptions, and to the feminist critics, such as Stevie Davis and Patsy Stoneman, who have widened our understanding of Emily Brontë in recent years.

I should be very sorry if anything I have written in this book should be taken in any way to degrade Emily Brontë's work. There is still something of a preference for artists whose genius appears to be wholly inspired and who do no work for their God-given results. This is a false and pernicious view of art. As we struggle with Emily Brontë to 'walk where my own nature would be leading', we have to realise that the walk is over rocks and through muddy mosses, and that producing her inspired poetry and prose was for Emily the work of a sculptor, not a magician.

Edward Chitham
Harborne

Part I
Emily Brontë and the Craft of Literature

Part 1

Introduction

The idea of birth suggests labour. This book will be about that labour. I hope to show how Emily Brontë worked on *Wuthering Heights* to produce the novel we now have. Before we reach the detail of this project, however, we need to stand back a little from the topic and view the Brontës' literary creation whole in comparison with that of other nineteenth-century writers.

The problem of the Brontës arises from their splendid accessibility to and popularity with twentieth-century readers, combined with the very little they left of their own personal thoughts and literary intentions. Dickens was an entrepreneur, guiding his own public image; Hardy was a long-living writer known to many, however he tried to shun publicity. Even Mrs Gaskell wrote voluminous letters. But Emily and Anne Brontë's work found success almost entirely after their deaths. Interest in them as authors was largely posthumous; even Charlotte did not enjoy mixing with the London literary set. By the time journalists would have liked to interview the famous family, its only living representatives were Ulster country people whose connection with the Brontës of Haworth was hardly credible.

But books on the Brontës were in demand. They had to be based on second-hand memories of the sisters' lives, or extrapolated from the novels. There are shelves full of early twentieth-century books on the Brontës, and some have value, but it was not until the 1960s that serious scholarship was directed towards the texts of letters, poems and novels. Only now since the 1990s do we have a thoroughly accurate text of all these to work from. Readers new to Brontë scholarship need to be aware of this situation, and of the still existing poverty of primary material when compared with that available for other authors. The scanty nature of the evidence makes it inevitable that following Emily Brontë at work, trying to look over her shoulder, is a tentative, hazardous process, and a conscientious commentator will have to hedge in conclusions with qualifying adverbs.

But we *can* look over Emily's shoulder. Years ago I skirmished with this attempt in *Brontë Facts and Brontë Problems*, and in the same book Tom Winnifrith set out a preliminary discussion of the way in which *Wuthering Heights* may have reached its final form. There are major theoretical as well as logistical problems about *Wuthering Heights*. The book is an acknowledged masterpiece, but appears to have no antecedents. It has strong internal cohesion and appears to have been written to a strict chronological plan, but who taught Emily Brontë to control her fiction in this way? This question raises the issue of the relation between inspiration and conscious art in the production of masterpieces. My understanding of this is that both are needed, but this is not a popular concept in the early nineteenth century, and it is in the shadow of the Romantics that the Brontës are working. The notion of Emily Brontë as brooding genius has persisted. Of course she was a 'genius', but she also 'worked like a horse' as Charlotte said of her in Belgium.

It is said that Emily's narrative skills were honed in writing such childhood epics as 'Gondal's Queen'. But this so-called epic was written by Miss Fannie Ratchford in 1955, weaving together fragments of Gondal poetry round the theme of the life of Emily's teenage and adult heroine, 'A.G.A'.[1] Miss Ratchord felt that almost all Emily's poetry could be located in a Gondal context and that a coherent whole could be made from it. We shall return to this question, but it needs to be said now that any such reconstruction misunderstands the way, as teenagers, Emily and Anne treated Gondal. For years, perhaps about seven, perhaps up to nine, they wrote as they liked and thought nothing of coherence. In 1841, they decided to cajole the disparate material into order, rewriting some poems in ways which help to tidy up the story, perhaps discarding others. After 1841, there was a chronological framework, but it was an afterthought, as I shall suggest was the case with the chronology of *Wuthering Heights*.

Even if we were to accept that Gondal sagas included carefully crafted stories with fully developed characters, to judge by the work of Charlotte and Branwell the Brontës had given no close thought to structure in the development of their fictional countries. After 1841 these works were called Gondal *Chronicles*, and they may have been as formless as Anglo-Saxon ones. It needs to be stated firmly that there is no surviving prose from any coherent Gondal narrative which might have existed. The titles of such stories as we hear of in diary papers ('the first wars'; 'the Emperor Julius' Life') do not sound like works of imaginative fiction. We can gather a certain amount about some figures from poems which have recurring characters, A.G.A., Julius, etc., but these are poetic figures. It is helpful, as we shall see, that some of these poems are narratives, but we simply do not know whether Gondal gave Emily and Anne any practice in dealing with fictional conventions.

It is often remarked that *Wuthering Heights* is a sport in nineteenth-century fiction. Perhaps that is because its author (while much enamoured of Scott) is not predominantly concerned with the fiction of the ages in which she lives and which preceded her. She comes to fiction writing as a fully-fledged poet, steeped in historical romance and enthralled by mystery, but she has not considered the problems of narrative technique in fiction writing. *Wuthering Heights* is therefore apprentice work *and* consummate masterpiece. In writing it Emily Brontë calls on an interest in chronology that began at least as early as 1841, and a strong interest in literary composition, theoretical as well as practical, but this theory is not necessarily novel theory. She is interested in form, in words and in poetry, but these considerations do not lead her to ask the question, 'What is a novel?' What we have, therefore, is the working out of a non-theoretic answer to this question, and the subsequent total revision of this provisional answer as the work goes on, in response to the demands of publication.

At a late stage, Charlotte enunciated the extraordinary opinion that 'Ellis' (Emily) 'will not be seen in his full strength till he is seen as an essayist'.[2] What she seems to be saying is the Emily is interested in ideas. In the same letter she says she considers her sister somewhat of a theorist: 'now and then he broaches Ideas which strike my sense as more daring and original than practical'. Emily's novel is full of *content*; the writing is almost unbelievably economical and spare. Everywhere we find an almost Tacitean compression and compactness. The book is endlessly discussed not only for its poetic qualities and intense imagery, but also for its world view. It appears to have something fresh to say to many who are not sophisticated readers. Style is made to fit the vivid content and is driven by it.

But we can go further. The attraction of the book is in part due to its mysterious allusions, as if the author knows much more than is being plainly revealed. Casually, Nelly refers to 'the old gate', Lockwood asks whether Heathcliff isn't related to the preacher Jabes Branderham, old Earnshaw buys a fiddle which gets broken, housekeepers appear and disappear. The whole texture is dense, posing questions and giving half-answers. It is typical of the book that it only gave up its chronological framework in the 1920s. Emily

Brontë is Sibylline, writing clues on variously scattered leaves, so that a hint in Chapter 3 may not be followed up until Chapter 32. (The image seems even more appropriate when we study the poem manuscripts, which are literally composed of scraps of paper, distributed at the moment around the world as if blown by the four winds.)

To understand Emily Brontë's book we need a powerful and accurate memory. How did she herself recall all the nuances we fail to see? She combines electric emotion with fierce intellectual control; how does she achieve this balance? The thesis of this book will be that the emotional intensity comes first and is not initially under control. As for the memory, her memory is indeed strong, but we may be able to discover places where it fails, or where she sacrifices total consistency for poetry. There will turn out to be inconsistencies, and one cause will be the way in which I suggest the novel was written, drawing analogies from what we know of her poetic composition.

Broadly, we shall see that it is impossible that *Wuthering Heights* was written, as it were, in one sitting. Just as we shall see that some narrative poems written by Emily Brontë went through several stages, sometimes at very distant intervals in time, so the novel also underwent radical change, and had to be recast long after its first production. This process gave its author the opportunity to reflect on her aims and allowed a more balanced, mature outcome. Neither the emotional impact nor the intellectual organisation suffered during this process. Both were enhanced and a balance retained. This balance can in fact be discerned throughout the book, and contributes greatly to its great stature.

1

Physical Conditions of Work

After the rather negative conditions mentioned in the last chapter, it might be supposed that there is little we can do to recreate a knowledge of the circumstances in which Emily Brontë worked. However, we shall begin by looking at some evidence for the physical conditions of Emily Brontë's work, since the thesis of this book is that we shall be able to deduce information about the writing of *Wuthering Heights* from a study of Emily Brontë's practice in other contexts.

A good deal can be discovered about the ways in which the Brontë sisters carried out their youthful projects in writing, painting, drawing and music. This is partly because others described the practice of the sisters, and partly because enough physical evidence has survived, especially from their childhood and youth, to make some tentative deductions. A major gap is the manuscript of *Wuthering Heights*, which has never been found; nor are there manuscripts for *Agnes Grey* or *The Tenant of Wildfell Hall* (which I shall shorten to *Wildfell Hall* in the rest of this book). It is perhaps surprising to discover no notes on the novel, no first drafts, no outlines of plot, etc. In the second part of this book we shall discuss why this is so.

Meanwhile, we shall approach the topic by looking carefully at what exists of Emily's work which might give clues to her working methods physically, and so form a picture of her habits of study and production. There is one further pitfall to be mentioned. Branwell and Charlotte left a good deal of writing from their childhood, though Emily and Anne left almost nothing. It is tempting therefore to extend the application of evidence from the manuscripts of the older pair of children to the younger pair. This may not be totally wrong, but we do have to exercise caution, since Emily was a strong-willed and innovative young woman, who seems to have led a breakaway from the imaginative invention of her older sister and brother, and from about 1831 pursued a different line with Anne. Their new imaginary world of Gondal did not follow that of Charlotte in all ways, and we must beware of supposing that the methods of work followed Charlotte's either.

Surveying Emily's remaining manuscript output we find a host of poem manuscripts, some small pieces of paper on which single day journals or diaries have been written, drawings and sketches, the remains of an account book, some *Devoirs* done in Belgium, a tiny clutch of short letters, a very few short notes or lists attached to poems or found with poems, names and annotations in music books and possibly some marks on blotting paper. There is very little else, and these pieces are sometimes very damaged, very small and almost illegible.

From a very early age the whole Brontë family adopted the practice of writing in a tiny script meant originally to mimic the print of magazines and newspapers, which the Brontës were trying to imitate in the production of their own journals. In *The Art of the Brontës* Christine Alexander and Jane Sellars call this script minuscule, but I shall continue to use the phrase Brontë small script, as there is a clear convention being followed by all the family, and indeed there can be cases where it is hard to tell which member of the family wrote a word or phrase. This is particularly so in the pencil notes occurring on the later poem manuscripts, added either by Emily herself or Charlotte during editing processes in 1845–6 and after Emily's death. There is also some doubt about manuscript additions to Goldsmith's *Geography*, which look to me like Anne's but which Dr Juliet Barker thinks are Emily's.[1] For many years these very similar small script styles caused utter confusion in attributing poems to members of the family, and at times, false attributions still cast a shadow.

The poem manuscripts give us a considerable amount of evidence as to how Emily Brontë composed. At a later stage I shall be using these to talk about content. At the moment I wish to discuss their physical appearance and qualities, in order to deduce information about the author's ways of working. There are various ways of classifying the poem manuscripts, and I shall need to return to them to discuss this classification from a different angle. Meanwhile, we can say that there are three notebooks which are clearly copy-books, two from 1844 and one from (probably) 1839, of which the two first mentioned are in small script, and the

1839 book in normal cursive, but crabbed and constricted to save space.

The remaining poems are to be found on 46 small pieces of paper. These small pieces can again be divided into copies which seem to be part of a collection and earlier drafts, possibly in some cases early copies, sometimes first drafts. A few are in pencil, most in ink. Clearly, an examination of the physical properties of these small slips of paper will help us to understand how Emily Brontë worked on her poems. There are also two or three small sketches of Emily at work, to be found on the journal papers, or diary papers as they have previously been called, specifically those from 1834, 1837 and 1841.

These journal papers are said to have been derived from those of the poet Byron, who was somewhat of a hero with the family.[2] They seem to relate to Brontë birthdays, but whose is not quite clear, as the earliest appears to commemorate Branwell's birthday and later ones Emily's. Anne was expected to write such papers, but not on her own birthday. This scheme throws light on Emily's interest in marking the passage of time, and also her assumption that she was the dominant partner in the enterprise in which she and Anne collaborated: the creation of the world of Gondal.

The 1834 paper seems to have been a collaborative effort, and includes 'a bit of lady Julets Hair done by Anne'. This may be an ink blot which Anne has transformed into a wavy drawing. This is the whole of the licence given to Anne, however, and apart from her signature she adds nothing else to the paper. The paper already exhibits a characteristic which will be common: it uses up all available space. It is very untidy, with crossings out and false starts. Most of Emily's writing will be like this. Two or three words revert inconsequentially to cursive style but Emily corrects herself and goes back to Brontë script. 'Apples' gets a capital letter in the middle of a sentence, but Sir Robert Peel seems to have a lower case P. A 'phaesent' and the 'kitchin' are wrongly spelled and there is little punctuation. Emily is 16. This is the work of a scatterbrain whose interest does not include neat or well-formed writing. The content is quite different, showing dash and flair, exuberance and observation, but the production is such that Emily Brontë would not survive the National Curriculum: indeed school was a burden to her. As yet Emily Brontë has not studied words and their manipulation, and there is little in the technique of writing to suggest that she will produce compositions of the first rank.

The 1837 diary paper shows both Emily and Anne at work, and includes a dialogue about the inspiration for work. On a scrap of paper $2\frac{1}{2}'' \times 3\frac{1}{2}''$ she draws the table in the parsonage drawing room, with apparently the piano in the background. Emily and Anne are sitting at the table, each writing. The text of the diary paper quotes the first line of Anne's poem, still known today ('Fair was the evening and brightly the sun'). Emily says she herself is writing a Gondal piece. Papers are scattered about the table in disarray, but their container, labelled 'The Tin Box', is visible. Alexander and Sellars point out that there is such a tin box in the parsonage collection, and this may be the very box. The Gondal story seems to be called 'The papers', for such is the label on them.[3] This label might be worth remembering as we come to discuss novel writing; for these 'papers' are not thought of as fiction, but as documents about Gondal. Even if we still had the Gondal accounts, they might not throw any light on Emily Brontë's ideas about how to present a novel.

Emily and Anne are using the table as a writing support here, without the intervention of portable desks which they sometimes used. The diary paper is written in ink, and the pens and an inkpot are visible in the drawing. Emily was not happy with a pen. Many of her manuscripts show places where the pen has dug into the paper or has run out of ink. She clears it by drawing it over the surface of the paper when sediment at the bottom of the inkpot gets on to the point of the nib. Her blotting paper has holes in it where the pen has been pushed through to clear such sediment.[4] Emily sometimes drops blots and her writing will penetrate to the other side of the paper, interfering with the poem on the verso. It has to be said that Anne's penmanship is not much better. Neither is interested in calligraphy.

Emily draws herself from the back in this picture. However, she is an excellent artist and is able to suggest the pose and the concentration of her subject as she draws. Anne is not writing, but has her head resting on her hands in thought. Emily's head is bent towards her paper, but her pen is on the table, beside her left hand. This point supports my conjecture, printed in *A Life of Emily Brontë*, that Emily was left-handed. After I had suggested this, I had support from Stevie Davies, who had also come to the same conclusion.[5] This will account for some of the untidiness, since left-handedness was likely to lead to struggles with the paper then as now. It is interesting that no school teacher had yet succeeded in changing Emily's handedness, which will have been another reason for her dislike of school. She has chosen the seat nearest the window to get the best light; Anne has to do with the darker seat. But Anne's pen is by her right hand.

Once again this diary paper makes use of all the space, writing extending to the very bottom of the page and providing us with a crucial problem of interpretation, since the last, added, phrase is giving details of a discussion the sisters have been having about whether to go out in the evening, or whether to write. The last sentence seems to say 'if we get into a humour we may stay in', but the last word is right on the corner and could possibly be 'out'. Thus we are deprived of a clear answer to the question of whether poetic inspiration was obtained by going out for a walk or by staying in. Emily gives the time of all this as 'past 4 o'clock', but in other material the girls are said to be writing in the morning. Time of day does not seem a crucial factor in the writing of Gondal or other compositions. However, some poetry seems to take its rise from inspirations gained outside on the moors behind Haworth, and it would be rash to make any certain deductions from this confusing conversation between Emily and Anne.

If the apparent internal evidence of the poems is accepted, composition could take place at any time. Later I shall discuss a poem 'How long will you remain?' (No. 60) which seems to have been written at midnight, to judge by the scene described and the report of a chiming clock, described as 'the minster', but surely that of Haworth church. This particular poem is one of a number of Emily Brontë's poems which seem to indicate that composition could take place at a very late hour, or during the small hours of the morning.[6]

In addition to the diary paper of 1837, two other similar papers give evidence of Emily Brontë's working methods. They are dated 30 July 1841 and 30 July 1845. The first was done while Anne was in Scarborough with the Robinson family, her employers. This meant that each sister had to produce a separate diary paper, so far as we know for the first time. Emily presents us with two pictures, tiny thumbnail sketches, at the top of the page. The location of the paper is at present unknown, and reproductions, e.g. that in *The Art of the Brontës*, are from secondary sources.[7] These sketches are very small and rushed, and I should not like to assert with total confidence what is depicted. It appears that Anne is in the top left-hand corner, apparently looking out of a low window (possibly at the top of the Scarborough hotel?). Outside the window are some scrawls, which may represent either boats or rocks. Her portable writing desk is on the table, and she writes with concentrated attitude, her chair pushed back a little from the table.

In the opposite corner Emily depicts herself, not writing, but looking out of the window. The window is a large sash window, and seems most likely to be that of her small bedroom, since a line parallel to it may mark the beginning of the side wall. On a similar table to Anne's rests Emily's portable desk and there is a chair behind. The chair seems to be pushed back, so we may conjecture that Emily has taken a rest from writing. There may be something in her hands as she gazes out of the window, but this area to the right of her may simply be a blot. (It is typical of the uncertainty surrounding the interpretation of these sketches that Alexander and Sellars see the two pictures as both of Emily, the first showing her working, the second looking out of the window.[8] This may be right, but I can't quite reconcile the two windows – if they are windows – with this. I also wonder if the two figures are wearing similar clothes.)

Perhaps from this confusing diary paper we may deduce that Emily sometimes wrote in her bedroom, and used her portable desk resting on a small table. The 1845 sketch is somewhat larger and clearer.[9] This time we are plainly in the little bedroom over the hall at Haworth parsonage. Emily's bed is across the large Georgian sash window, and she is writing on her portable desk, which is this time on her knee. The question of left-handedness might be able to be settled by this sketch. It seems to me that she is writing with her left hand, but the pen strokes are confusing, and the matter is not totally determined. Emily's upright sitting position is interesting; she does not appear to be shortsighted. On the other hand, the writing desk cannot have been very stable with no firm base, and the blotting and untidiness of some of Emily's manuscripts may derive from the habit of putting the desk directly on her knee. Altogether, this far corner of the room may be a slightly dark place to write. It is certainly formal, when Emily could have been lying on her bed with the two animals depicted there. For the third time Emily has drawn herself from the back, an extraordinary length to take concealment, considering that no one but herself and Anne would have been expected to see the picture.

None of these diary papers, though most are written in summer, show Emily or Anne writing out of doors. I shall presently mention a report which seems to indicate that they sometimes did so, but meanwhile we can notice that the balance of probability is that to write, if one is in the humour, one will need to 'stay in', and that the other pictures support this idea. Charlotte emphasised Emily Brontë's outdoor enthusiasm with her well-known words 'My sister Emily loved the moors', but this does not mean that she actually carried out the act of writing in such a context. Undoubtedly she walked out to gain inspiration, or was unexpectedly presented with poem material while out of doors, but the gazing out of windows is also part of her 'work' to gain in day-dreams her initial ideas. In these small sketches, except for the 1837 paper, we do not see piles of papers, though they are again mentioned in the text of the 1845 paper. The writing desks are too small to contain a great deal, and we can assume the Gondal papers went on being kept elsewhere, in a tin box or boxes.

Contradicting the evidence that Emily Brontë preferred to write indoors is one scrap of detail from Mrs Ellis Chadwick. She writes:

> Whilst they were going about their domestic duties, their novels were simmering, and they kept odd bits of paper on which to chronicle their thoughts. Emily's favourite spot for writing was in the little front garden, sitting on a small stool in the shade of the currant bushes, or out on the moors, far away from any habitation, and in company with the birds and the few sheep that wandered about the moor.[10]

Mrs Chadwick gives no reference or primary source for this, but her informant may have been the servant Martha Brown, whom she mentions in the previous paragraph. Martha would have been in an excellent position to see the front garden, but less capable of knowing what exactly happened on the moors. The words 'in the shade of the currant bushes' suggest the summer, and this may be a memory from 1847, when *Wuthering Heights* was being recast. There is little to underpin such a conjecture. The paragraph does isolate Emily, in a book written about the whole family, and we should be justified in supposing that Emily liked to write alone and undisturbed.

Nevertheless, it is known that the Brontës commented on each others' work as it was being produced. If we are looking for literary influences on Brontë novels the most potent is probably the nearest. As children, they had worked jointly. As adults, they still read out their work to each other in late evening colloquies as several early sources explain. Mrs Chadwick notes that they paced the sitting room 'and compared notes' after nine o'clock when the servants and Mr Brontë went to bed. Mrs Gaskell had also noted the same thing, presumably obtaining her information from Charlotte herself.

> The sisters retained the old habit, which was begun in their aunt's lifetime, of putting away their work [sewing, etc!] at nine o'clock and beginning their study, pacing up and down the sitting room. At this time, they talked over the stories they were engaged upon, and described their plots. Once or twice a week, each read to the others what she had written, and heard what they had to say about it. Charlotte told me, that the remarks made had seldom any effect in inducing her to alter her work, so possessed was she with the feeling that she had described reality: but the readings were of great and stirring interest to all...[11]

Charlotte herself confirms this in the well-known passage from the 'Preface' to the 1850 edition:

> If the auditor of her work when read in manuscript, shuddered under the grinding influence of natures so relentless and implacable, of spirits so lost and fallen; if it was complained that the mere hearing of certain vivid and fearful scenes banished sleep by night, and disturbed mental peace by day, Ellis Bell would wonder what was meant, and suspect the complainant of affectation.

In the earlier passage Charlotte is thinking of the effect her words will have on her own readers. She wishes to assert her own independence from her sisters, and is doing so correctly; it was not their objections which changed *The Professor* but its initial failure to find a publisher. The second quotation is bold, since Charlotte is concerned in the various vignettes she presents of Emily to exhibit her to the public as an equable and moral writer. Despite her feeling of being a mother to her sisters, even after their deaths, she admits Emily's intransigence. I shall later give reasons why Emily could not in the end maintain this obduracy, and suggest the causes for a revision of *Wuthering Heights*. Despite

Charlotte's firm assertion that she was not influenced by her sisters, such an influence was impossible to avoid. The family likeness of *Jane Eyre*, *Wuthering Heights* and *Wildfell Hall* was so strong that Newby could pretend with some success that they were all written by the same author. But doubtless Charlotte is right in maintaining that much of the influence was subconscious and not registered.

Returning to Martha Brown's evidence that the Brontës worked on small scraps of paper, we have already discussed some of these scraps, on which poems are found in draft and copied. It needs to be emphasised how small some of these scraps were. The smallest measure only about 2″ × 1″. Many seem to be the result of dividing notebooks originally about 7″ × 4 $\frac{1}{2}$″, first pulling apart quires, then tearing the two sides apart, then dividing the leaves by four and even dividing these quarter pages again in unorthodox ways. Derek Roper points to poem No. 102 written on a piece of mourning stationery and two on bits of card.[12] Doubtless part of the reason for such parsimony was the cost of paper, but there is a secretive air about Emily Brontë's writing which is underlined by this host of tiny leaves. Some similar small sheets exist for the other Brontës, but Anne at any rate prefers notebooks, though her writing too uses every spare millimetre. Martha Brown's phrase 'odd bits' expresses the situation exactly from a servant's point of view. There may well have been occasions on which searches were organised for lost 'odd bits'. However, we must bear in mind the possibility that Martha is largely referring to poems, and that *Wuthering Heights* and the Gondal saga must have needed longer spans of writing. It seems likely that *Wuthering Heights* too would need its 'tin box' or equivalent.

Precisely how *Wuthering Heights* was first presented to potential publishers in 1846 we cannot be sure, but it might be worth commenting on the physical characteristics of Charlotte's novel *The Professor*, which was intended at this time as part of the same package. It is likely that the three sisters would agree on a common format for presentation, as they had already been involved in the necessary common decisions in presenting their volume of *Poems*, 'by Currer, Ellis and Acton Bell'.[13] It would be hard to argue, for example, that they presented their final copy in booklets of anomalous sizes. At this point in their thinking, they were considering the three 'tales' as amounting to one whole, even perhaps somewhat linked in theme.[14]

The manuscript of *The Professor* still exists, and has been described for us in considerable detail in the introduction to the Clarendon edition, by Margaret Smith and Herbert Rosengarten.[15] Of this manuscript, ff. 13–338 seem to date from a time of revision and are on clean white paper, which Smith and Rosengarten suggest shows similarities to the paper on which *Jane Eyre* was copied. This copying took place between 16 March and 19 August 1847. The remaining pages of the manuscript of *The Professor* are folded, and the verso of the final sheet (339/340) is reported to be yellowed. We might presume that these sheets are contemporary with the first presentation of *The Master* (as it was then perhaps called), i.e. with the first presentation of *Wuthering Heights*. We may therefore be justified in assuming that the manuscript of Emily's novel was inscribed on similar paper.

The Professor was originally written in 'brownish ink' on sheets of paper approximately $9'' \times 7\frac{1}{2}''$. Charlotte is happy to present her final copy to the publisher with a quantity of final alterations made but not recopied on to a clean sheet. These precise sheets must have been sent to a publisher in 1846, and even if we suppose they then lay dormant and a neat copy was made to be sent out on other occasions, yet Charlotte evidently thought this was an adequate copy when she made a final submission to Smith, Elder. It is likely that Emily, less tidy than her sister, would be less scrupulous about sending a finely written manuscript, and we can perhaps envisage the manuscript of *Wuthering Heights*, even in its final form, as looking rather crabbed and still with erasures and substitutions on it. To judge by Emily's copy manuscripts, she would start quite neatly, but the writing would decline and the crossings out become less tidy and more frequent as the novel went on.

2

Learning's Golden Mine

At some time before 1839, but probably in 1838, Emily Brontë
wrote,

> All day I've toiled but not with pain
> In learnings golden mine
> And now at eventide again
> The moonbeams softly shine
>
> There is no snow upon the ground
> No frost on wood or wave
> The south wind blew with gentlest sound
> And broke their icy grave
>
> Tis sweet to wander here at night
> To whach the winter die
> With heart as summer sunshine light
> And warm as summers sky...[1]

We may plausibly link this poem with the first of three sheets of
Latin translation from the library of The King's School, Canterbury
(Walpole Collection) which will be the subject of this chapter. This
first sheet is signed and dated 'E J Brontë March the 13 1838.' It
consists of a version of the first 18 lines and probably spurious
introduction of Virgil's *Aeneid* Book I, with linguistic notes. Before
giving details of this work, and showing how Emily proceeded, it
may be best to remind readers of the degree to which the Brontë
family understood the Classical languages.

Until recently there was clear evidence for a knowledge of Latin
only for Patrick, Branwell and Anne.[2] Charlotte's work, both adult
and juvenile, includes many Classical references and there are
some overt ones in Emily's work. The problem has been to see
how, in an age when Latin was thought to be men's sphere, these
young girls could have learned the language. Anne's Latin *Delectus*

was explained by her need to learn Latin in order to teach Edmund Robinson.

However, here we need to invoke Patrick Brontë's well-known enthusiasm for the education of girls as well as boys, shown early in his career by the testimony of Elizabeth Wilson, one of his pupils at Glascar.[3] Patrick consistently sought to give his five daughters a systematic education at reputable schools. The characters of Charlotte and Emily, eager, determined and very quick to learn, suggest that they would demand to be taught Latin like Branwell; we have no evidence on whether this enthusiasm extended to Greek.

Juliet Barker reports that Patrick used a structured programme of reading in Latin and Greek to try to steady Branwell in 1839.[4] This suggests that he shared the nineteenth-century view of Classical studies as a moral stabiliser. This programme mentions three of the Latin books we know Emily to have read: Virgil's *Aeneid*, Horace's *Ars Poetica* and *The Four Gospels*. The precise extent of her reading and knowledge of these books will be the subject of this chapter.

It will first be necessary to look at the previously mentioned dated and signed version of a small part of the *Aeneid*. I hope Latinless readers will persevere at this point, since it will be necessary to deal with this text in some detail. The point here is that the degree of linguistic perception and discrimination required for the detailed comment Emily makes on these lines is considerable, and we can assume that this linguistic training affected her attitude to her own native language as well as French and German, which she also studied. This short translation reveals sharp, accurate attention. When there is discussion of the clear, dramatic, economic nature of the English style of *Wuthering Heights*, we need to bear in mind the characteristics shown in the detail of the work we are now to examine.

Virgil's epic work *The Aeneid* begins with the well-known phrase which Bernard Shaw adapted, 'Arma virumque cano': 'I sing of arms and a man...' But traditionally these lines are prefaced by four introductory lines generally thought to be spurious, explaining who Virgil is, and purporting to be by him. Eagerly Emily Brontë omits these lines and moves straight on to the epic itself, translating the first line 'I sing arms and the hero who First From the coasts of Troy'. She then rearranges the Latin words under the English to explain how she has obtained the translation: 'Cano arma que vir qui primus ab Oris Trojae'; in doing so she gives the nominative case of 'vir – a man' though the rest of the words retain their form in the verse. It looks as if she has intended to translate without explanation, but in these first two lines she becomes increasingly interested in explaining how she has reached her conclusions. Alternatively, we could see this translation as carried out for a specific exercise, but the variation in principle suggests that Emily Brontë is studying at her own rate for her own benefit.

She notes further (I have expanded her abbreviations) 'mas[culine] 2 D[eclension]' referring to *vir*, 'relative pronoun' [referring to *qui*], 'adject[ive] 3 Term' (meaning that the adjective can have three different terminations according to whether it is masculine, feminine or neuter); 'prep[osition]' (*ab*), '1 D[eclension]' (*Oris*) and the same abbreviated note for *Trojae*, which is also a first declension feminine noun. So far one line of Latin has been translated, necessitating three lines of work by Emily. She then translates the next line 'driven by Fate comes to Italy and the lavinian shores' and rearranges the Latin words in the order of English translation, placing them under their English equivalents: 'profugus Fato venit Italiamque lavinia Littora'. In this line she has made her first, understandable, mistake, since *venit* in Latin can be translated either present or past according to the length of the letter e. Emily Brontë has chosen present instead of past. She confirms her error in the notes below, writing '4C[onjugation] venio/present'. The rest of her parsing notes on the line are accurate apart from a copying slip where she writes profug*i*s instead of profugus.

We cannot follow her through the whole translation, which must have engaged her concentration for some time. I shall extract some lines and passages, however. The next line in the Latin continues (it had begun with 'Litora') 'multum ille et terris iactatus et alto/ Vi superum'. This Emily translates 'much he was tossed both on the lands and on the sea by the influence of the heavenly powers', and after carefully parsing each word, comments 'I think superum abbreviated', which indeed it is. Both the translation and the comment are interesting.

The contraction *superum* is relatively unusual for a beginner, though strangely there is another example in this passage. The accurate identification of the parts of speech of the words in the passage, and their accurate classification into declensions of nouns and conjugations of verbs suggests that this is not beginner's work. *Vis*, of which we have the ablative, *vi*, can mean 'power, might, strength, force' as well as 'influence', and Emily Brontë has had to seek carefully for her alternative. It is perhaps worth adding here that one of the values of the slow translation exercise from Latin to English is that it forces the student to revolve various alternatives in her or his mind, so that it soon becomes a habit not to write so speedily in English that the words haven't been given adequate careful consideration. The choice of 'influence' adequately describes how the gods acted on Aeneas' life in the epic and how powers outside their control will later act on Heathcliff and Catherine.

The term 'heavenly powers' for *superum* is not likely to have been in Emily's dictionary. A little of the nuance has come from the word *vi*, but 'heavenly' is slightly poetic, as indeed are a number of Emily's choices in the rest of the passage. For example, in line 7 the word *altae* means 'high, tall', but she translates 'lofty', and she also writes 'distinguished by piety' for *insignem pietate* and for *quid dolens* chooses 'wherefore greiving' (sic). She goes beyond the meaning of *casus*, initially writing 'mischances', then crossing this through and substituting 'perils', though 'mischances' is nearer to the root. Just before finishing the first piece of work on the epic and returning to the introduction, she chooses 'resentments' for *irae* (anger), once again exploring the full meaning of the Latin in a way which would earn her bonus marks in modern practice.

At line 7, Emily stops translating and draws a colophon consisting of a series of loops similar to those at the ends of some of her poems. Then or later she begins again: 'Introduction' and returns to the four dubious lines, using the Brontë spelling 'greatful' and finishing with another colophon consisting of a set of differently formed loops and the previously mentioned signature and date, thus reaching the end of side one, and presumably of the day's work in 'learning's golden mine'.

Her next burst of work, on the verso, covers lines 11–18. Once again, all words are parsed and both Latin and translation are fully written out. She substitutes 'far of[f]' for her earlier idea 'distant' in translating *longe*, but there are no more significant changes of mind. The bottom part of the verso of this sheet is blank, as though she did not continue at this time. Some months later, though we are unsure exactly when, Emily would go to Law Hill to begin her work as a teacher. At the time of writing the page we have been discussing, she was just under 20.

We need to try to deduce as much as possible about the circumstances surrounding this translation before proceeding to the more extensive Horace. It is certainly not beginner's work, though the detailed commentary on every word translated shows that at this point Emily considered it necessary to show how the translation was arrived at. Nevertheless, what she was entering on was a complex piece of literature, one of Mr Brontë's favourites, and the accuracy of her parsing shows that she had already worked through grammar and vocabulary, and understood the concept that words in one language are not the precise and only equivalents of words in another language.

Let us turn aside for a while to another Victorian novelist, born one year later than Emily Brontë, George Eliot. Precise details of her early acquaintance with Latin seem not to have survived, but we know that she took steps to learn it, and we might not be mistaken in relating a passage in *The Mill on the Floss* (Book Two: School Time, Chapter I) to Marian Evans' own situation, since the relation between Tom and Maggie is generally thought to reflect that between Marian and her brother Isaac. Tom is introduced to Latin via the 'Delectus' but later in the chapter the method is said to be 'the Eton grammar'. He begins with declensions and conjugations and will later call the whole process 'a bore' and 'beastly stuff'. He is given no explanation as to what Latin is, though it is said that girls might be given such 'smattering, extraneous information'. When Maggie comes to visit, Tom tells her that girls never learn such things as Latin, 'They're too silly.' She looks into his grammar book and finds the English key at the end, but it is clear that this is a book of elementary sentences for translation, not a Classical text. Tom begins to say over his grammar rules, which he has learned by heart, but he flounders and continually has to be prompted. Latin, it seems, begins with lists of contextless words to be committed to memory but 'It was really very interesting – the Latin grammar that Tom had said no girls could learn – and she was proud because she found it interesting.'

Without going too far beyond our evidence, we might reasonably consider that the intellectually demanding Emily Brontë would see Branwell's apprenticeship in Latin in very much the same light as Maggie sees Tom's. Though Branwell was not a dullard like Tom, he was certainly not of Emily's calibre and the sibling rivalry illustrated in *The Mill on the Floss* might well have been felt in Haworth parsonage. Just as with George Eliot's character Maggie, Emily did not need to pretend to be interested in words: they were a lifetime study. The *Aeneid* translation is well beyond the stage we have been describing, and implies that it has been undergone some time previously.

Three questions remain: Why choose the *Aeneid*? How far did Emily get with her translation, and what effect did the epic have on her writing? The first is easy, the others much more difficult. Clearly, Emily read *The Aeneid* because Mr Brontë owned it and valued it. Quite possibly, despite the note of 1839, Branwell had already begun on it. We have no evidence to help us guess how far the translation of *The Aeneid* continued. In the poem 'Written in Aspin Castle', begun 20 August 1842 and completed 6 February 1843, Emily writes of 'Sidonia's deity' (line 76)

> There stands Sidonia's deity!
> In all her glory, all her pride!
> And truely like a god she seems...

The word Sidonia (adjective formed from a noun) is used many times in *The Aeneid*, e.g. at Book IV, line 545 and Book XI, line 74, where it completes a line 'Sidonia Dido'. The god-like 'Sidonian Dido' (Queen of Carthage) is first directly seen in Book I, line 446, where she is described in the same phrase we have just quoted from Book XI. But line 78 of the above quotation may descend from a description of Venus, as she leaves her son Aeneas after a monitory conversation in Book I, line 405. Virgil writes 'et vera incessu patuit dea', which might be translated 'by her walk she reveals herself as a true goddess'. The collocation of the unusual word 'Sidonia' and the description of the deity as being 'truely like a god' surely indicates that Emily Brontë read thus far in Book I, more than halfway through the book, even if we doubt about Book XI.

The power of two goddesses in *The Aeneid*, Juno and Venus, and the organising energy of Queen Dido, may well have contributed to Emily's imaginary figure 'A.G.A.'. Alexander and Sellars describe the right-facing female head drawn on 6 October 1841 as having a Greek or Roman appearance because of the hair style and tiara, though they think this portrait may derive from an engraved plate.[5] Possibly this is so, but whether Emily imagined the profile or merely chose to copy this because it chimed with her idea of A.G.A., we can see a link which emphasises her interest in a Dido-like figure.

In general, I am inclined to consider it almost certain that Emily read and translated much more of *The Aeneid* than the 18 lines originally discussed, and that the evidence above indicates knowledge of Book I at least. Whether she read as far as Book XI it is impossible to say. The third question then becomes entangled with the second. In *The Aeneid* Dido and Aeneas fall in love and Dido at least considers herself married. Aeneas receives a message from the gods that he must leave Carthage and fulfil his destiny, to found Rome. He leaves Dido surreptitiously, and she builds a funeral pyre on which to commit suicide. Her speeches, impassioned and rhetorical, bitterly cursing Aeneas, remind us of those given both to Catherine and Heathcliff. The emotional heat of these descriptions of desertion accords very well with those in *Wuthering Heights*. If we suspect that this is evidence of Emily Bronte's reading up to Book IV of *The Aeneid*, this must unfortunately remain a suspicion only. The concept of epic does seem to inform her work, but we must leave a consideration of this until we have examined the rest of her Latin translations. It is time to look at Emily Brontë's understanding of Horace's *Ars Poetica*.

Emily Brontë's major Latin translation is a large portion of Horace's poem *Ars Poetica* (not so titled by the poet). What remains consists of a large part of one sheet, torn at the side after writing had been completed on both sides, and a smaller part of another sheet, the remains of a sheet of similar size to the other, again with writing on both sides. The extant translated lines are lines 61b–85, part of one word from line 89, part of line 132, lines 133–92 followed by a sketch, lines 193–232 (mutilated), traces of line 233, lines 234–77, 278–316 (mutilated); the translation runs right up to the bottom of this page. The torn-off part of the first, smaller sheet corresponds to lines 1–61, leaving no space at the top for heading, comments or introduction. There would have been another 160 lines in the remainder of the poem, which would have precisely occupied a further sheet of the same size as the larger extant sheet. We cannot be absolutely sure that Emily Brontë wrote out these lines as well, but the fact that her extant translation reaches to the very bottom of the sheet suggests that she is likely to have done so.

There can be no question that this is Emily Brontë's writing, but all other inferences are subject to some degree of uncertainty. The obvious question is whether she translated this herself, copied it from an existing published translation, or whether it was dictated by Branwell. We are also at a loss about its date. However, it is easy to show that it was not visually copied, e.g. from a printed source. There are spelling errors such as indiscreetly, feild, affectionatly, breif, deviners, novalty. Some of these are typical of Emily's spelling. There are also errors or infelicities in translation at times, and almost no punctuation. This, then, is a Brontë translation, in Emily Brontë's handwriting.

However, *Ars Poetica* forms part of the list of works Mr Brontë proposed to read with Branwell in 1839. Could this translation be Branwell's? If we did not possess the Virgil translation, showing Emily's competence in 1838, we might have to suppose so. But since we do have that earlier work, there is less need to bring Branwell into the situation. It is possible that Branwell and Emily cooperated in the work, leaving Emily to write it up. We cannot rule this out, but in places there are alternatives which may suggest Emily thinking as she writes, or rows of question marks which imply that she was not sure of a suitable translation. Let us take one of each of these as specimens, so as to examine the kind of thought processes which may be present. A relevant passage occurs near the start of the remaining copy. Here Horace is discussing (lines 46–72) vocabulary, linguistic change and the way in which writers can enrich a language. He illustrates this by the use of several images, comparing words to (i) leaves on a tree and (ii) the construction works of mankind. Though there is still dispute about precise nuances, we may join Horace at the point where he refers to a drained marsh:

> [palus]
> vicinas urbes alit et grave sentit aratrum,
> seu cursum mutavit iniquum frugibus amnis
> doctus iter melius, mortalia facta peribunt
> nedum sermonum stet honos et gratia vivax.
>
> (lines 65–9)

('the marsh [now] feeds neighbouring cities and feels the heavy plough, [whether] the river unfavourable to crops has changed its course, after being taught a better way: mortal deeds will perish, not even the standing and lively charm of words remaining longer.')
Emily Brontë writes,

> [a marsh ... fitted for oars] nourishes neighbouring cities
>   being taught a better path

and feels the heavy plough/ or the river has changed its
course   persued
injurious to the corn being-/ mortal deeds perish
much less may the honour of words endure [?] and their lively
??????
reputation

She initially omitted the phrase 'being taught a better path', and
has provided two alternatives, 'changed' and 'persued'. A row of
question marks hangs over 'reputation'. (I am uncertain about the
word 'endure' which is partly cut off.) This is not a copy, but
Emily's own struggling translation.

As with many of Emily Brontë's manuscripts it is hard to tell
how far this is a first attempt and how far a revision. On one or two
occasions she begins a word she is unable to finish on that line, for
example in translating 'nodus' in line 191 by 'difficulty', she writes
'diffic', then realises she cannot squeeze the word on to the line,
and begins again on the next line, 'difficulty'. In line 186 she splits
'im' and 'pious' before Atreus, and she appears to leave only the
last letter of 'conscious' for another line at line 242. Whether
these errors result from visual or audial miscalculation may be
disputed. In the passage already quoted, she seems to write 'has
changed its course' straight after 'or the river', but realises she has
omitted the participial phrase and folds it in over the top. This
could be a change of mind resulting from a copying process, during which she decides to relocate the phrase in the sentence order.
The question marks at 'reputation' seem to precede a translation,
though the word 'honos', which I have translated with the modern
equivalent 'standing', is quite close to 'reputation'. She is not therefore questioning accuracy, but appropriateness. In a passage where
Horace is discussing word approprateness this seems fitting.

At a subsequent point question marks seem to indicate a grammatical query. In line 238 Horace writes, 'Pythias emuncto lucrata
Simone talentum' which Emily Brontë translates 'Pythias *having
gained*??? [*sic*] the talents from cheated Simon...' She appears to
register doubt about whether the past participle can be active in
this particular verb, mindful of the important rule that in the over-
whelming majority of verbs it can only be passive. (In her perplex-
ity she turns the Latin 'talentum', singular, into 'talents', plural.)
There are other places where grammar does not seem quite secure,
as for example in the previously quoted passage where 'mortal

deeds perish' translates a future tense ('peribunt'), without apparently adequate reason for the change.

Two or three more examples must suffice. On the manuscript sheet which covers lines 159–232 there are four places at which alternatives have been written in. One is worth leaving for detailed discussion. The other three consist of 'timidly' or 'fearfully' for 'timide' (line 171); 'slower' or 'more slowly' for 'segnius' (line 180) ('more slowly' is more accurate English); and 'however' or 'nevertheless' for 'tamen' in line 182. The more interesting passage is Horace's famous phrase 'laudator temporis acti' (praiser of time gone by) at line 175, used of the 'typical' old man as opposed to the youth. This is combined in the passage with a short idiomatic Latin phrase 'se puero' which literally means 'himself being a boy' and is normally translated 'when he was a boy'. Emily Brontë is unsure how idiomatic to be. She tries both 'with himself a boy' and 'himself being a boy' but is not prepared to choose between them or go further in adopting an English idiom. For 'temporis acti' she tries both 'finished time' and 'time finished'; these are both correct but stiff and bald.

There is one other point which we might examine to assess the state of Emily's knowledge of Latin at this time. In line 160 Horace writes of a young actor 'mutatur in horas'. This phrase introduces two points which Emily is not quite master of. First, 'mutatur' is like 'luctata' above, and can be translated active though passive in form: 'changes', not 'is changed'; second, 'in horas' is idiomatically translatable 'hour by hour'. She misses this point and actually makes a translation mistake, writing 'in the hours'.

To summarise these findings about Emily Brontë's expertise in translating a very difficult Latin piece, full of compressed expression and dense phrasing: she is amazingly skilful in most places, producing an accurate if dull rendering and very rarely being outwitted by hard passages. This work is undergraduate standard, and even if it was prepared with Branwell's help or intervention, it shows remarkable application and energy. 'Learning's golden mine' has produced treasure which is not yet sparkling, but which will afford a great deal to think about for an aspiring author.

We now move into the realms of informed speculation about this evidence of Emily's interest in Horace. We cannot date the work exactly. It must be later than the Virgil of early 1838, because it shows a great deal more complex understanding of the language. Emily is moving freely along the lines, no longer feeling the need for parsing. By September 1838 she had gone to teach at Law Hill.

It might just be possible that this Horace translation dates from the summer previous, but such progress looks too great to be achieved in a few months, and I would prefer to place the work after her return from Law Hill. Law Hill was a stimulating experience, and left Emily in 1839 keenly writing and organising poetry. Possibly two attempts to collect her extant poems can be located in this year. I take it that the implication is that in 1839 she was quite seriously thinking of herself as a poet. Where should she turn for guidance as to how to write?

It was in 1839 that Patrick Brontë proposed a programme of Latin reading for Branwell. Among the works he indicated was *Ars Poetica*. The title literally means 'the poetic art' or 'The Art of Poetry'. If Emily was now taking herself seriously as a poet, this was just what she was seeking. On the whole, it seems likely that it would be in 1839–40 that this translation was written. I should be inclined to put it at the latter end of this period, and suggest that Emily worked at her Latin while Branwell was in Broughton and Anne at Thorp Green. Branwell will then have been the instrument by which she was led to Horace, but not an assistant. Obviously there is no proof of this, and one could see the translation taking place after Branwell's return. The point is, however, that Emily was very keen to know what gems could be retrieved from 'learning's golden mine' concerning the method of poetic composition. As she translated, she would soon find that more than poetry was being dealt with: Drama (always a Brontë preoccupation) was at the forefront of Horace's work. Major considerations of literary form are discussed in great detail, compared with the other arts (in which the Brontës were also acutely interested) and positions taken up. While it is clear that Emily Brontë did not accept Horace's advice wholesale, his precepts do seem present when she comes to write both her poetry and *Wuthering Heights*.

To have read a book does not guarantee having thought about it, but it is harder to translate without being forced to think. Even if we remain unsure why Emily Brontë wished to translate Horace's *Ars Poetica*, possibly looking for a commercial motive such as planning to produce a publishable verse translation, or providing the raw material with which Branwell could do so, the sustained effort of translating could not be carried through without posing the questions posed by Horace. Even if Emily Brontë had no particular reason for choosing this work to translate, she would inevitably have absorbed the ideas in it.

The first way in which *Ars Poetica* might be seen as influencing *Wuthering Heights* is the way in which it begins by highlighting anomaly and muddle.

> Friends, if a painter decided to fit a horse's neck to a human head, and paint all sorts of feathers on limbs collected from various places, so that a beautiful woman above ended in a dusky fish, and if you looked at this sight, could you refrain from a smile?[6]

Horace illustrates this point by himself dodging misleadingly from point to point within his exordium. This is exactly how Emily Brontë behaves in the first two chapters of *Wuthering Heights*, though I shall suggest that it was only in the second version that she did so. Catherine the second is not Heathcliff's wife; the 'obscure cushion' is not full of small cats, but dead rabbits; Hareton is even less Catherine's wife than Lockwood thinks, but will be more so.

In a second section, including some lines in the extant part of Emily's translation, Horace discusses diction. Poetic metres are reviewed, and it is pointed out that different poets requiring to treat different subjects made an appropriate choice of metre. Emily Brontë's own poetic metres are very varied, and it seems she was aware of the need to choose appropriately. Horace talks about 'the muse' as inspirer, and if there is anything in Irene Tayler's thesis in *Holy Ghosts* it might receive support from such passages.[7]

The next paragraph, of which unfortunately we have no trace of Emily Brontë's translation, discusses style and emotion:

> It is not enough for poetry to be well made: it has to be affecting. Poetry must attract the thought of the reader in the desired direction. The human face expresses laughter with those who laugh and weeps with those who weep. If you want me to weep, you first have to be sad yourself: it's then that your misfortunes hurt me, Telephus and Peleus! If you speak your script badly, I shall either go to sleep or laugh. Sad speeches require a miserable countenance; if they are full of threats, an angry one, frivolous ones a light-hearted one, and serious remarks a grave one.[8]

Possibly Branwell was instructed to read this work, and perhaps that was right for him. Emily chose to read it for herself, translating painfully phrase by phrase. These precepts weighed solidly in the scale for her, and they were not forgotten.

In the Introduction I suggested that Emily Brontë had no theory of the novel as such to work on. *Ars Poetica* does not present such a theory. It is, however, extensively concerned with Drama. It must never be forgotten that the Brontës' imaginative explorations began with Drama, and as late as 1845 on the journey to York Emily and Anne acted parts as they journeyed along. They *'were'* the parts they played, said Emily. From the toy soldiers and Mr Brontë's strange early stratagem to this expedition of grown women, Brontë voices spoke through masks like the masks in Greek tragedy. Emily, taciturn in front of strangers, writes her poetry in metaphorical inverted commas. For all the pages of Brontë small print, written descriptions are not Emily's forte: most of her work, and almost all of *Wuthering Heights*, can be heard or seen. Horace's emphasis on Drama can be seen as a second way in which his interests coincide with those of Emily Brontë.

In lines 153–78 Horace discusses character, in 179–88 the question of action and reported action on stage, in 189–90 and 192 acts and actors, and in 193–201 the role of the chorus, before moving away to such matters as Music, which were not so germane to Emily Brontë's purpose, though she does have a number of references to this art in *Wuthering Heights*. In 191 there is a precept about the 'deus ex machina'.

It will be useful to discuss these sections in the light of the view that Emily Brontë, while translating, is necessarily having to spend mental energy on the concepts being studied, and is metaphorically discussing them with the Roman author as she writes. Horace begins by insisting that actions should be appropriate to age, in lines which may be precursors of Shakespeare's 'seven ages' speech. He insists that the young person 'is eager to go and play with his peers, is reckless in the way he bursts into anger or lays it by', and 'finally escaping his guardian enjoys his horses and dogs, and the grass in the sunny fields'. This (though one does not wish to tie the point too tightly) is exactly what the second Catherine does.

The role of the chorus in Greek plays has been disputed, but Horace sees it as holding together the action of the play. It will be suggested later that the role of Nelly in *Wuthering Heights* was discovered after the narrative had been begun, and that she developed further in the revision process. Let us see how Horace considers the chorus should control the narrative.

> The chorus should maintain his identity as an actor and his active role. He should not interpose material between the acts which is irrelevant to the main theme, and is not inherently appropriate. He should support the worthy and give them friendly advice, control the angry and favour those who are loth to do wrong. He should approve feasts involving a modest table, wholesome justice and legality and the peace that allows city gates to be open; he should be discreet about matters entrusted to him and beg and pray to the gods that fortune should return to the underprivileged and depart from the overconfident.
>
> (*Ars Poetica*, lines 193–201)

We cannot firmly assert that Nelly is moulded on this pattern, but her role in the plot of the novel seems modelled on Emily's meditation over this passage.

There follow two sections which might be of less interest to Emily Brontë, on music in Drama and on satiric poetry. Though *Wuthering Heights* and her poetry do reflect Emily's interest in music, in the novel it can hardly be said that music plays a pivotal role. At line 251, however, Horace returns to the matter of poetry, exploring the appropriateness of poetic metres and urging a very careful process of learning about foreign (Greek) practice in these matters. Greek examples are to be considered day and night: the recommendation to burn the midnight oil was one which was very congenial to Emily Brontë. She takes on board the need for varying metres throughout her poetry. We shall later encounter Emily in Belgium, allegedly objecting to M. Heger's very classical method of learning by imitation. The evidence suggests that within her poetry she was prepared to learn from her predecessors.

In the following short section Horace deals with Greek tragedy and comedy speedily, discussing ways in which Roman writers have taken on the tradition in a following passage. Our surviving part of Emily Brontë's translation includes the first part of Horace's traditionalist explanation of the nature and function of poetry (lines 295–316). The discussion is concerned with the balance between *ingenium* (innate ability) and *ars* (learned skill), which is central to our understanding of Emily Brontë's work, set as it is against the background of the Romantic revolution and Charlotte's espousal of this in her public pronouncements on her sister.

The notion that poets are mad is well known to us from such passages as Theseus' speech in *A Midsummer Night's Dream* and Coleridge's *Kubla Khan*. These would surely (though we cannot prove it) be known to Emily Brontë. Horace discusses the question (lines 295–308) and humorously suggests that because he himself refuses to behave like a madman, he can't write real poetry, but must restrict himself to teaching other poets. The irony in this section reassures Emily Brontë that the narrator need not always be ingenuous, and also develops in a humorous way the notion that effective poetry owes as much to *ars* as to *ingenium*.

'Wisdom and taste' are the basis of poetry (the verb *sapere* has overtones of both), according to the line that begins the next sub-section:

scribendi recte sapere est et principium et fons
(*Ars Poetica*, line 309)

We are nearing the end of the part of Emily's translation that remains, and it is very unfortunate that part of this line is missing. She certainly writes 'To know/be wise is both the...' ('be wise' is written as a second thought above 'know'), but the first words of her next line are missing and she appears to write '...the secret of writing well', which would be an imaginative translation, but unfortunately I cannot be quite sure of the reading. The next lines explain what is meant by *sapere*. Learning from the philosophers is advised so that the student learns 'what he owes to his homeland, what to his friends, with what kind of love a parent, brother and guest are to be loved,' what is the duty of a senator and a judge and what is the role of a leader sent to war'. At this point (line 316) Emily's translation fades out, though I have given reasons earlier for thinking she is likely have completed the work.

Continuing with his underlying theme, Horace advances his discussion of the 'mad' poet. He claims a high place for the poet in advancing civilisation, through the mythical Orpheus and the less mythical Homer. The story of Orpheus charming animals with his verse is an allegory for the way in which verse has civilised brutish mankind. To the end the problem of inspiration versus skill is pursued in colourful verse and allegoric image. It is possible that when read and translated perhaps between 1838 and 1842 these final sections of the poem seemed to be the most important. From 1839 onward Emily's poetic effort becomes serious: she sees herself as a member of a poetic fraternity. Her two first serious attempts at collecting her work date from 1839, first the nucleus of the D manuscripts, then her transcriptions in C, using normal cursive writing. Though we have considered *Ars Poetica* as contributing to *Wuthering Heights* through Emily's adaptation of tragic convention, its first effect seems to have been on the importance with which she viewed her role as poet.

3
Inspiration and Labour in Emily Brontë's Poetry

In *Brontë Facts and Brontë Problems,* Chapter 4, I tried to show how Emily Brontë's perceptions and emotions became transformed through imaginative labour into some of the poems we have in complete form. This work has been carried forward by Derek Roper, whose authentic Clarendon edition makes it possible to see precisely how Emily arrived at a final text and how she reached a point in some poems where she felt it necessary to abandon the poem. Before exploring some of these poems in the making, there are two or three technical points which require mention.

Until the advent of the Clarendon edition, it was usual to refer to Emily's poems by the numbers given by Hatfield in his 1941 volume, *The Complete Poems of Emily Jane Brontë.* These numbers have now been superseded and I shall use the Clarendon numbering. However, Hatfield's manuscript classification is still the best and requires restating with some small changes. There are two manuscript copy books dating from 1844, one marked 'Gondal Poems', which have been conventionally called A (the untitled book) and B (that marked 'Gondal Poems'). The other copy book, C, uniquely in normal cursive rather than Brontë small script, probably dates from 1839 and represents an earlier interest by Emily Brontë in making her poetry accessible.

In addition to the copy books, there are 46 small slips of paper on which other poems have survived. These are known as groups D, E, F and T, though the division into these groups may not necessarily be traceable beyond the sale by Arthur Nicholls to Clement Shorter in 1895. Some of the D slips and one or two others are themselves early copies, perhaps dating from 1839. On the other hand some of the slips are very early attempts at poems, probably first drafts.[1] In a number of cases these slips present us with alternative readings to what appear to be Emily's final thoughts, and these can obviously be used to try to understand her thought processes. An examination of these poems with multiple manuscripts will form the core of the chapter which follows. It should perhaps be stated that there is no real problem with a decision over the chronological priority of manuscripts over others, though there is no space at present to explain why this is so.

A further area of discussion will also require attention. It has been known since about the 1920s that part of Emily Brontë's poetic output is related to her imaginary kingdom of Gondal. This was, of course, not known by, because not revealed to, the original readers of Emily's poems in the 1846 poetry edition by Currer, Ellis and Acton Bell.[2] The root question is to decide what is the relation between the poems copied into the 'Gondal poems' notebook of 1844 and those copied into the other booklet, and a further question is whether we can divide the poems copied into neither of these books into categories as Emily did in 1844. Gondal is a fictional place, and the Gondal poems participate in a fictional world. *Wuthering Heights* constitutes such a world, and we are entitled to suppose that an analogy might be drawn between ways in which Emily Brontë produces her fictional poems and her fictional novel.

If the poems in the untitled 1844 copy book are different from 'Gondal poems', then what are they? At one extreme, Dr Juliet Barker thinks the A manuscript is 'a notebook containing many Gondal poems', and Fannie Ratchford in *Gondal's Queen* wrote '...all of Emily's verse, as we have it, falls within the Gondal context'.[3] Derek Roper has not quite gone so far, but he sees no reason why the poems in the A manuscript cannot be thought of as containing fictional elements.[4] At what might be thought of as the other extreme, such writers as Romer Wilson use the A poems and others as a biographical quarry. In one sense a precise answer to this conundrum is not entirely germane to our present investigation, but since we are trying to discern the way in which Emily Brontë's imaginative creativity leads her from perception to artefact, we do have to pay some attention to this question. 'Gondal poems' are poems which have developed and been integrated into part of a systematic narrative, or perhaps sometimes have been created specifically for that narrative, while the other poems are, at the very minimum, by implication 'other poems'.

Manuscript A contains no poem with a Gondal name, reference or signature. Manuscript B contains such signs in 40 out of 45 poems. Manuscript A appears to have no subject heading.[5] Manuscript B is headed 'Gondal poems'. The contents of the manuscripts surely supports the view that Emily Brontë was classifying when she copied these poems, and classifying consistently. I cannot see how we can escape the logical conclusion that she saw a distinction, wished to preserve a distinction, and understood that it mattered.

As we shall see, the Gondal poems did not all clearly start as Gondal poems. Some of them develop fictional elements on top of the verifiably observed elements with which they began their lives. We have no data about the genesis and development of others. Some of the poems which end up in the non-Gondal booklet also have earlier versions which may help us to understand the process by which they grow. Some poems which reach neither book are also very illuminating in the way in which they hover between observation and fiction.

Part of the problem is caused by an assumption that if the A poems are not-Gondal, they must be an accurate record of direct personal experience. This is naive, but not completely misleading. Let us examine two poems which are most clearly 'not-Gondal', Clarendon Nos. 39 and 40, both (as we know now, though Miss Ratchford did not) written at Law Hill school. No. 39, 'Loud without the wind was roaring', exists in an earlier version in fragment MS E 12 as well as in its copied form. In its final form it is dated 'November 11th 1838', but the earlier manuscript reads merely 'Nov 1838'. The poem contains many references to November weather: 'the waned autumnal sky'; 'the cold rain pouring/Spoke of stormy winters nigh.'; 'the gloom of a cloudy November'; lines 23–30 describe the late autumnal scene. It also contains many references to the situation in which we know Emily Brontë found herself, teaching in a school at a distance from Haworth, as does No. 40. In line 52 she talks of 'exile afar' and in lines 55ff of the heather growing in a scattered, stunted patch surrounded by 'grim walls'; in poem 40 'A little while, a little while', Emily writes of the school children being temporarily 'barred away' so that her 'harassed heart' can choose where to 'go'. She asks whether she shall go where 'The house is old, the trees are bare ... But what on earth is half so dear – / So longed for as the hearth of home?'; or on the other hand, she wonders whether to seek 'another clime [Gondal]' and indeed ('Yes') the room passes away and she finds herself in 'A little and a lone green lane', a lane in Gondal.

It is not possible here to analyse fully these personal poems, but if the reader will examine them carefully, I believe some of Emily's

imaginative technique will become plain. In these poems she tells
us precisely about her imaginative habit. In doing so, she uses
imaginative vocabulary, as we have seen her do in her Latin
translations: the hills round Haworth are 'the mountain' (39, line
27) and the valleys 'glens' (39, line 34). These are not the only
contexts in which the Brontës described geographical features at
Haworth in terms which sound slightly Scots.[6] Yet surely it would
be perverse to deny the direct link between current, present experience and feeling and the poem created from them. Poem 39 does
indeed go through stages in its production, as we can see from the
earlier version, but the original motivation does not vanish. Doubtless No. 40 also goes through a process of development, though we
cannot see it because the earlier drafts and versions are lost.

The non-Gondal booklet is full of emotional experience, often
attached to a first person narrator. Here is No. 38:

> O Dream, where art thou now?
> Long years have passed away
> Since last, from off thine angel brow
> I saw the light decay –
>
> Alas, alas for me
> Thou wert so bright and fair,
> I could not think thy memory
> Would yeild me nought but care!
>
> The sun-beam and the storm,
> The summer-eve devine,
> The silent night of solemn calm,
> The full moons cloudless shine
>
> Were once entwined with thee
> But now, with weary pain –
> Lost vision! 'tis enough for me –
> Thou canst not shine again –

It is dated 'November 5th 1838' and is copied from the earlier copy
book, C. Two changes are introduced during the copying, in line 3,
where 'thine' is substituted for C's 'thy' and in line 13 (at which
point C has been destroyed) where initially Emily Brontë wrote
'Where' and corrected herself.

Who is the 'I' of the poem? On one hand, we may wish to be cautious in asserting that this is undisguisedly Emily Brontë as visionary. On the other, it is hard to see how it can be a Gondal character, since none of the elements of Gondal is present. There are no Gondal initials, no names, no Gondal geography. This poem was copied into the booklet which is not headed 'Gondal poems'. As we have seen, this 'other than Gondal' booklet begins with poems which can be shown to relate directly to experiences which Emily Brontë was undergoing at the time she wrote them. (This, incidentally, was not so clear to Fanny Ratchford's generation of commentators, since the biographical chronology of the Brontës was not accurately known for this period of their lives.) It seems fair to deduce that the A manuscript contains such poems as Emily felt would not fit a Gondal context, but reflected her own personal imaginative life more directly. Even Gondal reflects Emily Brontë's imaginative life, of course; but these poems are closer to her personal spiritual vision and lyric understanding.

We shall see in later examples how cautious Emily Brontë is with the first person singular pronoun. I have already shown ways in which her overall personality is consistent with this, such as drawing herself from the back. In Gondal and *Wuthering Heights* she is able to use the pronoun lightly, creating characters rationally to talk in their own right without any implication that their author shares their views, though it will later be suggested that it was the creation of the persona of Ellen Dean which enabled Emily Jane to pursue a coherent organisational viewpoint in the novel. Yet this imaginative creation of coherent figures who do not share her presuppositions seems harder for Emily than for Anne. Psychologically the Gondal figures seem to share facets of Emily's character; she objectifies herself in them, whereas the youngest Brontë sister seems more interested in observing dispassionately and reporting to her public what she has seen.

Though in Gondal Emily hazards portraits of people very unlike herself, she often seems unable to escape from the world of Scott, Byron and the ballads. We may enjoy such Gondal poems as 'Douglas's Ride' (No. 31) for its verve and energy, but not for its psychological penetration. Often Gondal seems an avocation for Emily, which can be entered to relieve the pressure of her own dense thought and feeling. In the non-Gondal booklet we encounter poems which engage with such experiences in a direct way. It can be assumed reasonably that the 'I' in the non-Gondal booklet is describing and meditating on experiences that Emily Brontë has personally internalised.

The three chosen here to examine are three which I have looked at on previous occasions. The issue is worth re-examining, however, because Derek Roper has studied them with great care in producing his Clarendon edition, and his additional points are important. These three short poems are Nos. 60 (12 August 1839), 82 (27 February 1841) and an undated poem No. 192. In each of these Emily Brontë seems to have made changes to what is essentially a first draft, or at any rate an early draft. We shall begin with the last mentioned, No. 192, to which no date can be accurately assigned, though I have an idea that poems among the E group may include some later ones, and this might possibly date from 1841. It is printed in the Clarendon edition as follows:

> She dried her tears and they did smile
> To see her cheeks returning glow
> A fond delusion – all the while
> that full heart throbbed to overflow
>
> With that sweet look and lively tone
> And bright eye shining all the day
> They could not guess at midnight lone
> How she would weep the time away

Derek Roper follows his principle of using manuscript punctuation. The lack of this in the present case reinforces the notion that this is a very early draft, for however light Emily Brontë's final punctuation, finished work is usually graced with some stops.

What Emily Brontë actually started by writing was 'I've dried my tears and then [did smile]'. The emotional tone is not radically changed but it is modified in the light of Emily's disinclination to reveal what might be her own feeling and reaction on paper. This may be a Gondal poem; since it is not copied into the B manuscript, and there are no initials, we cannot tell how it would have ended. As it stands it is not classifiable as Gondal, though equally we cannot take the subject of the description as a real figure. It might of course be the poet, reflecting on an actual event, but it is impossible to assert this on the face of it.

In line 3 the words 'A fond delusion' replace 'How little dreaming' and in line 7 'could not' replaces 'cannot'. In line 8 'would' replaces earlier 'had' and 'will', the former implying a change of verb form which was not written. In this poem, the poet has removed the subject a little from immediacy with her changes; the weeping girl is, in the second attempt, seen as an object, still sympathetically, but no longer as the speaker unframed. The onus of misunderstanding is now on the bystanders: '*they* did smile'. These onlookers are, in the revised version, deluded. Even in this early tinkering with a poem Emily Brontë fears to express herself nakedly: she replaces the first person with a third person and we watch as distanced bystanders. In some ways this is a more complex, and certainly a somewhat remoter approach. When the narrative of *Wuthering Heights* becomes surrounded by the well-known 'framing' narrators, similar processes are at work.

Certainly from 1841 is No. 82. The Clarendon edition prints:

> And like myself lone wholey lone
> It sees the days long sunshine glow
> And like myself it makes its moan
> In unexhausted woe
>
> give me the hills our equal prayer
> Earths breezy hills and heavens blue sea
> I ask for nothing further here
> But my own heart and liberty
>
> Ah could my hand unlock its chain
> How gladly would I whach it soar
> And ne'er regret and ne'er complain
> To see its shining eyes no more
>
> But let me think that if to day
> it pines in cold captivity
> To morrow both shall soar away
> Eternaly entirely Free

Derek Roper is responsible for the reading in line 5, replacing earlier suggestions of 'her' and 'us'. The poet has established her empathy with the creature woefully pining, often taken to be a hawk.

In lines 7 and 8 there is further evidence of change. What seems to have happened is that the poet originally wrote 'We' (for 'I') and 'our' (for 'my'). Her change of pronoun to singular is possibly set off by a decision to write 'me' in line 5, precipitating a corresponding change throughout. However, in fact this would not be a necessary consequence of the alteration. In line 10 the original words were 'see thee soar'. The change to third person is again slightly distancing. One could call these slight alterations retreats from immediacy, though in these instances the feeling of retreat is not strong. As in 'She dried her tears' we do experience a slight withdrawal. Though this poem did not reach publication in Emily Brontë's lifetime, we see a perfectionist working to build up an artefact which has attracted critical and public notice. It was never copied into a copy book, but nevertheless appears to be complete.

Poem No. 60 is written on a single sheet of paper which contains writing at first neat, but soon faltering and ending in less clear writing, with doodles and symbols drawn on it. The tone of the first line sounds like a real question, 'How long will you remain?' though there is in fact no punctuation. I consider it probable that the poem was actually written at midnight, the time mentioned in the first and second lines, and almost certainly in the Haworth sitting room. One cannot clearly prove this, and it is not certain whether this work, done in ink, is a draft or an early copy. The doodles include a pencil one which may date from later, but the snake with wings and the dreamily repeated 'Regive' is repeated below, appearing in a very strange form which I once considered to be a fresh word, but which is actually one more instance of the same verb. 'Regive' is an unlikely formation, and Emily's verbal interest causes her to repeat it wonderingly.[7]

This sheet of paper, with its initially Haworth-based, but subsequently Gondalised poem, gives an idea of how Emily Brontë's creative imagination works. The 'minster' in line 2 is surely Haworth church clock, and the 'shadowy room' (line 13) must be in the parsonage. But in line 19 we are surprised to find 'woods' appearing, not a prominent feature of Haworth landscape. The poem is about to be translated to Gondal. Though no Gondal initials or names appear, 'childrens merry voices' were certainly not to be heard in the parsonage in 1839.

Two other hypotheses deserve consideration. It might be argued that Emily Brontë (and possibly Anne) had another fictional world as well as Gondal. 'Gondal poems' would then mean poems about their Gondal world, with Gondal geography and characters, and the non-Gondal notebook could contain characters and geographical references from the other fictional world. But there are no fictional names, initials or references at all in the non-Gondal book. Whereas we can discern some degree of coherence in some of the Gondal narrative, with recurring initials and sometimes names (albeit contradictory in many places), there are no such constructs at all in the non-Gondal book. Even if we see this other, A manuscript as a mixed bag, with some personal poems like Nos 39 and 40 and some fictional poems which would not fit the Gondal saga, it is surely strange that not one of these alleged fictions bears any name at all. Characters, indeed, do seem to be hinted at. As I showed in *Brontë Facts and Brontë Problems* A 13–A18 seem to constitute a coherent group with a central figure, quite without name. Can this non-Gondal figure be from another saga unrelated to Gondal?

If so, why conceal the name of the figure? It is nowhere mentioned. It may be that these poems are some of the ones Dr Barker considers to be some of the many Gondal poems in manuscript A. But why are these poems separated from B and purged of names? The second hypothesis is that such looming, recognisable but anonymous figures are creations which have either never been included in Gondal or else have been removed from the main saga and have acquired their own independent existence.[8] On this view, the 'I' of the poems is a fictional character about whom we know nothing, but who is composing a poem cycle the references to which are outside the frame, so to speak. This is certainly true of some Gondal characters, of whom we are given only tantalising glimpses, but about whom Emily Brontë clearly knew more. The dispute then rests on the question whether the visionary experiences narrated by this character are separate from Emily's own experiences, or whether they actually are her own: whether the 'I' of the poem is in any sense Emily herself.

In *Brontë Facts and Brontë Problems* I have suggested a possible real person who might have provided Emily with the basis of her vision in poems A13–18. I have made it clear that this is a hypothesis. I am asserting that Emily Brontë is recording a real imaginative experience here, which might be described as emotional or spiritual according to philosophical orientation. For the purposes of this exploration of Emily's working methods, it is necessary to accept that poets cannot write about imaginative processes, dreams, visions, mystic visitants or other experiences which might be associated with the subconscious unless they have been through such experiences. It is not really helpful to suppose that Emily Brontë is describing in her poems experiences she has not had through the medium of fictional characters whom she does not name or refer to. In discussing Heathcliff, it would be rash to suppose she had met a prototype in real life, but contradictory to think she had not met him in her inner life. Just as Haworth church becomes 'the minster' in two poems, a real poet may become a vision, and a real man may contribute to an element of Heathcliff. It appears that objections to agreeing that the A manuscript is a collection of personal poems aim to guard against using these poems as a biographical quarry. This is a useful point, but such caution should not be employed to overrule clear distinctions made by Emily Brontë herself in her copying.

We can now proceed to examine more of Emily Brontë's poetic output, seeking to understand her methods of composition in the hope that there will be some analogy between this and the methods of composition in prose, first in Gondal (of which we have no prose remains) and then in *Wuthering Heights* and any other novel she might have written. Seven longer poems may be included in this examination. They are 'There shines the moon' (4); 'Loud without the wind was roaring' (39) which has already been mentioned; 'The night was dark' (43); 'Thou standest in the greenwood' (130); 'The Death of A.G.A.' (81); 'Silent is the house' (123) and 'Why ask to know the date?' (126/7). From these longer poems, we may hope to deduce how Emily Brontë worked on narrative and with complex material. These poems will be considered from the point of view of construction. Before venturing on them, however, it will be as well to turn the spotlight on the minutiae of poetic composition by examining short drafts of poems.

'There shines the moon' occurs in the B transcript, begun in February 1844. I agree with Derek Roper that a version of the poem was probably in manuscript C, but we have no means of recalling that version. The poem begins with eight lyric lines:

> There shines the moon, at noon of night.
> Vision of Glory – Dream of light!
> Holy as heaven – undimmed and pure,
> Looking down on the lonely moor –
> And lonlier still beneath her ray

> That drear moor stretches far away
> Till it seems strange that aught can lie\
> Beyond its zone of silver sky –

This is a static and intense description of the moon-flooded moorland. The rest of the poem after a gap of about a line in the manuscript consists of a lengthy reverie by 'A.G.A.', Emily's Gondal heroine, plainly in a Gondal mode and including three Gondal proper names, Elnor, Elbë and Augusta. Though there are landscape references the reverie is personalised and directed by 'A.G.A.', whose initials are at the top of the whole poem, with a date, 'March 6th 1837'. The eight-line stanza at the beginning seems to serve to remind A.G.A. of this past occasion and sets her off on her reverie. The reader may think that there is a qualitative change beyond line 9, when the verse sinks towards the conventional. The space left in the manuscript between the first eight lines and the rest seems to imply a change of focus. It may also imply a different composition date.

The moon did not actually shine on 6 March 1837, though a careful examination of Emily's poems concerning weather and climate suggests that she normally described the weather conditions she was experiencing.[9] This suggests that the first eight lines were already composed when the Gondal narrative was added. Many of the fragment manuscripts contain small detached stanzas on weather, and it looks as if this may have been one such which had been stored by Emily Brontë and then used as the prefix and inspiration for her Gondal poem by A.G.A. This Gondal work will probably have been produced on 6 March 1837, and have subsumed the lyrical fragment, which may have been composed at any time previous to that date.

We have already looked at 'Loud without the wind was roaring'. The earlier copy, in E 12, gives no day in the month of November for the composition. It looks as though E 12 was an early attempt by the poet to save fragments from previously written scraps, but she does not finish; the pen seems to have been damaged, as is shown by a series of parallel pen marks suggesting an attempt to clear the ink flow. Perhaps the copy in the A manuscript was made from the earlier version, which may have shown the precise day of the month. This supposed early version would have been destroyed when the A version was produced. E 12 could not be scrapped because it contained uncopied poems.

On the other hand, there was no wind on 11 November, and it might be better to guess a date some days later when the wind roared more enthusiastically. In line 6 of E 12 a careless error is introduced, 'without' being substituted for 'within', though this is against the sense. What we can deduce from this non-Gondal but partially narrative poem is that there were at least three stages in its composition, the times of these stages widely separated. First there was the original, possibly made on 11 November 1838 (or a date which contained numbers that might be confused with 11, e.g. 14 or 17), the E 12 copy introducing at least one error and unfinished (E 12 may date from about 1839), and the final version of 1844. The development of the poem lasts in all six years or more.

'The night was Dark' (43) exists in one copy only and is not recopied for the B manuscript. It is very directly related to the ambient weather:

> The night was Dark yet winter breathed
> With softened sighs on Gondals shore
> And though its wind repining greived
> It chained the snow swollen streams no more

In mid-January 1839 there was a weather change. 10 and 11 January had been cold, but on 12 January, the composition date of the poem, a period of four warm days began, providing 'a little rain' instead of the frost of the previous days. In line 27 of the poem the feet of the strange tutelary spirit are compared to 'melting sleet', an image surely derived from immediate observation on 12 January 1839.

There are few changes in the manuscript, D 7. In line 1 Emily Brontë originally wrote 'but', and changed it to 'yet'. In line 17 she wrote 'distrest' in an archaic spelling, and in 25 she originally wrote 'the' for the second 'her', but changed this to the present text. In line 40 she changed 'If my cheek grew pale in the loudest gale' to '*its* loudest gale', substituted a 'thy' for 'Your' in line 53 and turned 'in toilsome pain' to 'of toilsome pain' in line 62. A more substantive change occurs at line 52, where the poet originally wrote

> And I save them with my single arm

which she changed to

> And I save them with a powerful charm.

The change from second person plural form to singular in line 53 is followed by 'thou' and 'thee' in lines 57 and 59 and 'thy' in line 61. It is possible that the draft had 'you/your' at these points. Presumably the spirit is seen as talking in an oracular non-modern style, though the Gondal character in whose name the poem was written (the name is not actually given) uses 'you' when addressing the spirit in line 29. The form 'distrest' perhaps indicates that Emily had been reading archaic or archaising poetry, and indeed 'The Rime of the Ancient Mariner' seems not far from this poem. The change from the image of the single arm to that of the charm is much more interesting. This female tutelary spirit is unique in Emily's writing, and perhaps she felt it anomalous that a spirit, and a female one at that, should be said to have a 'powerful arm'. Flesh and blood Gondal women, however, sometimes did have powerful arms.

Poem No. 130, 'Thou standest in the green-wood', is found in its latest form in the B manuscript, where it is headed 'To A.G.A.'. It would be reasonable to date this final version to about March 1844, having regard to the fact that it is the fourth poem in the manuscript, which was begun in that February. It consists of one five-line stanza and eight four-line stanzas, a total of 37 lines. As it stands it cannot be detected that it was a composite, and we should not know its history if a version of lines 1–27 were not found in D 3 and a version of lines 26–33 in D 8.

The D 3 manuscript contains on one side 'Come hither child', an interesting poem which has been dealt with elsewhere.[10] This is dated 19 July 1839. Much of 'Come hither child' is composed onto this small piece of paper, though it cannot be asserted that this was the very first attempt at the poem. Even if this very much altered copy is not the first draft, it must be dated to 1839, not very long after the date assigned to it by Emily Brontë. The neat writing at the start is superseded by more roughly added words as second thoughts. 'I'm standing in the forest' occupies the verso of this sheet, and so probably dates from mid- to late 1839. It is the origin of six of the nine stanzas of No. 130. It contains, as stanza four, a stanza dropped entirely from the final version, and after stanza six a couplet which was not incorporated into 130. At this point the paper ran out and we do not know whether Emily continued on a sheet now lost. Because Emily seems not to have destroyed any fragments of length, we might deduce either that there were few if any further lines in this version, or that the version began to approximate much more closely to the final one: however, this would be a difficult conclusion in view of the lines next to be mentioned, on D 8.

D 8 is a most interesting fragment, containing a list of Gondal names (as is normally supposed to be the case) and part of a poem 'It was night and on the mountains', unfinished. At some point after August 1839 Emily folded this small piece of paper and reused the front for two drafts, the writing of which follows the irregular fold line. The year of the date is hard to read, but 26 July 1842 seems almost certain. Two pencil stanzas follow the fold in the paper:

> I gazed upon the cloudless moon
> And loved her all the night
> Till morning came and radiant noon
> And I forgot her light
>
> No not forgot – eternally
> Remains its memory dear
> But could the day seem dark to me
> Because the night was fair

These stanzas are added to the stanzas from D 3 and with two changes ('ardent' for 'radiant' and 'Then' for 'And' in line 4) become stanzas 7 and 8 in the poem copied into the B manuscript. The B poem is indisputably a Gondal poem, in which the 'I' of D 3 has become 'Thou' and applies to A.G.A. The 'cloudless moon' stanza may represent an original observation; perhaps the 'I' of the observation is Emily Brontë, but this would not be clear if we did not have the fragments. In line 35 we see why 'radiant' was dropped from the fragment stanza and replaced by 'ardent': 'radiant' is to be the epithet of the sun in line 35.

The couplet at the end, which may or may not have been continued on a following sheet, begins to expand the fiction:

> I dreamt one dark and stormy night
> When winter winds were wild [...]

In the final poem the lines chosen from D 8 indicate different weather: 'I gazed upon the cloudless moon'. Clearly Emily Brontë had not fully planned the poem; it had developed in her mind through the versions. This poem is a patchwork, the inspiration for which came from several sources and which is sculpted into consistency at or before the 1844 copying. It is not possible to see this from the finished poem, and we should not be aware of it if it were not for the survival of the early pieces. The genesis of this poem is an important clue to the development of the novel.

'The death of A.G.A.' (81) is a Gondal narrative of some complexity, introducing allusively a number of Gondal characters about whom we can only make guesses. It bears two dates, January 1841 and May 1844. It was, then, either completed differently from its final version or left incomplete until in 1844 Emily Brontë came to tidy the Gondal narrative. The context may suggest that the 1844 portion begins at line 139, when the action fades before the lyrical and the verse pins down the time to summer (line 146). It contains reminiscence and flashback, particularly in the form of Angelica's account of her childhood friendship that resembles in its intensity the link between Catherine and Heathcliff. There are gaps in the story (e.g. at line 139) similar to the space in which Heathcliff is away and we never learn where he has been. When the narrative resumes after the break, Lesley and Surry have apparently been mortally wounded by Douglas, but as in Greek tragedy the final blow is not seen 'on stage'.

The effect of the allusions and omissions makes this a hard poem to grasp, as *Wuthering Heights* also has its difficulties. It may be that lessons were learned from the poem so that eventually the narrative of the novel was clarified, but the scattering of narrative strands through the artefact is certainly not dissimilar.

The next narrative poem for our consideration is headed in the manuscript 'Julian M and A.G. Rochelle'. It has always proved a problem for critics, and apparently also for Emily and Charlotte Brontë as they considered how to present it in the 1846 poem edition. It was first published entire in Helen Brown and Joan Mott's *Gondal Poems* in 1938. A version had been printed in the 1846 edition of *Poems*, entitled 'The Prisoner', consisting of 15 stanzas based on the manuscript and an extra stanza designed to round off the poem. In Charlotte's new poem edition, retrieving more unpublished poems of Emily and Anne, published in 1850, she printed three more stanzas as a separate poem, entitled 'The visionary' and rounded off by two more stanzas not found in the manuscript, which I regard as written by Charlotte herself. The poem has been a thorn in the flesh of subsequent editors,

who have often printed plural versions. Maureen Peeck-O'Toole
writes interestingly about it and makes an attempt to reintegrate
the pieces.[11] Because of its apparent (and I think, real) lack of
homogeneity it is worth looking at the poem with some care to
see whether it throws light on Emily Brontë's attitudes to composition and thus on *Wuthering Heights*.

Derek Roper performs a useful service by printing the whole
poem as found in the B (Gondal) manuscript. It is not possible to
reprint it here in full, but I shall summarise it, quoting significant
stanzas to help us see the way in which it fits together.

As we have it the poem begins with the three stanzas used as
part of the 1850 poem:

> Silent is the house – all are laid asleep;
> One, alone, looks out o'er the snow-wreaths deep;
> Watching every cloud, dreading every breeze
> That whirls the wildering drifts and bends the groaning trees –
>
> Cheerful is the hearth, soft the matted floor
> Not one shivering gust creeps through pane or door
> The little lamp burns straight; its rays shoot strong and far
> I trim it well to be the Wanderers guiding star –
>
> Frown my haughty sire, chide my angry Dame;
> Set your slaves to spy, threaten me with shame;
> But neither sire nor dame, nor prying serf shall know
> What angel nightly tracks that waste of winter snow.

After these stirring and audially fluent stanzas it comes as a
surprise in the 1850 version to find a stanza trying to explain
them:

> What I love shall come like visitant of air,
> Safe in secret power from lurking human snare;
> What loves me, no word of mine shall e'er betray,
> Though for faith unstained my life must forfeit pay.

These and the next four lines are not in the manuscript. It seems to
me that they are explanatory not of the preceding lines, but the core
section of the original poem, which we shall soon reach. They have
no particular place in the thought of the original writer, and it

seems likely that they were added by Charlotte, who quite sensibly wanted to rescue the first three stanzas of 'Julian M and A.G. Rochelle' and perhaps to comment, less sensibly, on its central portion.

Stanza four in the original begins a narrative in the first person:

> In the dungeon crypts idly did I stray
> Reckless of the lives wasteing there away;
> 'Draw the ponderous bars, open Warder stern!'
> He dare not say me nay – the hinges harshly turn –

We have not been told, nor are we ever told, who was the one looking out over the snow-wreaths in the first stanza. The word 'serf' may help us to expect a medieval dungeon, but there is little else to prepare us. The shift to the first person is not explained, but in the original the title referring to Julian may suggest that he is the prison visitor. Twelve stanzas then pass in which Julian talks to a fair prisoner, whom he knew many years ago as his playmate in childhood. These are reduced in the 1846 version to seven. The thirteenth stanza in this section in the manuscript reads,

> Yet, tell them, Julian, all, I am not doomed to wear
> Year after year in gloom and desolate despair;
> A messenger of Hope comes every night to me
> And offers, for short life, eternal liberty –

The eighth in the 1846 version reads,

> Still, let my tyrants know, I am not doomed to wear
> Year after year in gloom and desolate despair;
> A messenger of Hope, comes every night to me,
> And offers for short life, eternal liberty.

Punctuation changes would be an interesting study here, but the more interesting point is the way in which the specific Gondal reference has been erased, as in other Gondal poems published in 1846.

There next follows a passage of six stanzas agreed by most critics to be examples of Emily Brontë writing at her best. They cannot be fully quoted but begin,

He comes with western winds, with evening's wandering airs,
With that clear dusk of heaven that brings the thickest stars;
Winds take a pensive tone and stars a tender fire
And visions rise and change which kill me with desire –

The poem ends in the 1846 version with a further stanza which clearly has the function of completing (peremptorily) the story of the captive. It is not in the manuscript (except for its first words, 'She ceased to speak', Homeric or Virgilian in form). In the manuscript, there are 15 further stanzas to conclude the narrative, making 152 lines in all. The instinct of Charlotte in the 1846 editing process to trim the poem severely seems right (it is disputed how far the process was a prime concern of Emily herself, or whether she ceded authority to Charlotte).

Maureen Peeck-O'Toole defends up to a point the welding together of apparently disparate elements in the poem.[12] Length, she points out, was not a sufficient reason for editing this narrative severely, since Charlotte's own 'Pilate's Wife's Dream', published in the same volume, is longer. She regards the manuscript version as just as authentic as the published version, while retaining an open mind on how far Charlotte exercised influence or authority on Emily's editing process in 1845–6. She believes the prison context is essential to the meaning of the poem, though she does not claim its poetry to be exalted.

Turning to the first three stanzas, she considers whether they are a sequel to the main narrative, bringing it up to the present. 'It was spring and summer then, and it is winter now.'[13] She considers that Julian, after liberating Rochelle from prison, took over the role of the messenger of Hope, and that Rochelle is the wandering angel who tracks the wastes of snow. The interpretation continues very interestingly, and cannot be fully summarised here. However, I do not see how the text quite squares with the view expressed. The varying nature of the elements in this poem suggest to me much more a conflation of several existing pieces, which in 1845, as part of her revising and tidying process, Emily Brontë feels can be made into a superficially homogeneous poem.

In arguing this, I need to point to the eventual presentation of the poem in 1846. It was very much modified, specifically for print. There was, then, no objection on the part of Charlotte, and either Emily agreed or acquiesced, to a radical revision of the material in the notebook. The overall impact of the poem was changed, as anyone can see by reading both versions. The process also repeats editing processes we have already looked at. We have seen several poems where different sections have been welded together, and a composite poem produced. It makes much more sense, I think, to see 'Julian M and A. G. Rochelle' in this light. Both 'Silent is the house' and 'He comes with western winds' are poems of high quality, recognised as such by critics, and indeed by their author. But they lack context. Emily Brontë is not averse to supplying such a context, but she cannot provide this out of her inspiration, and has to seek intellectual means to fill in the gaps. The result is verse rather than poetry.

Evaluating the quality of the various parts of 'Julian M and A. G. Rochelle' will clearly involve some degree of subjective opinion, and the only way to do this is to read and think about the poem in the manuscript version. It appears to me that it consists of about three stanzas, 'Silent is the house' and the next two, which have a personal origin, and were probably abandoned on a small sheet of paper until they could be linked with the later material; a central section written out of Emily Brontë's own burning experience, beginning 'He comes with western winds'; and linking or explanatory stanzas probably composed in 1845 when she wanted to make a poem out of the pieces. The way in which this poem came to be assembled is therefore similar to ways in which *Wuthering Heights* took shape, as I shall be suggesting in Part II. It seems to me pointless to deny that 'Julian M and A. G. Rochelle' contains anomalies, does not quite tell a coherent story, and proved hard to edit. It began from fragments, was welded into an unlikely whole, and was dismantled.

The material of this poem is not so disparate that it cannot be made to yield coherence, but its mystery is partly due to the way in which it was created, piecemeal and without a clear plan at the start. There is absolutely nothing wrong with creating a work of art in such a way, but it should not be made to answer to values it cannot provide. Though *Wuthering Heights* is a far cry from this poem, it too will provide anomalies, the explanation of which will be similar to that just discussed.

We shall need to return to look at 'Why ask to know the date?' begun in September 1846. What is important at this stage is to note that here again we have a narrative which Emily Brontë has to labour over and which she cannot compose fluently. One part of the poem was apparently written in late 1846 and then copied into the B notebook, while the second part was added much later. The manuscript shows us a poet who is toiling rather than inspired, though where lyric imagination is concerned there is much of value, and the moral development is subtle and interesting.

In these long narrative poems Emily Brontë does not construct a plot so much as discover the bones of a plot from the dramatic or lyric qualities of the poetry. She sometimes starts in uncertainty: 'Were they shepherds who sat all day...?' 'Why ask to know the date, the clime...?', sometimes in a lyric dream, 'Silent is the house, all are laid asleep...'; 'There shines the moon, at noon of night.' Such small notes as we have about her Gondal planning do not suggest that she was primarily interested in the actions of characters. A small fragment we shall later examine lists characters, apparently, by their initials and physical characteristics.[14] Diary papers list characters also, and give general vague information about the whereabouts of the principals. If Emily Brontë is interested in action, it is in emotional action, produced by violent feelings and leading to treachery, strife, murder and suicide. She has obviously been stirred by the romances of Scott and the stark feelings in Byron's characters, but swift and consecutive action is not foremost in her mind.

In the prison poem the story is conveyed in conversation, as Julian talks with the captive Rochelle. The core of the piece is the lyric passage explaining how Rochelle's 'messenger of Hope' comes to her at evening. There is violent action as Julian strikes off the captive's fetters, but overwhelmingly the poem is a dialogue, heard not seen. In 'There shines the moon', a traveller returns and muses over the death of a loved one: the narrative is simply a reminiscence of that death scene. 'Why ask to know the date...?' is more complex, but both this poem and 'The death of A.G.A.' provide unclear narrative focused on the feelings of the characters. There is a great deal of scene-setting and much self-analysis.

These poems, like Gondal itself, begin with incident and emotionally charged characterisation.[15] The implied causes of the emotional fervour may be explored, but this is an afterthought. There is certainly some swift action, but it is usually the result of feelings that have welled up and spilled over. We cannot argue that because no plot outlines of Gondal have ever been found, there were none, but it is worth noting that the few indications we have outside the poems, both from Emily and Anne, suggest an interest in geographical location, physical personality and an exploration of the being of the characters rather than their consecutive actions.

In pointing to this, I am really only returning to the observations of Inga-Stina Ewbank, who heads her section on Emily in *Their Proper Sphere* 'The Woman Writer as Poet'. She notes that the poetry 'suggests particular emotional intensity around certain imaginative experiences'. She instances 'intense longing for one who was beloved and is dead' and 'a desire to be liberated – by death, by nature or by the imagination – from the bonds that enslave the spirit'.[16] Just these intense emotions pervade *Wuthering Heights* and as in the poems, the narrative is subsidiary. The drama is *not* subsidiary, but Emily Brontë, unlike Anne, is careless about the narrative framework for her drama. In exploring the stages by which the novel came to be written, we should not be too disappointed to see this emphasis retained and enhanced, though through sheer intellectual struggle the poet author finally overcomes her problems of construction.

As a result of this investigation we can make some deductions about Emily Brontë's methods of poetic composition.

1. She had a habit of beginning to write with a current impression or 'inspiration' clear in her mind. In the 1837 diary paper she discusses with Anne whether to go out so as to get 'into a humour' for writing.
2. She then often carried out small-scale modifications which had the effect of distancing the experience from herself. In 'And like myself lone', she changes the pronouns so as to generalise.
3. When she ran out of inspiration she often stopped writing (e.g. in 'I gazed upon the cloudless moon') and seems to have stored the fragment of poetry until it could be expanded or integrated with further material. Many of the small fragments we have on some of the 46 manuscript scraps are such unfinished but hoarded lines.
4. Her revisions paid careful attention to nuances of meaning and to the effect of sound.
5. Many of her poems indicate an observation of the ambient weather conditions, and overwhelmingly the weather described in the poems is real weather; even the time of year is generally consistent with the manuscript date. When this is not so this is sometimes, though not universally, because the fragment has been adopted for another poem of inappropriate

date. It is fair to say, however, that Emily Brontë finds it hard to write about weather that is not actually present to her perception.

6. The process of constructing poems out of fragments can take years. Efforts are made to make new additions and sections conform to what has been selected from other contexts, but anomalies may persist.

7. Some of the most successful stanzas found in the narratives are less narrative than lyrical or meditative, and they frequently seem to derive from an actual experience, though we have little objective evidence for this. Examples are the moonlit description in 'There shines the moon' and the 'mystic' section of 'Silent is the house'.

4

Drafting, Correction and Fair Copy: Emily Brontë in Brussels

Why did Emily Brontë go to Brussels? There is really no primary evidence for an answer. Ostensibly the germ of the idea seems to come from Charlotte's employers, the Whites of Rawdon. In a letter of 29 September 1841 (MS untraced) Charlotte discusses the task of fitting herself for opening a school. She has been recommended to spend six months 'by hook or by crook' in some school on the Continent. If they do not do so, the sisters will have difficulty competing with other schools in England. In Brussels Charlotte considers she will be able to 'acquire a thorough familiarity with French. I could improve greatly in Italian and even get a dash of German.'[1] If Emily (not Anne) could share these advantages, 'we could take a footing in the world afterwards which we can never do now.'[2]

It is beyond the scope of this book to guess what Charlotte may have intended at this point; whether the school idea was the real reason for her interest, or whether she was trying to equip herself for authorship. But Emily hated being away from Haworth so much that we must look for a pervasive motive for her decision. Considering her projects of fair-copying her poems in 1839, it seems quite probable that she thought of this chance to extend her education as a means towards writing. It is likely that the writing of poetry was uppermost in her mind.

The full effect of the Brussels experience on the writing of the Brontës has not yet been examined in detail. Enid Duthie's *The Foreign Vision of Charlotte Brontë* is a useful contribution, though she is not so concerned with Emily.[3] In the following pages I am less concerned with the content of Emily's work as its method, but some of the questions touching content will inevitably be raised.

There is a great deal of difference in the views of commentators, from that of Juliet Barker, who considers that her air of misanthropy has been 'vastly overstated', to Stevie Davies, who emphasises the view of one of the *Devoirs* that the universe is 'a vast machine constructed solely to produce evil'.[4]

We can dimly perceive the routine at Brussels from the few letters by Charlotte which have remained for this period, reminiscences by M. Héger told to Mrs Gaskell, and the memories of later pupils at the Pensionnat. Of these, the major source is Frederika Macdonald, writing in *The Woman at Home*.[5] She seems to have experienced a system which if we take some accounts at face value, could have been invented specifically for the Brontës. Mrs Gaskell, far the earliest biographer, gives details which I propose to follow closely. After a few weeks, M. Héger perceived that

> with their unusual characters, and extraordinary talents, a different mode must be adopted from that in which he generally taught French to English girls...After consulting with his wife...[he] told them that he meant to dispense with the old method of grounding in grammar, vocabulary, etc., and to proceed on a new plan, – something similar to what he had occasionally adopted with the elder among his French and Belgian pupils. He proposed to read them some of the master-pieces of the most celebrated French authors (such as Casimir de Vigne's poem on the 'Death of Joan of Arc', parts of Bossuet, the admirable translation of the noble letter of St. Ignatius to the Roman Christians...), and after having thus impressed the complete effect of the whole, to analyse the parts with them, pointing out in what such or such an author excelled, and where were the blemishes. He believed that he had to do with pupils capable...of catching the echo of a style, and so reproducing their own thoughts in a somewhat similar manner.
>
> After explaining his plan to them, he awaited their reply. Emily spoke first; and said that she saw no good to be derived from it; and that, by adopting it, they should lose all originality of thought and expression.[6]

Frederika Macdonald confirms this approach:

> He...read aloud some eloquent, pathetic, or amusing passage from a classical French author. He would then analyse this

passage, and signalise its beauties or criticise its defects. Afterwards he would either himself suggest, or allow his pupils to select, a subject for composition...sufficiently different...to make anything resembling unintelligent imitation impossible.[7]

She then notes that these were written on paper with wide margins, and copied for M. Héger on paper with equally wide margins. M. Héger would make comments in the margins, and the work would be returned to the pupil, who was expected to follow up the comments, but need not submit her work again.

This method of teaching is extremely Classical in tone. It assumes that writers will need to cast and recast their thoughts, partly so as to find a totally acceptable vehicle for them, but partly to produce 'beauties' of style. It is wholly inconsistent with the 'inspirational' school of composition which the Romantics appeared to favour. That they did not actually work on this principle is quite clear from the notebooks of Shelley, Coleridge and others. Nor can we think of Emily Brontë believing in this mode of composition, as is evidenced by her various versions of poems and her interest in Horace. What precisely, then, was her objection to M. Héger's proposed method, and when 'she would have entered into an argument on the subject', what points would she have raised?

We might note here that on this occasion we have an Emily animated, engaged with the subject and potentially voluble. M. Héger 'had no time' for such an argument, and apparently cut her short. It seems as though he considered that she posed a threat to Charlotte's learning (he thought Emily exercised 'a kind of unconscious tyranny' over her sister). Emily and he 'don't draw well together', said Charlotte, adding that she cried when M. Héger was very ferocious, but implying that Emily did not. Despite his ferocity, M. Héger liked Charlotte, but his awed remarks about Emily suggest that he disliked her 'strong, imperious will'. Throughout her poetry, we find Emily both forcefully assertive and at times contradictory. In this case, after her protest, she allowed herself to take part in M. Héger's experiment. Perhaps she saw herself bound to object in the name of Romanticism, but able to understand the practical need for the kind of serious analysis of literary spadework which she had used herself.

The literary examination of these passages was directed towards character, action, finding the *mot juste*; it did not deal with plots. Passages for imitation (which must not be 'unintelligent') seem to have been character studies, rhetoric, philosophical discussion. There is plenty of each in *Wuthering Heights*, wrapped up in the narratives of Lockwood and Nelly Dean. It is interesting that Catherine often justifies her actions, and Nelly herself at times provides justification, though it is of a conventional tendency. Attention to the exact word needed in the context is extremely strong in the novel. We may reasonably see an influence from Brussels in these areas. It is now time to consider this influence more carefully.

We may start by noting the audial medium used. M. Héger read passages aloud. Perhaps it would not be necessary to stress this if our own culture was closer to that of the nineteenth century. 'Silent reading' seems always to have been subsidiary to actually hearing words, even those patiently waiting on the page to be brought to life. Victorian reading was a communal, family affair at times. The Brontës read their works aloud to each other, not just left them with the other sisters to peruse at leisure. During these late evening sessions, each sister commented on the work of the others, and amendments were made accordingly, though 'Ellis Bell' was not anxious to make them. Neither M. Héger nor his pupils, however, could avoid listening to the extracts and hearing words from a sound point of view: they were not just 'reading for meaning' as the strange educational jargon has it, but reading for the sound and essence of the piece. Héger's personality entered the reading, without doubt. Emily's sharp ear caught it, and (dare one propose it?) some of the 'lineaments' of this 'insane tom-cat' may have merged with Heathcliff's.

M. Héger fully understood that he had an extraordinary personality in front of him. He compared her (chauvinistically, we might say now) to a *man*. He uses words like 'powerful reason', 'a head for logic', 'show of argument' (this perhaps a little slightingly), and talks of the vividness of her view of scenes and characters. Perhaps he had at this later stage read *Wuthering Heights*, but it is not certain and we must suppose much of this is based on his memories.

However, in contrast to the audial medium by which work was to be initiated and judged, Frederika Macdonald makes it clear that the medium for composition was written, and viewed as such: it was a *literary* style that was sought. She mentions six rules which M. Héger applied to the writing process.[8] Let us first take those with a strong written application. Rule 6 was 'One must not read, before sitting down to write, a great stylist with a marked manner

of his own; unless this manner happens to resemble one's own.'
Rule 5 was 'One must not fight with a difficult sentence; but take it
for a walk with one; or sleep with the thought of it present in one's
mind; and let the difficulty arrange itself while one looks on.'
Though Emily Brontë did wrestle with difficult sentences (we see
her doing so in the final parts of 'Why ask to know...?') often she
did leave incomplete poems to simmer in her mind. This was not
due to M. Héger's precept, however, because we have many examples of this from dates before Belgium.

The emphasis on style to be seen in rule 6 underlines what we
have said about Emily Brontë's Classical approach, despite her
Romantic inclinations, to the problem of perfecting expression.
The fourth maxim of M. Héger also dealt with style; he warns
against neglecting what the ear can hear as a fault in style, but
also against trusting the ear exclusively. Many alterations in the
poetry are made to avoid repetitions without meaning or intended
emphasis, but this process too begins before M. Héger's influence.
Héger's third maxim is harder to understand: 'one must never
tolerate the employment of a literary image as *an argument*. The
purpose of a literary image is to illuminate as a vision, and to
interpret as a parable. An image that does not serve both these
purposes is a fault in style.' A difficulty here is the understanding
of the word parable, which suggests a tight analogic relationship
akin to an argument. For the most part Emily Brontë appears to use
images to explore emotional weight rather than intellectual, but in
the French *Devoirs* she does seem to argue analogically.

Two maxims borrowed from Voltaire and turned into Héger's own
words complete the list. 'Il faut donner a son âme toutes les formes
possibles' and 'J'admets tous les genres, hors le genre ennuyeux.'
These do not deal specifically with writing technique, but they offer
an interesting additional light on Emily Brontë's learning in Belgium.
Finally, a series of invocations, which surely Emily remembered,
since they seem to surface in Anne's 'The Three Guides':

Esprit de Sagesse, conduissez-nous:
Esprit de Vérité, enseignez-nous:
Esprit de Charité, vivifiez-nous:
Esprit de Prudence, préservez-nous:
Esprit de Force, défendez-nous:
Esprit de Justice, éclairez-nous:
Esprit Consolateur, apaisez-nous.

Mme Héger confirmed this list to Frederika Macdonald for her 1916 book *The Secret of Charlotte Brontë*. Early in 1845 Emily wrote 'The Philosopher' in which she describes a spirit reconciling the streams of three rivers. This would not seem to have much to do with the foregoing invocation if it were not for Anne Brontë's 'The Three Guides', in which she serially invokes Spirit of Earth, Spirit of Pride and Spirit of Faith, and in each case makes a request of the invoked spirit. Other elements in Anne's poem seem to pick up the content of 'The Philosopher'. All M. Héger's lessons apparently began with this sevenfold prayer, not to a particularly Catholic God, but to eternal truths which sound Platonic.

It would clearly be useful to find outlined a theory of poetic inspiration adopted by Emily Brontë. We have already considered Horace's contribution to such a theory, but attempts to go further are severely hampered by lack of evidence and I do not wish to read into the poems what is not there. The precepts given above clearly relate to any form of composition, but this is perhaps thought of as dominated by prose. Both 'The Three Guides' and 'The Philosopher' are poems about life rather than about the subject of literary composition. M. Héger sees a total coherence between the two, but Emily Brontë is not able to do so, as the internal evidence of some poems suggests. A typical example is No. 9, with its third stanza,

> I asked my self O why has heaven
> Denied the precious gift to me
> The glorious gift to many given
> To speak their thoughts in poetry...

and the fifth stanza,

> But now when I had hoped to sing
> My fingers strike a tuneless string
> And still the burden of the strain
> Is strive no more 'tis all in vain[.][9]

Inspiration would not issue in poetry. However, this poem dates from August 1837, before Emily Brontë studied *Ars Poetica*.

Three poems from 1844 almost deal with the problem. They are Nos. 103 'My Comforter', 108 'To Imagination' and 110 'Plead for me'. In these poems, perhaps especially the last two mentioned,

Emily Brontë seems to be discussing her reliance on imagination, but she does not press this to the point where she translates her belief in inspiration to its material epiphany on paper. The poems themselves are more integrated than No. 9, but they do retain a strong element of conflict. No. 108 begins,

> When weary with the long day's care
> And earthly change from pain to pain
> And lost and ready to dispair
> Thy kind voice calls me back again –
> O my true friend, I am not lone
> While thou canst speak with such a tone!

Typically this poem is about something heard, not seen on a written page. M. Héger's inspirational prayers are not far away, but there is no answer to the question of transmission of these ideas to a blank sheet via pen and ink. No. 110 sees Imagination (though it is not named) as a kind of drug, whose influence may not be benign. On the one hand, she sees this entity as a 'Slave because I rule thee still', but yet it is also a King. Imagination is a 'Darling Pain that wounds and sears'. Certainly her Belgian experience is not responsible for producing thoughts of this kind; they are well documented in the early poems, of which No. 9 is a specimen. Although, according to Charlotte, at Roe Head school, which Emily attended very briefly for a few weeks in 1835, she encountered a life of 'disciplined routine' and fled from it, Emily was aware of the need for such a routine, or she would not have allowed herself to be persuaded to go to Brussels, but she certainly found it hard to sustain such a routine, and despite her formidable intellect, she does not write in an orderly fashion.[10]

It appears that the remaining manuscripts of French *Devoirs* are of two kinds: some are drafts in process, with M. Héger's comments on them, and some are fair copies. It appears that such copies were expected at the end of the composition period, and that M. Héger would retain these fair copies. One also gets the feeling that M. Héger softened his prescriptive attitude to subject matter as time went by. It really would be very useful, but it seems almost impossible, to know how exactly the subjects for composition were eventually chosen. We have one helpful comment from Mrs Gaskell, who talked to M. Héger concerning his use of Victor Hugo's description of Mirabeau. It is worth quoting Mrs Gaskell in full.

He told me that one day this summer [1842]...he read to them Victor Hugo's celebrated portrait of Mirabeau, 'mais, dans ma leçon je me bornais à ce qui concerne *Mirabeau Orateur.* C'est après l'analyse de ce morçeau, considéré surtout du point de vue du fond, de la disposition, de ce qu'on pourrait appeler *la charpente* qu'ont été faits les deux portraits que je vous donne.' He went on to say that he had pointed out to them the fault in Victor Hugo's style as being exaggeration in conception, and, at the same time, he had made them notice the extreme beauty of his 'nuances' of expression. They were then dismissed to choose the subject of a similar kind of portrait. This selection M. Heger always left to them; for 'it is necessary,' he observed, 'before sitting down to write on a subject, to have thoughts and feelings about it. I cannot tell on what subject your heart and mind have been excited. I must leave that to you.'[11]

After this lesson, Emily Brontë is said to have written her study of Harold before the battle of Hastings.

Charlotte Brontë transcribed sections of Hugo's 'Sur Mirabeau', though we cannot, of course, be sure that her transcriptions represent exactly what M. Héger read aloud. She focuses particularly on Sections III and VI of the essay. In Section VI Hugo contrasts Mirabeau as a speaker with Mirabeau as a writer.

It seems likely that the passage on which Emily Brontë based her portrait of Harold consisted of the paragraphs beginning 'Mirabeau à la tribune, c'est quelque chose de magnifique', and the following paragraph beginning 'Tout en lui était puissant'.[12] Read aloud by M. Héger, what in these paragraphs caught Emily's imagination sufficiently to be reflected in her *Devoir*, and to provide a model for her later writing? Three elements seem to be comparable. They are the heroic character of the principal figure, expressed in restless movement across the metaphorical stage; the contrast between his demeanour there and in other circumstances; and the rhetorical style in which all this is expressed. Each of these finds an echo in Emily Brontë's work.

The Brontës had been attracted since childhood to the solitary male hero, all the better if he were somewhat misunderstood. Possibly this derives from the well-known episode in childhood when Branwell was presented with a box of toy soldiers, and each child claimed a hero from among the set. The Gondal story is full of lonely men, slightly apart from their fellows, exiled or in position.[13]

Mirabeau would therefore appeal to Emily Brontë as an unusual hero, complex and deep, whose oratorical appeal wins friends despite objections and difficulties. These facets appear in her King Harold, who walks 'éloigné du camp' and dreams of the reasons for his superiority: 'une expression sublime illuminait son pale visage'; as in various places in the novel expressions convey a true or false impression of the inner musings of the character. Hugo stresses the difference between Mirabeau as a writer and as an orator. As an orator he is in his element; he has the assembly captivated by his speech, whereas when he is seen as a writer he is 'quelque chose de moins que Mirabeau'. His speech is like flowing water, frothing waves, sparkling firelight, a bird in flight (one simile piled on top of another). Hugo emphasises this contrast over and over again. Emily Brontë enjoyed contrasts. She too sees a different Harold facing real battle from the one cosseted in his study, surrounded by servants 'abimé en plaisirs, trompé par les flatteries'. The real hero comes into his own when he is freed from constraint and challenged by enemies. Neither Mirabeau nor Harold can be seen as a model for Julius Brenzaida or Heathcliff, but they both partake of the lonely, challenged quality that appears in both the Gondal and the Yorkshire hero. We can see how Emily Brontë adopts a favourite archetype in working on her *Devoir*, stimulated by M. Héger's reading about a powerful and singular Frenchman.

Thirdly, the Hugo passage is full of rhetoric. Emily Brontë does not follow out her exemplar closely in the *Devoir*, but she does try to please M. Héger by some elements of her sentence construction:

Harold, sur le champ de bataille, sans palais, sans ministres, sans courtisans, sans faste, sans luxe, n'ayant que le ciel de sa patrie au dessus de lui....
    Une multitude de passions humaines y éveillant en même temps, sont exaltées, sanctifiées, presque deifiées.

Such rhetoric is hardly new for Emily Brontë. A great deal of her English reading would contain similar structures. When she comes to write *Wuthering Heights* she adopts two voices which are very different in their oral patterns, those of Joseph and Nelly. Yet what we remember of the novel often centres on strong oral passages, bolstered by careful considerations of sound and pattern. It is anticipating our examination of *Wuthering Heights*, but still a good opportunity to look at a famous speech of Catherine's (and this powerful passage must be a *speech*; we can imagine no other successful method of conveying such material):

> 'This is nothing,' cried she; 'I was only going to say that heaven did not seem to be my home; and I broke my heart with weeping to come back to earth; and the angels were so angry that they flung me out, into the middle of the heath on the top of Wuthering Heights; where I woke sobbing for joy. That will do to explain my secret, as well as the other. I've no more business to marry Edgar Linton than I have to be in heaven; and if the wicked man in there had not brought Heathcliff so low, I shouldn't have thought of it. It would degrade me to marry Heathcliff, now; so he shall never know how I love him; and that, not because he's handsome, Nelly, but because he's more myself than I am. Whatever our souls are made of, his and mine are the same, and Linton's is as different as a moonbeam from lightning, or frost from fire.'[14]

This is sharp, clear, lively. It conveys the feeling of natural speech with the colloquial 'I was only going to say...', 'I've no more business...' the interjection at a crucial point of the vocative, 'Nelly'. These carefully chosen colloquial features persuade us that a country girl is speaking. They reflect Emily Brontë's sharp ear and her sustained thought about oral language. But rhetorical contrasts are also an important part of the structure of this paragraph. Everywhere there are comparisons and balances. 'I've no more business...*than*...'; '...*if* the wicked man in there...I shouldn't have thought of it'; 'he's more myself than I am'. Some of this patterning may go back to working from a Latin grammar, but the tuition of M. Héger, examining the craftsmanship of Hugo, appears to have had its effect.

The final sentence is not, when we come to think of it, a typical utterance of a country girl in a farm kitchen, either in content or construction. We have the accurate positioning of 'his and mine' in the first half of a compound sentence, with Linton pushed into the second half; we have the double image in part two, emphasising and balancing the double in 'his and mine', we have the pivotal 'and', and the progression from vague concessive ('What*ever*') to sharp image ('fire'). Such a sentence is a product of very thorough linguistic exploration and practice, to which M. Héger's forceful tuition on rhetoric (part accepted by Emily and part rejected) has contributed as much as her ear for common speech and her study of Horace on imagery and appropriateness.

Emily Brontë did not go back to Brussels with Charlotte after returning for Aunt Branwell's funeral. One could look at this action in several ways. We know now that Charlotte had particular motives for going back to where she could be near M. Héger. Emily plainly did not share those motives, but perhaps her refusal to go back suggests more. As Charlotte said in a letter to Ellen Nussey (May 1842), 'Emily and he don't draw well together at all.' In the same letter she describes Emily as working 'like a horse', but though this was doubtless the case, the immediate direction of M. Héger and his continual criticism seems unlikely to have made Emily more subservient.[15] Opposition (as she saw it) generally hardened her will.

Whereas for Charlotte the experience of French culture is felt positively in her novels, this does not seem true for Emily. When she returns to Haworth she is seen to be reading German books in the kitchen, not French ones. In 'No coward soul', she damns the 'thousand creeds' that have exerted influence against her instinctive belief in a supernatural power, albeit a pantheistic one. One of those creeds may well be Catholicism as she saw it in Belgium. If anything, her antipathy towards authority perhaps receives impetus from this experience.

On the other hand, her work on her poetic vocation is not set back by M. Héger's classical methods, and Emily clearly recognises a common background with that of Horace, the master she has chosen for herself. M. Héger's insistence on a rhetorical model, his enthusiasm for the 'charpente' of language, were not lost on Emily; she saw the value of this approach, and doubtless this is why she worked 'like a horse' as Charlotte's letter puts it. After Belgium, Emily's craftsmanship intensifies. Her thirst for knowledge and understanding is far from declining. Her dedication to the art of poetry remains paramount, despite the call of Gondal invention. The poems of the year following the return home are a mixed group, of which the Gondal ones do not suggest great progress in poetic technique, but a few do seem to give evidence of greater confidence. For example, 'Self-Interrogation' (No. 93) involves a poetic dialogue of a kind found also in Anne's work, but well-handled and still recognising the primacy of labour, yet its weary frustrations too ('...labour hardly done – ...little gained at vast expense...'). This sounds like the poet whose craftsmanship is uppermost in her mind, the sculptor of Charlotte's description of her sister, rather than the inspired Romantic prophet.

5

Organisational Skill: The Poems from 1844 to 1846

We have already looked at the content of Emily Brontë's poems, confirming the view that there was a distinction in her mind between Gondal poems and non-Gondal. We need now to revisit the work of copying to see how Emily Brontë's mind was moving in the years between Belgium and the birth of *Wuthering Heights*. The question to be addressed is *how* she organised poetry on the page and in the notebooks, making the assumption that a major classification is implied by the division into two notebooks as shown by our previous discussion.

Derek Roper has made the most recent investigation of the order in which poems are transcribed into A and B manuscripts, and I shall base my comments in part on his work.[1] Before looking at this aspect of her arrangement, we need to consider another characteristic of Emily's approach to poetry, and I shall further precede this by a reminder about what we actually have as evidence.

The two copy books A and B are certain to have been begun in February 1844. A is unavailable to the public, but has been photographed well on at least two occasions. It is not possible that the heading 'Transcribed Febuary 1844' (sic) could be faked. B is in the British Library, frequently on view in a showcase, and can clearly be seen to be headed with words which include 'Transcribed Febuary 1844' (again the mis-spelling). In almost all cases in A manuscript, the date is written above the poem (there seem to be two exceptions) and there are no initials to record the fictional 'writer' of the poem. These are Emily's own, written *in propria persona*. Most of the poems in B also have dates, and indeed many of the earlier poems, not copied from earlier manuscripts, are also dated in Emily's hand.

Dates, then, are important to Emily Brontë (and indeed to her siblings). In the Gondal poems Gondal dramatic or internal dates are occasionally added both by Emily and Anne after a clear chronology has been worked out, beginning in 1841 and at least seven years after Gondal had been created. But Gondal poems were not written in order of Gondal date; like *Wuthering Heights* the Gondal narrative (so far as we can dimly trace it) ranges over time now forwards, now back, just as in *The Aeneid* there are flashbacks and forward leaps. In other words, epic arrangement is not linear, adhering to the reality of human consciousness in recalling and forecasting time rather than dealing with it in linear mode. Emily and Anne did the same in Gondal, imposing a rigid timescale on the material only after committing it to paper. This is because they live partly in Gondal, their minds developing already existing events and occasions, not simply forging ahead into the linear future.

It seems possible that Emily felt a tension between linear time and the time of the mind. She is always impressed by time, has to be reminded of it, and then reacts. This is evident in the 1834 diary paper where Emily records that it is 'past Twelve o'clock' but she and Anne 'have not tidied ourselv[e]s, done our bedwork [or] done our lessons' (sic).[2] Time passes in a dream for these two whose characters are 'discovering the interior of Gaaldine', yet every now and then they make an effort to link with local time in Haworth. This interest in time and chronology is not totally alien to them: the whole idea of marking anniversaries with diary papers seems congenial and natural. The celebrated 1837 diary paper is littered with times and dates: headed by a date, it calculates the exact age of the four young Brontës in four years' time, gives the date of Queen Victoria's coronation, and reiterates the time of day ('4 o'clock'). Emily Brontë is shown as conscious of local time and yet willing to annul time in imagination and memory. This whole syndrome of responses is very clear in *Wuthering Heights*.

Amazingly, the word 'time' in the poems can attract an inappropriate initial capital (e.g. poems 105, 112, 116 in Derek Roper's edition). It is not quite the only word to do so (most appear to be abstract nouns), but the initial may be significant. To Emily Brontë (and perhaps her siblings) 'Time' is a concept to be explored. As we shall see, in *Wuthering Heights* Emily Brontë does not seem to realise at first how necessary close chronological control is going to be. But the workings of time are a subject for the novel, and after a while she understands the importance of the accuracy of her frame. As often in the case of literary composition, we need to look for a cause in personal experience, this time the proximity of the chiming church clock.

In the poem manuscripts under discussion (and probably some earlier manuscripts) poems are grouped by subject. Derek Roper analyses the way in which this happens.[3] In the non-Gondal manuscript, he shows, there is first a section on moorland scenery and 'Earth', then a short Stoic section, then a section on an apparently lost lover. Other topics follow. But within the subject grouping it seems that the poet wanted a specific order to prevail. Over No. 84 she has written a number '2' and over the following poem '1'; Derek Roper considers this is to correct an inappropriate order. Both the inappropriateness and the correction are typical. Emily is initially inclined to be careless about time, but then wakes up to its importance. She enforces the rule of time upon a reluctant artist. There is a similar example in the Gondal manuscript.

This process of intellectual discipline in arranging her work is obviously important to Emily Brontë. There is a good deal of 'untidiness' in her approach to creativity, but again and again we encounter this intellectual organisation, questioning order and arrangement. This has already been shown and discussed in the content of the poems, and the topic will be thoroughly explored when we get to the novel. Despite her ritual objection to M. Héger's point about the need for practice as well as inspiration, she is extremely well aware of the need for tight control of form. What does emerge, however, is her reluctance to be thoroughgoing in her planning at the beginning. She certainly does not sketch out the way in which she will order the notebooks, and it is only in retrospect that she changes the order to comply with a plan that has emerged during the interplay between imagination and structuring.

I should now like to reconsider a small Gondal fragment which may constitute useful evidence on how Emily Brontë thought about fiction and its creation. As has been noted on many occasions the dramatic basis of Gondal story was sometimes acting by the sisters, first as children, but carrying on into adult life. So in 1845, when Emily and Anne went to York, on the journey they 'were' Juliet Augusteena, Rosabella Esmalden and others. Fictional actions simply arose in this way, and were added to the story at an appropriate point. How far such episodes were written up is unsure.

A question might be asked, how did Juliet Augusteena come into existence? Part of the answer lies in the inspiration of such moments as the journey to York. But in the fragment mentioned, we see such characters in a very early stage of development. Later, it will be suggested that Nelly Dean appears from nowhere in mid-1845, and that her creation solves major problems in both the plot and the narrative mode of the novel. The fragment I wish to discuss is manuscript D 8, which contains a short list of characters which we may reasonably suppose to be part of Gondal, and which has small fragments of writing from various periods on it.[4] It seems likely that the list in question dates from 21 August 1839, a period of fruitful work with the Law Hill experience in mind.

Five characters are listed on this small fragment. They may all be Stewarts, written as 'Stwart'. The two men have this surname added to their first names, 'Ronald Stwart' and 'Marcellus Stwart'. The three women, Regina, Flora and Francesca, do not have a surname appended, and indeed Marcellus receives his surname only as an afterthought. Each name is followed by a date, which may be the character's birthday. One can see Emily and Anne sometimes celebrating such birthdays and possibly even keeping a calendar of Gondal anniversaries. The importance of enduing these characters with chronological exactness is here built into the characterisation. Physical details are next given. This remains important for Emily Brontë in both poetry and novel; in the present case it is reasonable to suppose that the cryptic 'Brown H' stands for 'brown hair'.

Emily Brontë does not keep the columns of her abbreviated characteristics in line, and each character tails off at the end of the row so that we are left uncertain what the final details are about. This shows her usual infuriating mixture of order and muddle. Symbols are used without any key (this is quite understandable, as she most certainly was not producing this list for later enquirers). We can be fairly certain that '–6–' means '6 feet tall' and the next character's '–5 7–' will mean '5' 7″ tall'. Two characters have small drawings of castles towards the end of the row and this must mean that these people live in castles; but the others have a gap at that point, so we are unsure whether Emily would have come back and drawn a house or cottage by them.

There are unexplained asterisks and in one case a strange symbol which looks rather like the sign for dangerous electricity. This symbol is unparalleled in other cases, and we do not know what it could stand for. Its cryptic nature, however, as well as the allusive nature of the whole list, makes a valuable point about

Emily Brontë's mind: much of her thought is subterranean and closely guarded. Still, we can see how she works towards a clarification of the characters she is inventing. Physical appearance, height, age, where they live: all this is important. Nothing seems to be related to their trade or wealth, their politics or pets, and we cannot be sure exactly who is married to whom.

At the end of the list comes a treble colophon similar to those between poems in the manuscripts. This indicates that Emily has finished what she wants to write. She adds '21 Aug' laconically, and takes the small scrap of paper with her to use later for writing poetry. We note the emphasis on character: plotting is not a concern. As in *Wuthering Heights* events happen to people because of who they are, making narrative an unpredictable consideration. This is entirely consistent with what we have seen in the poems: static or timeless impressions are the root of Emily Brontë's imagining, and she sees in her mind's eye events happen to the characters, which her rational mind then has to shape into a story.

This scrap of paper was apparently taken to Belgium and back, a silent witness to Emily's concern with Gondal amidst the distractions of M. Héger's rhetorical approach. It returned to Haworth, and played its part in the reorganisation of poems in the 1844 notebooks. The emphasis in 1844 was certainly on Gondal. Thirteen poems were begun and completed that year (we have no unfinished scraps though 'The day is done' (102) exists only on a small sheet and is not recopied into the Gondal notebook). Of these 13, eight are in the B manuscript and are Gondal poems, four are in the A manuscript and are not Gondal, and one is the uncopied poem just mentioned. In addition, 'The death of A.G.A.' was finished in May 1844 and adds length and weight to the Gondal tally. As an exercise in how to deal with narrative, it may well have added to Emily Brontë's understanding, but it is an imperfect poem.

Two poems of the eight Gondal are concerned with A.G.A., who dies in May. Consciously restoring her in December, Emily Brontë writes in a dramatic date, 'Sept 1826', but without a precise day. Almanacks, which will soon be used to validate dates in the past, are not yet in evidence. A.G.A. apparently refuses to die in Emily's mind; a year later still she will be reincarnated as A.G. Rochelle in the prison poem we have already considered. These poems of 1844 are in copied form, completed and smoothed, as though Emily is preparing for presentation once again (as she seems to be doing in the early part of 1839). But just like *Wuthering Heights* they involve characters being killed and reborn. Just so does Catherine haunt Heathcliff on a spiritual plane and bequeath many of her characteristics to a younger Catherine, her daughter.

After the poem on A.G.A.'s death, Emily Brontë collected miscellaneous Gondal poems in her transcript book, then began to copy in other poems as they were composed, as we can see by the completion dates. This was a process of systematisation not completely coherent, but paving the way for work on publishable material. Even though according to Charlotte's account the impetus for such work came from her, the conscientious editing and arrangement of these poems in 1844 shows that Emily Brontë (and Anne was proceeding in a similar way) had glimpsed a possibility of authorship and was beginning again to see how her poems could be groomed for entry into such a world. One must therefore doubt the precise terms of Charlotte's account of the beginning of the publishing enterprise, though it seems probable that when the moment of revelation came, Emily shrank from it and tried to obstruct it.

We need now to digress from a chronological approach to discuss the poem edition of 1846. Unlike *Wuthering Heights* the published poems do have an observable manuscript source, the two notebooks we have been examining, manuscripts A and B. It is possible that traces of the way in which these were prepared for transcription to be sent to the publisher may be visible. We need to look at this possibility to see whether this will throw any light on Emily Brontë's methods, including ways in which she might have edited her manuscript of her novel.

There has been some controversy about how far Emily cooperated with Charlotte in the production of the poem selection. In *The Library* (sixth series, No. 6, 1984) Derek Roper discusses the controversy and examines the changes apparent in the 1846 edition when compared with the A and B texts.[5] This was a pioneering article, but as I wish to take the matter in a slightly different direction, I shall not quote from it in the present context. I shall first look at Charotte Brontë's evidence about the circumstances of the revision, then turn to the manuscripts and the 1846 text for comparisons.

The paragraph in which Charlotte describes the beginning of the poem project is well known:

One day, in the autumn of 1845, I accidentally lighted on a MS volume of verse in my sister Emily's handwriting. Of course, I was not surprised, knowing that she could and did write verse: I looked it over, and something more than surprise seized me, – a deep conviction that these were not common effusions, not at all like the poetry women generally write. I thought them condensed and terse, vigorous and genuine. To my ear, they also had a peculiar music – wild, melancholy, and elevating.

My sister Emily was not a person of demonstrative character, nor one, on the recesses of whose mind and feelings, even those nearest to her could, with impunity, intrude unlicensed; it took hours to reconcile her to the discovery I had made, and days to persuade her that such poems merited publication. I knew, however, that a mind like hers could not be without some latent spark of honourable ambition, and refused to be discouraged in my attempts to fan that spark to flame.

Later, I shall suggest that one reason why Emily was unwilling to divert her attention back to poetry was that *Wuthering Heights* had now reached an interesting and compulsive stage. Meanwhile, Charlotte's account evinces reluctance on Emily's part to the point where we can say that 'for days' she refused to cooperate. On the other hand, publication *per se* was not necessarily against Emily's inclination; the 1839 fair-copy (Manuscript C) in her cursive hand seems evidence that she had contemplated this, and the three-novel work on which the sisters were cooperating appears already to have been intended to be published. The difficulty is to know how far the alterations made to the poems in the A and B manuscripts when they appeared in the 1846 edition were due to Emily and how far to Charlotte's influence, if not her actual composition. Some of these alterations may represent 'Emily Brontë at work' but some may merely show the determination of Charlotte to present printable poems.

In the 1850 poem edition, and the corresponding version of *Wuthering Heights*, Charlotte introduced changes which must be hers. There are words written on the poem manuscripts which are identifiably in Charlotte's handwriting. This shows that she had no scruples in modifying her sister's work to take account of what she thought the public would want to read. The problem is that there is no way of telling precisely what influence she exercised in modifying the poems for 1846. We shall deal with these alterations as if they were Emily's, but in the knowledge that Charlotte may well have had an input.

Twenty-one poems were chosen for 1846, taken from manuscripts A and B. A number of different kinds of modification appears, including indentation, closing unclosed inverted commas, capitalisation or decapitalisation, and where necessary, deGondalisation of poems from the B manuscript. If we exclude these changes, there seem to be about 78 substantive alterations from manuscript to printed forms. Hardly any of these changes were made on the A or B manuscripts themselves. At which points they were made is unclear. Possibly they were even made in the final copy for the publisher, as there are still changes in Charlotte's handwriting in the manuscript of *The Professor*.

There could be various ways of classifying the changes made to Emily's poems at this time. We have to judge by the effect such changes make on the modern reader; we have no notes to explain from the poet's point of view why she changed her poems. It appears to me that the changes could be classified as follows: changes for the sake of *elegance, linguistic accuracy, strengthening, softening, clarification of an ambiguity, sound, consistency,* and a group where changes seem to be substantive and indicate a change of meaning. Most of these groups are small, and in some cases perhaps several motives are at work.

Take a substantive change to 'Stanzas', 'I'll not weep that thou art going to leave me...' (No. 75). In stanza 3 the manuscript reads:

> And I am weary of the anguish
> Increasing winters bear –
> I'm sick to see the spirit languish
> Through years of dead dispair

Line 3 is emended to 'Weary to watch the spirit languish' for the 1846 edition. The new version picks up the 'weary' of line 1, and increases the incidence of the mournful letter W. Perhaps 'sick' is also too abrupt and even perhaps unpoetic. The aim of the change seems to be to make the poem more cohesive, smoother and less startling. It is not clear whether this is a real improvement or not, and readers will doubtless hold divergent views. There is no sign of an alteration in the manuscript. We could categorise this change as for 'elegance' or for a softening process.

In 'Self-Interrogation' ('The evening passes fast away', No. 93) there are no fewer than 13 changes. The final stanza is much altered. In the manuscript it reads:

> The long fight closing in defeat,
> Defeat serenely borne –
> Thine eventide may still be sweet –
> Thy night, a glorious morn –

In the 1846 edition, with indentations and inverted commas, the stanza looks very different:

> 'The long war closing in defeat,
> Defeat serenely borne,
> Thy midnight rest may still be sweet,
> And break in glorious morn!'

The aim of the changes seems to be to soften the stanza, making it more conventionally elegant. In line 1 *fight/defeat* is harsh, but it does represent a clash in a way which Emily Brontë's instinctive ear approved. The word 'rest' in the later version of line 3 seems clarificatory, a softening and explanatory addition. The oxymoron in the final line is gone; the new text hints at resurrection instead of inversion. In the case of this stanza, the meaning itself is radically altered by the softening, civilising process. Derek Roper restores manuscript punctuation to these 1846 poems, while retaining the 1846 text, an interesting attempt at compromise.

There are other alterations to this poem, 13 in all (though quantifying changes in these poems is not easy, and the number will depend on the method of counting). Noticeably, there are no alterations at all in stanzas 1–3. The fourth stanza yields a number of changes, and it is worth noting that the stanza had caused Emily Brontë trouble before, to judge by changes visible in the manuscript. Line 3 seems to begin as 'Yet weak Repentance clouds my eyes', goes through a stage of 'still weak Repentance clouds mine eyes' in the manuscript, and ends in the 1846 version as 'Still, sad Repentance clouds my eyes'. The comma is helpful in determining the grammatical function of 'Still', which could possibly have been an adjective in the manuscript text. 'Still' is effectively taking the place of 'Yet' in Emily's first thought. The second change, 'my' to 'mine' back to 'my', is also a problem of grammar or word-form.

This line shows alterations very different from those of the previously quoted stanza.

Stanza six of the same poem ends with the couplet (in the 1846 text)

> ["]And where thy heart has suffered so,
> Canst thou desire to dwell?"

This appears in the manuscript as

> And where thy heart has suffered so
> Say would'st thou longer dwell.

This initial version is changed in the final manuscript version to the same text, verbally, as in 1846, but the change seems likely to have been made at the copying stage, not during revision for 1846.

Stanza nine contains another interesting change, made for purposes of clarification. The manuscript reads: 'Well thou hast fought for many a year'. This becomes: ' "Well, thou hast fought for many a year" ', turning the 'Well' from an adverb into an interjection. Again, the effect seems to be to soften the poem, and the pause makes a difference to the sound in reading it. Whether this final version is better or worse for the change is a moot point, but I do not see how it gains. In stanza eleven there is a further alteration which we shall take as the final example from this poem. The second couplet was published as

> It is endurance not to weep,
> If that repose seem woe.

The manuscript text is

> 'Twill be endurance not to weep
> If that repose be woe[.]

As in the final stanza we have an oxymoron softened. In the first line of the couplet it is not sure that 'It is' helps the line. It may be clearer, and less archaising, but the sense of the poem seems to require the future tense, which has been lost in the change.

A further selection of the 'softening' alterations may be worth looking at. Poem No. 95 ('How clear she shines') is interesting because one of the alterations subsequently adopted for the 1846 edition appears in Brontë small script as a correction in the manuscript, apparently made later than the copying of the original text. This is in line 2. The poem begins:

> How clear she shines! How quietly
> I lie beneath her silver light…

But the word 'gardian' has been written in, in handwriting which can hardly be anyone else's but Emily's (despite the fact that there are some words in this manuscript that are by Charlotte, dating, it seems, from her 1850 revision). It is worth noting here that there is a title ('Hope') added to No. 99 ('Hope was but a timid friend') also unequivocally added by Emily Brontë after the copy had been made. These two changes are the best evidence that the editorial process leading to publication in 1846 gained at least some of Emily's attention.

A second change in 'How clear she shines' is not visible in the manuscript. At this point we need to be cautious, recalling that the A manuscript is known only in photographs. They are excellent photographs, however, and it seems very unlikely that a word inserted in the text by Emily, even in pencil, would not show up in them. The change under consideration is in line 10, where the original reads 'Grim world, go hide thee till the day…' and the 1846 version 'Grim world, conceal thee till the day'. This seems a softening change, 'go hide' possibly having a provincial ring to it, the surely weaker 'conceal' fitting in with the kind of change Charlotte was later to make to *Wuthering Heights*. Emily's 'gardian' light is not so clearly softening 'silver' and indeed may be seen as adding a new dimension to the poem.

Four changes are made to 'A Day Dream' (No. 105). In lines 35 and 36 'its' and 'the' are reversed, so that 'Before a token of the fall/Is on its surface seen' becomes 'Before a token of its fall/Is on the surface seen'. Just possibly this avoids a colloquial use of 'Fall' to mean 'autumn'. In line 40, 'A thousand thousand glancing fires' used of the starry vision reported by the poet becomes 'A thousand thousand gleaming fires'. I cannot see an improvement here. The poet alone knows what her original vision should be compared with, but 'glancing' has speedier movement and seems to make perfectly good sense as the poet stetches herself on the moor and looks up above her. A change in 'To Imagination' (No. 108) also seems to soften the sense. In line 16 an 'unsullied sky' becomes an 'untroubled' sky. However, in line 14 of the same poem a change from *greif* to *guilt* has the effect of changing the stanza's meaning as the couplet finally presented is

> What matters it, that, all around
> Danger, and guilt, and darkness lie...

This is one of a small number of changes which actually alter the sense, another interesting one being in 'Faith and Despondency' (No. 111) where in line 22 'speechless pain' becomes 'hopeless pain'.

Returning to 'A Day Dream', an alteration is made in the form of the past tense of 'ring' and 'sing', the 1846 text reading

> And, while the wide earth echoing rung
> To their strange minstrelsy,
> The little glittering spirits sung,
> O [for 'Or'] seemed to sing, to me.

The manuscript forms of the verb are 'sang' and 'rang', which would be acceptable in twentieth-century English.

A number of changes involve altering plural to singular, apparently for clarification. Thus in 'Faith and Despondency' (No. 111) *Pillows* becomes *pillow* and in the same poem *roots* becomes *root*. It should be emphasised that none of these changes occurs on the manuscript we actually have, and they must have been introduced at a later state. Among alterations made for the sound, we note in 'Stanzas' (No. 75) a change from 'It closes with the tomb' to 'It closes with a tomb' (line 8), which appears to help a reader struggling to pronounce the double 'th'.

We cannot deal with all the editorial changes in this chapter. Enough have now been quoted to show the kinds of revision made during this process. It remains to discuss the evidence to determine how far these revisions represent Emily Brontë's poetic intentions, and how far they are governed by external factors, such as the need to please Charlotte, the publisher or the public. Such matters are germane to a discussion of how *Wuthering Heights* was prepared for publication during its final revision in 1846–7.

We have already established in earlier chapters that Emily Brontë frequently revised her poems (one is tempted to substitute a stronger phrase such as 'tinkered endlessly'). Examples have been given of immediacy lost in this process, but under the influence of such writers as Horace and demanding teachers like M. Héger improving changes are also made at times. The impetus for these changes seems generally to be the improvement, as Emily sees it, of the artifact. She has considered publication, we may consider, citing as evidence the cursive manuscript C, dating almost certainly from 1839. Now she is faced with the certainty of her work being seen by a remote publisher. She is being directed by Charlotte, as our quotation from Charlotte's own account shows, and she may well be fretting because this process is taking her away from composing her novel. It is a matter of judgement how far she cooperated willingly in this whole enterprise. Charlotte told Mrs Gaskell that she herself did not change what she had written (or at least 'seldom' did so) because of objections by the other sisters.[4] Emily's will was as strong as Charlotte's, to put the matter at its lowest.

Most of the alterations adopted in the 1846 text are not visible in A or B manuscripts. We have noted a good example of one that is so visible, 'gardian' in 'How clear she shines', and there are some titles. In addition to 'Hope' (No. 99) there is 'My Comforter' (No. 103) and 'To Imagination' (No. 108). Some titles used in 1846 are not in the manuscripts. Most alterations added in 1846 must have been made in another copy. We may suggest that Emily began the revision process on the two existing manuscripts, which she was still using to copy new poems on, and carried on the process on other paper, possibly rewriting the poems entirely, though we have no evidence for this.

There is an important point to raise, to which no clear answer can be given, and which does not materially affect how Emily Brontë revised *Wuthering Heights*. In whose handwriting were the 1846 poem texts finally presented? There seem to be several possibilities. Charlotte saw the poem edition, as she initially saw the production of the three novels, as a joint enterprise. The poems are arranged as a collection by three authors, each poem being identified by a name at the foot, Currer, Ellis or Acton. The order of the poems seems to be thematic, and at any rate it does not separate the three; the poems are interspersed. We might consider the practicalities of producing a text based on this kind of arrangement. Three separate sets of poems could have been sent to the publisher, leaving him to interleave the contents; the poems could have been sent to him in three different hands, interspersed as required; or they could have been written in one hand, in the correct order.

The first two methods involve complications. Though Charlotte was prepared, judging by the state of her existing novel manuscripts, to allow a publisher to work his way through emendations added near the original words, at least she put the leaves of the manuscript in the correct order. If the balanced arrangement of the 1846 text is authorial, as it surely must be, then she could hardly expect to present Aylott and Jones with three sets of poems with instructions as to how to order them. If the poems were in the published order in the manuscript, however, as surely they must have been, it would have been quite complicated for each sister to write her poem in turn before handing on the booklet to the next one. Such a rotation of the copy would have taken time. It could possibly have been done, for instance, during one of the Brontë conference sessions after nine o'clock in the evening, but even so the finished work would have presented a piebald appearance and might not have impressed a publisher favourably.

If neither of these alternatives seems likely, then Charlotte must have copied the whole text in her own writing. From the start she espoused the role of entrepreneur in the whole proceeding. So she did in the case of the novels until mid-1846, when they were rejected for the second, or possibly third time. After this there was a change, and Emily worked more closely with Anne, an echo of the change which had taken place earlier in their lives when Angria gave place to Gondal. If it is agreed that Charlotte did undertake the final copying task, it is quite possible that she introduced textual changes. In particular, some of the 'softening' and 'regularising' changes we have just examined may possibly be Charlotte's work, the work of an interpreter, going nowhere near as far as she did after her sisters' deaths, when she revised *Wuthering Heights* for the 1850 edition, but still with the idea of mediating the work of her sisters, especially Emily, to the public.

As we have seen, several changes later adopted in 1846 do occur in Emily's own writing in the A or B manuscripts, but most do not. Those that do show Emily wishing to improve her work artistically, but do not provide evidence of a temporising Emily, complying with a publisher's suggestions. Later, as we shall see, a crisis over *Wuthering Heights* faced her with the choice of remaining adamant and blocking Anne's opportunity to be published, or modifying her book. On the occasion of the 1846 printing, the choice was less stark. We might be justified in believing some of the changes to the A and B texts which appear in the published version have Emily's total acceptance, but it would be hard to be completely certain which she approved, which she suggested, and which she let go for the sake of the joint enterprise.

In one sense, as we are trying to discern the influences on Emily Brontë's handling of the final presentation of *Wuthering Heights* it does not matter how far the changes to the 1846 edition are her own or have her total backing (though it would be important if a poem text were in prospect). Whatever compromises she made in *Wuthering Heights* are foreshadowed here in the changes made before the poems could reach their public. Emily Brontë 'at work' includes Emily Brontë compromising with her sisters and with her publishers, even if in the case of so strong-willed an artist, such compromise is very strictly limited.

Part II
Wuthering Heights

6
Wuthering Heights: The Problem

We now arrive at the climax of our discussion of Emily Brontë's working methods. Our aim is to arrive at an informed view of the ways in which *Wuthering Heights* took shape in the light of the evidence so far adduced for Emily's attitudes to composition and having regard to the circumstances in which she found herself at the time of this composition, and the general aims of the three sisters, especially Emily and Anne. There has always been controversy about the nature of *Wuthering Heights*, from the days when early critics noted its power but saw in it the roughness of immaturity. Soon after this Charlotte defended the novel despite what appeared to be its faults.[1]

In 1926 C.P. Sanger discovered complex chronology underlying the confusion, and since then critics have tended to see a carefully organised work in which all the apparent problems have an intended solution and where the intellectual control of the author is paramount and exact.[2] In *Charlotte Brontë* E. F. Benson suggests that Emily had a change of mind during the production of the book, and that this led to anomalies that cannot be explained away.[3] In her 1969 essay, 'A Fresh Approach to "Wuthering Heights"', Q.D. Leavis raised the issue of what she calls a 'false start' based on King Lear, and refers to a previous essay in *Brontë Society Transactions* in which the first part of the novel is said to be different in style from most of the book. (This feeling of discrepancy may be one reason why there has been a minority view that Branwell had some hand in the initial stages of the novel.)[4]

In *Brontë Facts and Brontë Problems* Tom Winnifrith gave reasons for thinking that the book may have been rewritten and expanded before publication.[5] This point will now be followed up, continuing to advance evidence about working practices, the chronology of the lives of the Brontës during 1844–7, further topographical data and careful examination of the text to support Winnifrith's thesis and to suggest in detail how the current text was arrived at. There certainly *are* unresolved anomalies in the text, they can be used to show how it was written, but they do not preclude placing the book in the highest rank of fiction.

One structural point is worth noting before beginning to examine evidence more closely. The binary nature of the book (it is full of dualism) extends to a repetition in the second half of the book of the growth from childhood of a character called Catherine who is never as strong as her predecessor. Other second-generation characters also seem tamer; they shadow the great first-generation figures. On the whole, commentators on the book spend a great deal more space, *pro rata*, on the first half of the book and its figures and events. There is actually some difference in structural technique between the two halves. Film-makers often go so far as to omit all or most of the second part. They see the story concerning the relationship during and after life between Heathcliff and Catherine as the vital theme. Of course, they miss an extremely important element of the book as published and as on mature reflection conceived by its author. But one of my assertions in the following pages will be that, though Emily Brontë's concern with duality was visible throughout her early version of the book, her exploration of the life of a second Catherine was only made possible by a change of plan forced on her and Anne after the original version had been submitted and rejected.

Some readers may be deeply affronted by the suggestion that the version we now have of *Wuthering Heights* was not in Emily Brontë's mind when she started. But I have tried to show that in her narrative poems the final version was hardly, if ever, present when she started. In one sense Emily Brontë wrote quite quickly and at white heat; but she often re-read and redeveloped her own work, seeing further implications after she had put her first thoughts on paper. Critics are perfectly right to comment on *Wuthering Heights* as we have it in print; they are not obliged to account for the ways in which it was produced in a mixture of inspiration, doubt, sustained joy and then perhaps frustration leading to a major intellectual effort. Yet the perception of the popularisers and academic critics is to some extent united, as will be shown. The problem of the differences in tone between the first and second parts of the novel has been shelved and worse, not even noted. In the following pages some attempt will be made to address it.

Unlike the work we have been examining so far, there are no extant manuscripts of *Wuthering Heights* and no plans, notes or external information to be gleaned from notebooks. We cannot draw detailed analogies from other prose works, since the Gondal saga common to Emily and Anne has not survived. It would be fair, however, to invoke the knowledge we have now gained of Emily's earlier work habits to illuminate what she planned in *Wuthering Heights* and deduce how she proceeded. It is more contentious to compare Emily's novelistic aims and procedure with those of her two sisters, though this has been done incautiously. From the very first commentators on Brontë novels looked for originals, especially after Mrs Gaskell's *The Life of Charlotte Brontë* directed attention towards the three sisters' own lives.[6] In the case of *Wuthering Heights* these originals were hard to discover, and this led to attempts to suppose that Heathcliff had a basis in Branwell or other absurdity. One such 'original' which seems to have no basis, but has an enduring mythological life of its own is the identification of the rambling mansion of the Earnshaws with Top Withens near Haworth.

But all the Brontës used imagination based on the world around them, and Emily is no exception. Like the others, she had sharp observation and an almost unbelievable memory. It is quite fair to look for stimulus to her imagination from the surrounding world as well as books she read. One clear law of Emily's thought is her reluctance to abandon anything she has shown interest in; there is always more to be extracted from any scene, situation or personality. Another law of her thought, perhaps encouraged by the epic tradition of Virgil, is the strange flexibility of time, in which events recur slightly altered, cast their shadows before and comment on their previous occurrence. Muriel Spark, who had studied Emily Brontë carefully, used this aspect of her work brilliantly in *The Prime of Miss Jean Brodie*.[7]

My aim in this section will be to set out a careful chronology of the writing of the novel, showing the relation between Charlotte's ambition to procure financial stability by writing and Emily's inner exploration of conflict. It is hoped at the end to provide a likely month-by-month account of the book's progress from the original idea to the submission of the novels to Henry Colburn in July 1846 and beyond. Readers need to be reminded that the novels considered by Colburn cannot have been the texts as known now, and when they were wholly or partly rejected by a second publisher Charlotte and Emily both rewrote their books, though it seems that

Anne did not. This, of course, has implications for Charlotte's view of Anne, and also throws some light on Anne's rather surprising confidence which can be seen on several occasions between 1846 and her death. For those who did not follow the arguments in Tom Winnifrith's earlier discussion, his points will be reviewed.

Throughout this proceeding it is necessary to move with caution. Of the deducible events and stages of the production of *Wuthering Heights* some can be fixed with fair accuracy, others involve conjecture. At some points, therefore, this account is firmer than at others. I shall try to leave readers in no doubt precisely what is the evidence and what are the arguments I am using. It needs to be stressed that Brontë documents relating to biography other than those preserved by Charlotte and her friends are very scanty. Emily claimed never to have written a proper letter.[8] This was not strictly true, but the impression that the Brontës were recluses, wrong in the case of Charlotte and misleading in the case of Anne, is not unfounded with Emily. A nervous and retiring perfectionist, she would have been delighted to hear that thousands of readers 150 years after her death would still be enjoying her novel, but would have been reluctant to clarify what they found puzzling.

Among the points we might wish to question are the following: (a) Why does Catherine's ghost say she has been wandering on the moor for 20 years? (b) What is the significance of Lockwood's dream of Jabez (Jabes?) Branderham? (c) Who or what is Joseph, and why is he in the novel? These matters have been explored from a literary critical point of view and various suggestions given. Less frequently have theories been put forward to suggest why Gimmerden Sough becomes Gimmerton, what is the significance of the fact that *Wuthering Heights* does not appear in the 1845 diary paper, and why there are so many housekeepers at Wuthering Heights.

It will be as well to state the overall thesis immediately. Both on internal and external grounds it seems most likely that *Wuthering Heights* was written in three bursts of creative energy, namely (i) the beginning, largely now represented in Chapters I and III, with some of II; (ii) the story of Heathcliff's origin, love for Catherine, her betrayal of this, her death and Heathcliff's longing to be reunited until he too dies; (iii) the reconciliation of the warring forces and hope of renewal with a new generation. This is not to say that no written antecedents can be found: the reverse is the case, as both Gondal and non-Gondal poetry provides numerous examples of the ideas of the novel being explored. As Mary Visick says, the Gondal characters are transmuted to Yorkshire ones. It is impossible to show that Emily Brontë was not experimenting in this way in earlier years, but the motivation to produce the novel as part of a set of three belongs to the months following the end of 1844.

Our proposed month-by-month schedule cannot be underpinned at all points, though the reader is entitled to have conjecture supported as firmly as possible. It will appear that the likely periods of composition are January to March 1845 for the first creative effort; early autumn 1845 to June 1846 for the second; and September 1846 to May 1847 for the third. Charlotte Brontë's comments in the 'Preface to "Wuthering Heights"' support this view in likening her sister to a sculptor working 'with time and labour' on a block of granite. The implication is that the material was hard and took a great deal of shaping, which lasted a long time. Charlotte may not have been quite aware of the tripartite division of this laborious task, but her remarks do show how taxing and prolonged the work had been.

'Ill-success failed to crush us,' writes Charlotte of the failure of the joint poem venture of mid-1846; 'We each set to work on a prose tale.' This was not at all what happened, as a number of biographers have made clear, and in *A Life of Emily Brontë* I have corrected the chronology as far as was then possible. Charlotte must have known that by mid-1846 three 'prose tales', of which one was *Agnes Grey* and one a one-volume version of *Wuthering Heights* were already in existence. It has been suggested to me that Charlotte did not mean to deceive and was not to know that a later generation of literary scholars would find it desirable to fix the dates of the writing of these novels accurately. According to this theory, she was not interested in chronology, and forgot such details. However, allowance must be made for the impression Charlotte wanted to create, in romantic mode, of Emily as genius. Emily *was* a genius, indeed, but this does not mean that all her work flowed out of her painlessly, as Coleridge had claimed his 'Kubla Khan' came to him in a dream. Charlotte's picture of Emily as sculptor, labouring hard over her intractable rock, is a much better image. On this occasion, Charlotte is simply wrong: the 'prose tale' had its origins long before the failure of the poems.

In this chapter we shall examine the external evidence for the way in which *Wuthering Heights* came to be written, revised and published. Matters relating to the assembly of the subject matter will be left to a later chapter. As we have seen in the preceding paragraph, traditional ideas of the ways in which the Brontë sisters set about publication come from Charlotte, a woman of tremendous courage and determination, whose instincts combined an obstinate honesty with a romantic imagination and whose pronouncements have to be seen in the light of our understanding of those qualities. We have to rely on what she says, but attention to the subtext is important.

Why was *Wuthering Heights* written? 'Out of a burning need to explore just these themes, which had been in the mind of the author all her life' is one possible answer, but evidence suggests that Gondal had served quite well as the vehicle for such an exploration for many years. It can also be shown that Emily had previously tried to drag the fictional enthusiasms of her three siblings back to Yorkshire, and that even Gondal had a Yorkshire dimension.[9] But the need to try to put something saleable on paper did not begin to be pressing until very late in 1844. In 1842 Charlotte and Emily had gone to Belgium to perfect their French and general education with the aim of setting up their own school. On Charlotte's return at the end of 1843 she had worked hard at the idea, advertising and cajoling, but by November 1844 it was clear that nothing would come of the plan.[10] Anne was employed at Thorp Green, but neither Charlotte nor Emily had earned income and their father, now 67, could not be expected to live for ever. It was essential to look for alternative sources of finance now that the school plan had failed.

It is well known that the Brontë sisters cooperated in planning and developing their work; indeed they had done so from childhood. By this time, they may well have discarded Branwell's cooperation, but we are probably justified in supposing that there was a tripartite colloquy at some time during the Christmas holiday December 1844–January 1845 while Anne was at home. Twelve months earlier, Emily and Anne had apparently taken a decision to tidy and copy their poetry; now it was the turn of the prose to be put under scrutiny.[11] It is clear from Anne's bitter poem 'Call me away', written on her return to Thorp Green on Friday, 24 January 1845, that her heart was at Haworth where Gondal had been an important element of her holiday.[12] It seems likely that Charlotte had urged a re-examination of the sisters' prose stories to see whether anything could be made of them for publication.

This is not quite how Charlotte puts the matter in the 'Biographical Notice of Ellis and Acton Bell'. Here she seems to date the recovery of joint action to mid-1845, after Anne had returned permanently from Thorp Green.

> About five years ago, my two sisters and myself, after a some-
> what prolonged period of separation, found ourselves reunited,
> and at home. Resident in a remote district, where education had
> made little progress, and where, consequently, there was no
> inducement to seek social intercourse beyond our own domestic
> circle, we were wholly dependent on ourselves and each other,
> on books and study, for the enjoyments and occupations of life.
> The highest stimulus, as well as the liveliest pleasure we had
> known from childhood upwards, lay in attempts at literary com-
> position; formerly we used to show each other what we wrote,
> but of late years this habit of communication and consultation
> had been discontinued; hence it ensued, that we were mutually
> ignorant of the progress we might respectively have made.

She goes on in the next paragraph to describe in well-known words how she discovered a 'volume of verse' in Emily's handwriting; this is generally thought to have been the B manuscript. Charlotte deals next with the way the sisters moved on to publish their edition of poems in 1846. There is evidence, however, to suggest that she has conflated two events in these paragraphs, and that an attempt at novel writing preceded the change of mind which led to the successful publishing (but not successful sales) of the 1846 poem edition.

The chronology of the presentation of the novels needs to be re-examined; to do this we shall largely use Charlotte's accounts and letters. Here are the relevant passages:

1. '...We each set to work on a prose tale: Ellis Bell produced *Wuthering Heights*, Acton Bell *Agnes Grey*, and Currer Bell also wrote a narrative in one volume. These MSS were persever-ingly obtruded upon various publishers for the space of a year and a half; usually, their fate was an ignominious and abrupt dismissal.' ('Biographical Notice')

2. '[The Bells] are now preparing for the Press a work of fiction – consisting of three distinct and unconnected tales.' (CB–Aylott and Jones, 6 April 1846.)[13]

3. June 27th 1846. Date at close of MS of *The Professor*.

4.   'Sir –
     I request permission to send for your inspection the M.S of a
     work of fiction in 3 vols. It consists of three tales, each occupy-
     ing a volume...' (CB–Henry Colburn, 4 July 1846).[14]
5.   'The three tales had tried their fate in vain together, at length
     they were sent forth separately, and for many months with
     still-continued ill- success...Charlotte told me that her tale
     came back upon her hands, curtly rejected by some publisher,
     on the very day when her father had to submit to his opera-
     tion.' (E.C. Gaskell, *The Life of Charlotte Brontë*, Chapter 15.) [The
     date of Mr Brontë's eye operation in Manchester was 25 August
     1846.][15]
6.   'In July 1847...a parcel containing a MS – The Professor –
     reached our office...bearing the scored out addresses of two
     or three other publishing houses; showing that the parcel had
     been previously submitted to other publishers.' (George Smith,
     director of Smith, Elder, *Cornhill*, 1900).[16]
7.   '[The Professor] has now had the honour of being rejected, nine
     times by the "Trade" (three rejections go to your own share).'
     (CB–George Smith, 5 February 1851)[17]

Concentrating on the mathematics of these sources, and beginning with the letter of 1851, we may deduce that before Smith,
Elder received *The Professor* in July 1847 it had been rejected six
times. There were 'two or three' addresses of other publishers on
the parcel at that date, and it seems wiser to take the larger number
(if there had been only two, Smith might have been less inclined to
make the point). It seems fair to deduce that *The Professor* had been
rejected in a new, smaller brown paper parcel three times, and thus
it had been rejected at the most three times with the other two
novels, and at the least twice. We know something about two of the
rejections, which occurred between 4 July 1846 and 25 August 1846,
a matter of about seven weeks. It may always be impossible to
decide whether the rejections numbered two or three.

    The first rejection was by Henry Colburn. We cannot be quite
sure that the work was ever delivered to him. In an annotation on
Charlotte's letter, he requests that Charlotte should send details of
the nature of the stories before he will see the manuscript.[18] This
process will have taken a while, but seen or unseen *Wuthering
Heights* was turned down with the other novels. We know that
the other rejection took place in August, though we do not know

the name of the publisher, and I shall discuss the matter below. Emily and Anne, who were at Haworth, took their own books out of the parcel and sent *The Professor* on to Charlotte in Oxford Road, Manchester, where it arrived on 25 August just as Mr Brontë was preparing for his eye operation.[19] Later rejections were apparently at a slower rate, but we must also make allowances for Charlotte's revising *The Professor*; in any case, by this time *Wuthering Heights* and *Agnes Grey* were no longer travelling together with Charlotte's book.

In mid-September 1846 both the younger sisters returned to Gondal, each beginning a longer poem set in a Gondal context. The significance of this will be examined later. In the meantime we need to look at the other end of the process of submitting *Agnes Grey* and *Wuthering Heights* to publishers, their acceptance by Thomas Cautley Newby. Again we shall quote the sources verbatim:

1. '*Wuthering Heights* and *Agnes Grey* had been accepted by another publisher...It was lying in his hands, awaiting his pleasure for its passage through the press, during all the months of early summer.' (E.C. Gaskell, *The Life of Charlotte Brontë*, Chapter 16)
2. 'A prose work by Ellis and Acton will soon appear: it should have been out, indeed, long since, for the first proof-sheets were already in the press at the commencement of last August...'[20] (CB–WSW, 10 November 1847)

We are not likely to find chronological data more detailed than the above though the two passages are hardly satisfactory. What for example, are 'all the months of early summer'? Emily Brontë sometimes writes of May as a summer month and at the other end August is still summer, but not 'early summer'. It might be fair to guess that Newby had written accepting the 'work' in May, but had done nothing about it during June or July, producing 'proof sheets' from his press only in the first week of August. 'It' was published as a three-volume novel in the first fortnight of December 1847.

We now need to state the problem clearly: how is it that during summer 1846 three novels intended for publication as a three-volume set, *Agnes Grey*, *Wuthering Heights* and *The Professor* (then called *The Master*) are circulated to publishers, but then in summer 1847 two of these titles only find a publisher, and are ultimately published in December as a three-volume set despite having lost the third title? What would be the effect on Emily and Anne Brontë in August 1846 of Charlotte withdrawing her contribution and thus leaving the package of three unviable? The evidence seems to suggest that Charlotte began *Jane Eyre* immediately after *The Master* was returned to her, and though she did not jettison it completely, it seems likely that she had lost confidence in it for the moment and thus left the three-volume package short of material.

It is possible that the novels as sent off to publishers in July and August 1846 were in a state of imbalance so far as length was concerned. But consider Charlotte's careful approach to fairness in selecting (with the other two) the poems for the poem edition. The ratio of poems there is 19 Charlotte, 21 each Emily and Anne: but Charlotte's poems are longer on average, and each sister ends up with very similar bulk. It is very unlikely that the three novels would have been so divergent as must have been the case if *Wuthering Heights* as submitted in 1846 were its present length. We shall see later that it would have been quite difficult for Emily to have found time in 1845–6 to write a novel so much longer than those produced by her sisters. And Charlotte is careful in her letter to Henry Colburn of 4 July 1846 to describe her submission as '3 tales, each occupying a volume'. If one 'tale' was twice as long as each of the others, could she have said this?

Charlotte Brontë had nothing but contempt and dislike for Newby, the eventual publisher of *Wuthering Heights* and *Agnes Grey*. In a letter to her own publisher, W. S. Williams, she asks him to give her some background on him.[21] His confusion of the three Brontë sisters in his dealings with Charlotte during 1847 is generally thought to be deliberate, while on the other hand an apparent confusion in his letter to Emily concerning her second novel is thought to be accidental.[22] It is possible, however, that we are accepting Charlotte's view too readily. Newby was an astute businessman. He certainly seems to have wanted to pass off the work of Emily and Anne as though it were Charlotte's, once *Jane Eyre* had been published. But it is not clear that in 1847 he fully realised that there were three sisters behind the three novels published by the Bells. As with some reviewers, Newby may have been genuinely confused, a contributory factor being the pseudonyms used by the Brontës. By 1848 this confusion had gone, but the whole situation left Charlotte anxious to enlighten her own publishers, not only because she felt the dishonesty of the whole matter, but because she did not wish to have Emily's novel, or Anne's novels, ascribed to her. Newby's reputation with other novelists seems to have been quite good.[23]

Whatever her reason, Charlotte writes in December 1847 of Newby's edition that its 'orthography & punctuation...are mortifying to a degree'.[24] But a glance at Derek Roper's edition of the poems will show how unorthodox were Emily's own spelling and punctuation, and her writing is hard to read whether she is making an effort with cursive or using Brontë small script. In the case of *Agnes Grey* there is a copy belonging to Anne herself with her subsequent alterations in them. There are not many changes she wished to make. Quite possibly Charlotte's censure should fall on her sister rather than the printer, though certainly the Aylott and Jones poem version (1846) tidies up some apparently unorthodox spelling and punctuation in the latest available copies (but these are not copies sent to the printer). Practice at the time seems to have been to allow the actual compositors to add punctuation.[25] I therefore agree with recent conservative editors who have retained the punctuation and spelling of the first edition to a much greater extent than in previous editions, though this may seem confusing to a modern reader. I shall use such modern editions, with care, though I have checked many readings with those of the first edition.

What might be called the quantitative argument for the rewriting of *Wuthering Heights* was explored by Tom Winnifrith in *Brontë Facts and Brontë Problems*.[26] My own examination of the first edition shows that the two volumes of *Wuthering Heights* as printed by Newby contained 348 and 416 pages respectively, while *Agnes Grey* contained 363 pages. In a typical nineteenth-century edition, the Smith, Elder printing of 1889, there are 180 pages of *Agnes Grey* to a rather more tightly packed 305 of *Wuthering Heights*; this of course reflects Charlotte's revisions of 1850, where paragraphs were run together, as well as textual changes made. In this edition *The Professor* occupies 247 pages, though there is no way of knowing precisely how the length of the novel was changed in its transformation from *The Master*. In the Clarendon edition Herbert Rosengarten points out that the old title remained with the earlier version and was not changed until a major recopying exercise which replaced all but eleven folios in our currently preserved edition. It seems clear that Charlotte expanded the book before its final posthumous publication as a two-volume set in 1857.[27] Tom Winnifrith's figures for the lengths of the novels in the standard

Haworth edition are as follows: *Shirley* 666 pages; *Villette* 594; *Jane Eyre* 555; *Wildfell Hall* 502; *Wuthering Heights* 350; *The Professor* 269; and *Agnes Grey* 202.[29]

On the rejection of the three-volume set in August 1846 Anne moved towards writing *Wildfell Hall* and Charlotte began *Jane Eyre*. Emily did not write a new novel at this point, but it is here contended that she used the time to rework and expand *Wuthering Heights* so that when it and *Agnes Grey* were finally submitted to Newby he considered the length viable, and it was not necessary for the sisters to call upon Charlotte for a slim version of *The Master*. Whatever conclusion one wishes to draw from the quantitative evidence submitted above, it is clear that the length of *Wuthering Heights* as finally published is about twice that of *Agnes Grey*. This simply cannot have been the case when they were first submitted. Having looked at external evidence on the submission of the original three novels, and discussed the lengths of the versions eventually published, we have to move on to tackle the task of proposing viable theories to cover the discrepancies. Most of our evidence will have to be extracted from the text itself.

7

Wuthering Heights: The First Phase

It will not be possible to give a page-by-page account of the whole of *Wuthering Heights*, but since my view is, not surprisingly, that the first three chapters were the first section of the book to be written, it seems best to begin by giving an account of their content, in the light of the thesis proposed, namely that there was a major revision of the whole novel in 1846–7 and that though this did affect the first three chapters, some of the core of the story had been established in them, and was not susceptible of change. I assign the date of the first writing of these chapters, for reasons that will become apparent, to the months January to March 1845.

The whole book begins with a date, 1801. Once this date has been given it sets up a timescale which has to be maintained. In itself, however, it is not crucial. Though it turns out that Emily Brontë was using an almanack to perceive the phases of the moon during the progress of her novel, and indeed the same almanack had been used for Gondal before this and was also used by Anne in *Wildfell Hall*, the actual phases of the moon in 1801 were not the same as those in the 1826 almanack which she used.[1] If '1805' or '1810' had been chosen, would this have made any difference to the story? If not, why choose 1801? There are two possible reasons for this choice. One possible reason, which may have been subconscious, was that this date brings the substance of the action in the first generation to a time when Patrick Brontë was a child. He was born on 17 March 1777 when Catherine was about 12, and Hareton would be born the next year (1778). One of the lowest layers of *Wuthering Heights* is the 'Irish outcast' story, and Emily's choice of date may have enabled her to deal with her father's own memories and her own personal feeling of involvement with them.

The other, and perhaps more likely, point of origin for the date is Ponden Hall, which has a plaque on it describing its rebuilding in 1801 by one Robert Heaton, whose initials close the inscription on the plaque: 'R.H. 1801'. Ponden Hall was one of Emily Brontë's early haunts and it is most likely that the 1801 had stamped itself on her memory as a child, along with some stories from the hall's history which are also in her mind as she writes *Wuthering Heights*.[2] After its publication a coolness grew up between the Heaton family and Mr Brontë, and it seems probable that they thought Emily had derived some of her material from their history, perhaps even the character of Heathcliff himself. Nevertheless, it is not at all certain that the date, 1801, was in the earliest writing of the story. I hope to show that it was added later, at the time when it became necessary for Emily to systematise her chronology. As she began to write the 'tale' (after Anne went back to Thorp Green, perhaps) she need not have thought of any detailed time-scale.

By the end of the first page, some characters are being deployed. Lockwood, whose name could have had various Yorkshire origins, is, as Ian Jack notes in the introduction to the Oxford 'World's Classics' *Wuthering Heights*, a Waverley figure.[3] His function appears to be the stranger-observer, who will mediate the odd world of the Heights to the reader. As the chapter advances Emily becomes interested in his character, making him a fop, later enamoured of the young girl he meets, with a 'susceptible heart' and a good opinion of his own attractiveness. Lockwood's interest in the girl fades as the book proceeds and is not a live issue with the reader for very long. The girl, who turns out to be the second Catherine, does not appear in Chapter I and the possibility of a link between her and Lockwood does not seem to be integral.

Much of this first chapter is given over to a careful description of the house itself. It corresponds very closely with the old delapi-dated house near Halifax, High Sunderland, whose owners, the Priestley family, were no longer living there when Emily knew it in 1838. There are many ways in which Wuthering Heights reflects High Sunderland. An important one is its name, which Emily has reversed and modified, making:

It seems, then, that the name of the mysterious house which is to be the central dramatic locale of the book was chosen right at the start, and that the original intention was to explore associations formed in the Law Hill years. Within the next pages, written, it may well seem, in the first few weeks after Anne returned to Thorpe Green, in late January to February 1845, there are 15 or 16 characteristics of the mansion. These were briefly explored in *A Life of Emily Brontë*, but we shall now look at them again, considering whether they are possibly applicable to a whole group of West Yorkshire farmhouses, to only a few, or to High Sunderland particularly. It is clear that Emily Brontë visualises this old house with great clarity, and she makes no mistakes in portraying it, either in this introductory passage or later.[4] Either she had drawn out a plan of the imagined house, or she had a vivid recall of High Sunderland.

Here is the passage in which features of Wuthering Heights are detailed, omitting material that is not relevant to the topography of the house and its contents.

1. '[Heathcliff] sullenly preceded me up the *causeway*, calling,
2. as we entered the *court*:
   "Joseph, take Mr Lockwood's horse; and bring up some wine."
3. ... "No wonder *the grass grows up between the flags*, and cattle are the only hedge cutters." ...
4. *Wuthering Heights* is the name of Mr Heathcliff's dwelling, "Wuthering" being a significant provincial adjective, descriptive of the atmospheric tumult to which its station is exposed in stormy weather. Pure, bracing ventilation they must have up there at all times, indeed: one may guess the
5. power of *the north wind, blowing over the edge*, by the exces-
6. sive slant of a *few stunted firs at the end of the house*; and by
7. *a range of gaunt thorns* all stretching their limbs one way, as if craving alms of the sun. Happily, the architect had foresight
8. to build it strong: the *narrow windows are deeply set in the wall*,
9. and the *corners defended with large jutting stones*.
10. Before passing the threshold, I paused to admire a quantity of *grotesque carving* lavished over the front, and *especially*
11. *about the principal door*, above which, among a wilderness of
12. crumbling *griffins*, and *shameless little boys*, I detected the date '1500', and the name 'Hareton Earnshaw.' I would
13. have made a few comments, and requested a *short history of the place* ... but ...

14.   *One step brought us into the family sitting-room*, without any
       introductory lobby, or passage: they call it here 'the house'
       pre-eminently...I believe at Wuthering Heights the kitchen
15.   is forced *to retreat altogether into another quarter*...I observed
       no signs of roasting, boiling, or baking...
       ...to the very roof. The latter had never been underdrawn,
16.   its entire anatomy laid bare to an enquiring eye...'

It is my contention that Emily Brontë actually began writing her
story with a description of the house and the Gondal-like character
who is being naturalised in Yorkshire, discovered by a Waverley-
like interloper. At this point she has no idea how the story will
progress, but she sets her scene in intricate detail, summoning up
the memory of High Sunderland. Additional details consistent
with High Sunderland appear later in the novel.

Evidence on the architectural features of High Sunderland is
scattered and contradictory. A visitor to the site now can still see
what its situation was, can understand its geographical relationship
with Halifax and Law Hill. But for detail it is necessary to rely on
secondary material from Halifax record office and elsewhere. This
material should be treated with caution. One well-known book
prints its illustration back to front and the nineteenth-century
print drawn by Briggs and engraved by Wright includes fanciful
features of Gothic style which were not originally there. During its
demolition in 1950 photographs were taken and are now kept at
Shibden Hall, but they do not represent the hall as it was earlier,
and it is hard to discover exactly when various features were added
or taken away. An 1885 plan shows a barn which appears rarely in
illustrations, but an unidentified press cutting at the Brontë Parsonage reproduces a watercolour said to be in the possession of
Halifax Antiquarian Society. This shows the barn appearing to be
of stone and with drip-moulds over the windows which may be
seventeenth-century, or may be in the early nineteenth-century
cottage Gothic style. In either case, the barn will have been there
during Emily Brontë's stay in the neighbourhood. A large building
to the East of the hall (the right in most pictures) was built as a
slaughterhouse and would not be there in Emily's day.[5]

Horner (1835) shows that one way to the house was along a
flagged causeway to the West of the gateway. A photograph in
Raymond's *In the Steps of the Brontës* shows grass growing up
through the flags on the extension of this causeway along the

front of the house.[6] 'Entered the court' implies passing through a barrier such as a gateway, and the entrance from the West was through such a gateway. This disposes of points 1–3 above. The enclosure was not a court, but could well have looked like it, having a field or possibly garden on one side and the south wall of the house on the other. The relation between the name of the house in the novel and the house on which it is based has already been explained. The geographical situation and details of vegetation can be experienced on site, but the illustration in *In the Steps of the Brontës* facing p. 209 looks due North and shows the meaning of the word 'edge' in the novel. Horner's engravings and the later watercolours show a scattering of trees which do not look like thorns and are certainly not firs. They may be sycamores, which is also the case in early pictures of Top or High Withens. That has no thorns either, though many West Yorkshire farmhouses have. Old photographs of Old Ponden Hall show a gnarled oak tree. We may see the range of gaunt thorns in the light of a neglected hawthorn hedge, but it may be that Emily Brontë imported it into her decaying mansion.[7] (Ernest Raymond concludes his chapter with 'We can assert with some confidence, I think, that Law Hill and High Sunderland between them gave a first birth to *Wuthering Heights*'. Possibly the thorns may be from Law Hill.)

Points 8 and 9 above relate to the narrow windows and corner buttressing. The deep-set, narrow nature of the mullioned windows at High Sunderland is because of the stone casing, which is not original, but perhaps dates from the seventeenth century. There are two prominent buttresses at the hall. One is to the north of the west gateway, through which Emily seems to have passed on a visit to the house. Its function is not clear, but it is shown on Horner's drawing as well as later photographs. It is not precisely 'at the corner' and neither is the other prominent buttress, which is shown at the east end of the south front in the photograph in Bentley's *The Brontës and their World*.[8] There are no buttresses at Top Withens, and little to connect it with Wuthering Heights; the identification seems to stem from Ellen Nussey, who is most unlikely to have seen or known of High Sunderland.

The carving at High Sunderland seems a unique feature. It consists of both free-standing and relief carving in three main places: outside the west gateway, inside the west gateway and at the front door. Putting together the various illustrations, it seems to have included:

1. • a naked hairy giant, free-standing, on the buttress;
    • relief or free-standing heads over the gateway;
    • a frieze over the gateway, consisting of animals, perhaps stags, and faces;
    • patterns of relief sculpture including two flying birds, a coat of arms, a head on the keystone, and possibly five other human heads, all small in comparison; stylised plants and other architectural features. These are inside the west gateway.
2. • two naked male figures of large scale, twisted and grotesque, of which one still had its head in the first part of this century, while the other head is missing;
    • a relief carving of a stylised sun;
    • a lozenge shape and other minor abstract carving.
    These are over the front door.

During the demolition process in 1950, some of this carving was bought by a Mr West of Halifax, who intended to have the gateway rebuilt in his garden. This project was never fulfilled, but at least he saved some of the carving, and was subsequently able to return it to Shibden Hall, where part of the collection still is. If these identifications are accepted, we may see the Lintons in final ascendancy, incorporating some of the wildest elements of Wuthering Heights in their own lowland mansion!

These sculptured figures are prominent in the novel's description of the house, and even those who think Top Withens is a model for Wuthering Heights accept that this element is from High Sunderland. There appears to be no other West Yorkshire hall that Emily could have seen which has anything like these sculptures. Comparing the description above with Emily's words in the novel, we can surely see identity. The carving *was* grotesque, it *was* crumbling, it *was* above both principal doorways, there were birds, though they may not precisely have been griffins, the three naked male figures correspond to the shameless boys. The date 1500 and the name 'Hareton Earnshaw' are not on the front of High Sunderland, but there are some engraved Latin mottoes one of which was placed over the front door, and the sun sculpture occupied a position where a date might have been expected. '1500' is pure fiction, and not very accurate in view of the style of the house. However, most of the features in my points 10–12 are accounted for.

One interesting small point from *Wuthering Heights* links with a point above. In Volume II, Chapter VII, Catherine the younger is being taken on a tour of the house by Hareton. She asks him about the inscription over the door. He cannot read it and calls it 'some damnable writing'. 'Can't read it?' cries Catherine...'I can read it...It's English'. Behind this remark could possibly lurk a dim memory of Emily's when in 1838 she had been shown High Sunderland and looked up to see writing which was not English, but Latin, a language she could probably read but her companions could not. Otherwise there seems no reason to mention the language of the inscription, which would naturally be expected to be in English.

No one would ask for a history of Top Withens, but as point 13 above shows, Wuthering Heights looked as if it merited a place in the history books, just as High Sunderland has had a place in such books as Ambler's *The Old Halls and Manor Houses of Yorkshire* (London, 1913). The point is elaborated later in the novel, where Wuthering Heights is compared to a castle. This comparison would be out of place with any of the farmhouses nearer Haworth.

High Sunderland in the nineteenth century is quite badly documented so far, though we must hope more evidence will emerge. Photographs show a small porch, so that two or three steps would have been needed to take the visitor from the causeway to the living room (the 'house'). There is certainly no passage, but perhaps this might be considered a small lobby. High Sunderland kitchen was on the right of the living room, and this coincides with Wuthering Heights, as later descriptions show. A problem which seems hard to settle is the matter of the ceiling (point 16). Shibden Hall museum possesses photographs taken in 1950 when High Sunderland was being demolished.[9] These seem to confirm a plan of *c.* 1905 apparently showing separate chambers on the first floor. This is the only point in which the description of Wuthering Heights flatly contradicts the evidence about High Sunderland. It is possible that nineteenth-century alterations are responsible for this anomaly. We can certainly hope for more evidence to emerge.

The name of Thrushcross Grange is also found on the first page of our text, but there is almost no focus on it, or the contrast between it and Wuthering Heights for the first few chapters. I shall defer consideration of the name and the factual basis for descriptions of the house to a later stage. Though the name

Hareton Earnshaw stands over the door of the mansion, it is some time before we are told that the boor-like man who helps around the house is Hareton Earnshaw. Chapters 1 and 3 are mainly concerned with establishing the ambience of Wuthering Heights, while Chapter 2 concerns a series of blunders and confusions suffered by Lockwood and felt too by the reader. It does not seem to me to be quite of a piece with the rest of the opening section. However, Hareton's name is significant, and comes from a different strand of Emily Brontë's imagination.

'Hareton' sounds like a West Yorkshire name of the type of Hartley, Sutcliffe, etc., but in fact this is not so. Emily uses the same principle she has already adopted for the name of her mysterious house. She takes a local character and scrambles him: R. HEATON becomes in anagram HARETON. Quite probably she used more than just the name of the Brontës' neighbours at Ponden Hall, and this may be the reason for the Heaton family's antipathy towards the book. It seems likely that Robert Heaton of Ponden was particularly kind to Emily, so that the emergence of a young man with uncouth characteristics and a dubious history which coincides with elements of Heaton history seems inappropriate. Her use of the name, even in garbled form, seems less than tactful.[10]

For several reasons, the end of Chapter 2 and most of Chapter 3 seem to have been written during February and March 1845. Two major ones stand out. First, there is the snow. As has already been shown, Emily likes to portray weather that is actually present at the time of writing. It would certainly be rash to say she always does so, but the poems have shown us that this is usual. According to Shackleton, the Keighley meteorologist, February was 'very cold and dry'. Emily reflects this at the start of Chapter 2 with: 'On that bleak hill top the earth was hard with black frost, and the air made me shiver through every limb' (paragraph 3). By 3 March the wind had turned to the north-east, and a month began which Shackleton calls 'mostly severe'. On 3 March itself there was sleet and snow.

The second point is the parallel with Emily's poetry, especially the well known 'Cold in the earth', dated 3 March. This poem is ostensibly a Gondal piece, with the superscription 'R. Alcona to J. Brenzaida'. It laments the separation between the two, which took place 'fifteen wild Decembers' ago ('fifteen wild Decembers... have melted into spring' – again we note the precise timing). Emily's mood is very sadly nostalgic, and though the 'fifteen' may have to do with Gondal chronology, now reasonably well established, there is more to this than a light fiction. The pain of separation in the poem is exactly paralleled by the pain of separation from Catherine expressed by Heathcliff in Chapter 3 of *Wuthering Heights* when Lockwood cries out after seeing her ghost. This theme was on Emily's mind in the first part of March 1845, and we may reasonably date Chapter 3 to that month.

Chapter 3 continues the material of Chapter 1 and parts of Chapter 2. The Waverley figure, Lockwood, is ensconced in a rarely used chamber, dreams and suffers a strange experience. We first learn that Heathcliff has an 'odd notion' about the room from the housekeeper, whose name has been given as Zillah in the second part of Chapter 2. If Zillah had been in his employment long, she would have known why he had this 'odd notion', and we shall return to discuss housekeepers in the novel later. Organisation must by this time have been pressing Emily, and this section may be an interpolation. Of the earliest stratum, however, are Lockwood's two dreams.

First, he dreams about an affray at the 'Chapel of Gimmerden Sough'. This form of the name does not recur. Hilda Marsden has an ingenious suggestion about the derivation of 'Gimmerden', which if true makes Emily Brontë a philologist.[11] Whether we accept her point or not, the final element in the place-name, -DEN, does reflect Shibden and suggests that Shibden Hall was already in Emily's mind. When the name next occurs it is as Gimmerton. Lockwood's dream of a chapel riot introduces material which is never used again, and which has puzzled commentators. Why is it necessary to bring in 'Jabes Branderham'? What does Lockwood mean by his curious remark to the fevered Heathcliff a page or two later when he asks, 'Was not the Reverend Jabes Branderham akin to you on the mother's side?' What sort of first name is 'Jabes' anyway? Editions from 1850 onward have 'Jabez' suggesting an emendment by Charlotte, but these two strange and anomalous spellings are retained in 1847, and they do pose a problem.

It is Joseph who leads Lockwood to the old chapel. Joseph's part in the novel has been much disputed. His rough eloquence has been variously interpreted: he is a chorus, he balances Nelly, he is a canting sample of Christianity to pose against the paganism of the book's message.[12] What seems clear is that he is integral to the book from the start. He is as much a part of Wuthering Heights as the Earnshaws. It seems likely that he was taken over by Emily with High Sunderland and is based on actuality. Here he drives Lockwood, in this early written chapter, to dream about the harshness of a sectarian sermon.

The long sermon is not revisited; the pilgrims' staves remain in the dream. One can suppose that Emily Brontë left this episode in at revision because of its nightmare qualities, which allow it to lead up to the Catherine episode. Without it the novel would be paler, but it is not structural, it is part of the original conception of the book. Likewise the ghostly child is also part of the very first writing of *Wuthering Heights*, and is prepared for by the books Catherine has been using as a diary. Her habit is very like that of her creator, using every scrap of space on pieces of paper. Surely this episode of a dream of a lost child derives from Emily's experience in spring 1845 of the heartache at 20 years' separation from her elder sister, Maria? The 'twenty years' of the child's answer, the fact that this is a child not an adult, and therefore not the ghost at the time of her separation from Heathcliff (when she bears a child herself as a married woman), suggests that Emily's vision *started* with the frozen child. Catherine was not 'Linton' 20 years previously, according to the chronology which Emily was so carefully to work out, but had not yet apparently done. By the time she had worked it out, she may have realised that the child episode would not fit, but it was the germ of her whole book, and to lose it would have been disaster. The crucial illness and death of Maria Brontë took place *20 years* before this chapter in real time, and Emily was going to keep this in even though it was an anomaly in her chronological pattern. There seems no other explanation of this, and the consequences of the decision were far-reaching.

Heathcliff's arrival leads to a conversation which emphasises the primary material of this part of *Wuthering Heights*: the haunting of an old, derelict house which Emily had seen at Halifax. The haunted house at this point is, as Lockwood says, 'swarming with ghosts and goblins!' (The word has already been used at the beginning of the chapter of his vision of air 'swarming with Catherines'.) It is here that Emily first begins to suggest an origin for Heathcliff, whom she has created as an anomaly in Yorkshire. Lockwood suggests that Catherine might be a changeling. In the outcome it is Heathcliff whose life is portrayed as possibly that of a changeling, while Catherine is of 'the old stock', but we can suppose that it was at this point, probably in March 1845, that the changeling story became associated with the primitive 'desolate High Sunderland' story, which may be in focus because of a joint decision with Anne.

In the rest of the chapter Emily's imagination transfers the feelings she has over the loss and haunting of Maria and possibly Elizabeth to her created Heathcliff. The tone of this is very similar to the tone of 'Cold in the earth', as has many times been pointed out. The poetic intensity of this episode led to a period when Emily concentrated on poetry. It seems highly likely that these first three chapters, in an early form, now languished as so many poem beginnings languished, awaiting continuation. This would need to wait at least for the return of Anne from Thorp Green in June.

8

The First Version: Adapting Gondal

The second phase of writing *Wuthering Heights* lasts from about August or September 1845 to May 1846. This must be the case on any rational chronology and whatever we think the content of this section consisted of. The July diary paper says not a word about the novel. Nor does Anne mention *Agnes Grey*, though there have been persistent attempts to say that 'Passages in the Life of an Individual,' which she mentions, is the novel. This may be the case, but the matter remains uncertain.[1] *Wuthering Heights,* or whatever it was then called if anything, was set aside. Emily went back to Gondal. She was writing (both diary papers tell us this) the 'Life of the Emperor Julius'. His full name was Julius Brenzaida. Mary Visick suggests that he played a transformed part in the novel, and I see merit in this suggestion.[2] He did so initially by entering the story as Jabes Branderham, an authoritative and forceful character in the novel, soon abandoned.

It is hard to know how far the transformation of Julius is conscious. The name Julius could have been used in the chapel scene, though there is an assumption that Emily took the name 'Jabez' from Jabez Bunting, a strong preacher who had been active in Haworth. As we have seen, Emily's preacher's name was not strictly 'Jabez' and in Emily's appalling small script Julius looks much like Jabes. The very seed of the novel was the terrain where Emily had first taught, just as Anne's was Mirfield where *she* had first taught. High Sunderland had come into focus, and Julius had entered this haunted residence in a dream. Julius Brenzaida, Jabes Branderham, Jane Brontë: they are all versions of the same name. (We must not forget Emily's second name, developing into an *alter ego*; she did not do so, often signing her poems 'E.J.B.'. Charlotte used this name significantly in *Jane Eyre*, where some of the character of the heroine and some of her experiences are based on Emily.)[3]

Of course, there was certainly a sinister host at Wuthering Heights in the first version of the first three chapters. He need not quite have been Heathcliff, and the dream of Jabes may indicate that Lockwood (perhaps not yet so named) reinvented his host in the middle of the night. The question 'Who is Heathcliff?' is present as a mystery in the first layer of the book, but Emily may not have been able to answer it as she wrote the first few hundred words. Just the fact that she could not give a clear answer may have caused the pause in writing. It is quite likely that it is not until after the summer that she becomes clear about his origin and status. Liverpool was to play its part in crystallising this.

The astounding fact about July–August 1845, if my chronology is right, is that Julius and Jabes crystallised into Heathcliff, and that it was in those weeks that Geraldine from Gondal merged with Catherine the girl ghost. An element of *King Lear* was stirred into the brew, and origins were explored. Heathcliff, according to Lockwood, is kin to Jabes Branderham 'on the mother's side'. And of Heathcliff's mother we know nothing else. Q.D. Leavis, followed by other commentators, thinks he might be Earnshaw's son.[4] The idea has a good deal to recommend it, and appears to explain a lot about Catherine's relations to her foster-brother (he is her blood brother too, in part). Still, the idea does not need to be asserted too strongly. But what is Emily Brontë trying to say in this reference?

Branwell (also akin to Jabes Branderham) went to Liverpool in July 1845, feeling ill and claiming he had had an affair with Mrs Robinson. Would Mrs Robinson turn out to be the mother of a little outcast? (I think not, since I retain a good deal of scepticism about the truth of Branwell's stories about his dismissal from Thorp Green, which Charlotte and perhaps Emily believed.) It is important that he went to Liverpool, the single named town in *Wuthering Heights* (Leeds, Halifax, Keighley are not mentioned). It was at Liverpool that the racially and religiously hybrid Brontës first entered England in the shape of Patrick (also known as Papish Pat). This series of events in late summer 1845 stirred Emily and made it possible for her imagination to turn back to the abandoned novel. Feelings about the alienation of an Irish child in England, Branwell's wildness, Julius Brenzaida's love for Geraldine (herself half-Irish in origin), perhaps a reading of *King Lear*, placing the name Edgar nearer the front of Emily's mind than it had been: all these coalesced to produce a situation where she was eager indeed to get on with the shelved novel, as Anne was getting on with hers.

We can proceed a little further with *King Lear*, though supporting evidence is lacking. There are three Brontë sisters, just as King Lear has three daughters. Emily is generally thought of as her father's favourite, whom he taught to fire a pistol in the domestic year of 1843 when she was the only one at home. Emily took after her father in an obvious way. Unlike her sisters and Branwell, she was tall. Though he had not been able to make full use of it, Patrick's intellect was great. He had pinned his hopes on delusive Branwell, not a daughter, but Branwell had failed to bear the weight of expectation. In 1843 Emily had taken his place, and Branwell had now proved treacherous to Patrick's ideal. Emily, then, was Cordelia.

So the part of Emily's mind that was Julius and had been Jabes in the early spring was reborn as Heathcliff. But there was another important side to Emily Jane Brontë which was unrepresented by the passionate and uncontrolled exile from wild Ireland. This was Emily Jane the housekeeper, methodical and reasonable, an interesting sequential story-teller, with a mixture of Cornish and Irish antecedents, but above all one who could order things and (with Anne) impose sense in Gondal Chronicles on the chaotic mass of Gondal saga.[5] Emily (soon to be Ellis) the grand-daughter of Eilís or Alice (in English sometimes called Eleanor) became Ellen or Nelly, with her second name losing its voiced aspect and becoming 'Dean' instead of Jane.

Nelly Dean was a marvellous discovery, and it surely dates from that imaginative summer of 1845. Nelly observes the arrival of Heathcliff, of whom it might not be too much to suggest that in some shape or form he was 'always, always' in Emily Jane's mind in one guise or another. Nelly took over from the earlier housekeeper whom we know now as Zillah. Without this discovery, *Wuthering Heights* would have been a Gondal story, on the far side of the world, or a parody of Hoffmann. Nelly 'domesticates' the myth, in the words of one twentieth-century commentator.[6]

Emily begins Chapter 4 with the same sort of confusions we have seen in the revised Chapter 2. However, these may not have been in the original. The correction of 'eighteen' for 'sixteen' in the number of years Nelly has been here eventually has to fit a chronology that still does not exist. These three pages, it will be suggested, come from the final version, and Nelly's story now begins with 'Before I came to live here...'. These words mark the return to composition 'at the beginning of harvest' when the 'apples and pears' of the narrative really were ripening at Haworth. Later, an orchard came to be part of Wuthering Heights and fruit does not need to be brought from Liverpool. During August and September, it seems that Emily's writing went along smoothly, converting Gondal characters into Chapters 4 and 5. Julius' foils are Alfred and Gerald. We know little about the latter, though Alfred certainly strikes us as a mild figure.[7] It is Gerald, however, who is turned into *Edgar L*. 'Edgar L' has a tinge of *King Lear* in him, but his surname may come from Glascar, where a Linton family lived at the time of Emily's father's childhood.[8] One of the family was called Isabella Linton, and we may think Emily now recalled her from one of her father's breakfast table stories.

We may also note another name which may have been coined at about this time. It is Thrushcross Grange, a hybrid between Shibden and Anne's story of her life. (This coinage may even date from the earlier phase of the work, but perhaps Anne and Emily were specially preoccupied with the name of Thorp Green this summer because of its influence on Branwell's downfall.) *Thorp Green* was a lazy, lowland mansion, where effete gentry corrupted lively minds by their hypocrisy and cheese-paring luxury, while at Stump Cross, just north of Shibden, later to be called in as the site of a well-remembered signpost, was the location of an old house called Shibden *Grange*. Even in the first chapters Gimmerden seems to echo Shibden, and this suggests very close attention to the locale near Halifax. Perhaps the first three chapters were rewritten at this stage and the names High Sunderland and Shibden Grange/Thorp Green solidified, though I think it more likely that High Sunderland at least had metamorphosed before this.

Meanwhile Charlotte was looking for commercial viability. It is not at all clear how far the younger sisters would have kept her up to date with their work, and she seems to have decided that poetry was marketable. Was this really as a result of a chance discovery when 'One day, in the autumn of 1845, I accidentally lighted on a MS volume of verse in my sister Emily's handwriting'?[9] On the evidence of dating in the manuscript, Emily Brontë had been writing poetry in October 1845 – the poem 'Silent is the House' which we have already noted. It was a long poem, and a conflated one; does the date apply only to the conflation as in other cases and is the famous 'He comes with western winds' a record of experience earlier in 1845, not October?

We have already looked at the way in which Charlotte later explained the Brontës' decision to edit their poems for printing. There are many mysteries about this account which cannot ultimately be solved in the present state of our evidence. It is quite clear that Charlotte's change of tack interrupted the novel writing for all three sisters. Unless all we have said about the way *Wuthering Heights* developed in 1845 is far wide of the mark, the book had been proceeding well. However, Charlotte has one piece of objective evidence on her side, namely the existence of the prison poem, with its date of 9 October. This shows that Emily Brontë had turned aside from the novel that autumn. This in turn suggests some kind of hitch in *Wuthering Heights*.

In these last years Gondal tends to be used by Anne, and also perhaps by Emily, as a retreat when other composition is discouraging. (A classic example is in September 1846, after the return of the three novels.) On the other hand, the theme of the poem is not totally alien from Chapter 6 of *Wuthering Heights* in which Heathcliff and Catherine are imprisoned in the wash-house until they make their escape across the moors to Thrushcross Grange. A.G. Rochelle may be a version of 'A.G.A.', who in turn is a prototype Catherine. Julian's name sounds like that of Julius, who is a forerunner of Heathcliff. Emily's subconscious mind is working round the same motif: imprisonment and release for a fair captive. Catherine is once again virtually imprisoned by her illness and enforced captivity at Thrushcross. It is this captivity which seduces her from her previous freedom of spirit and overlays her natural careless girlhood with social concerns, the regard for status which will contribute towards her rejection of Heathcliff.

It therefore may seem best to interpret this episode as a meditative pause on the way to seeing how Catherine will behave. The immediately preceding chapter, number 5, is short and abrupt. It has important things to relate, but does not carry us on in a tide as subsequent chapters do. What the Gondal prison poem perhaps does is to provide a way back for Emily to delve again into her background material, looking for further links between her well begun novel and the Gondal saga of her youth, which expressed themes which would be at the forefront of all her writing.

So far, a good deal of this exploration has been concerned with the ways in which Emily Brontë's own observations from life were turned into story in the first and final months of 1845. According to the theory put forward, the initial impetus for the novel may have come from a joint decision with Anne, and this led on the one hand to recall of High Sunderland, a mansion Emily had seen and perhaps explored in 1838 while a teacher at Law Hill. During the same period a Gondal character called Julius Brenzaida and his lover Geraldine had occupied her mind. These two also formed part of the nexus of feeling stirred by memories of Law Hill. Julius Brenzaida, Jabes Branderham, Jane Brontë provide one aspect of the beginnings of *Wuthering Heights*.

It is now time to study this link a little further. As Anne wrote in her diary paper of July 1845,

> Emily is engeaged in writing the Emperor Julius's life she has read some of it and I want very much to hear the rest [.][10]

According to the theory developed, the first three chapters of the novel had been written, but we note the emphasis on poetry in early–mid-1845, and the emphasis on Gondal in July. On their outing to York the younger Brontës played at being various Gondal characters.[11] By about August the novel had been resumed. The Emperor Julius must have been transformed into Heathcliff about the beginning of August.

Julius Brenzaida first enters the Gondal saga (which was not composed or arranged chronologically) in 1838. He writes a song to 'G.S.' dated in Emily's timescale (not Gondal time) 17 October 1838. G.S. turns out to be 'Geraldine' (line 1). She is often assumed to be the same person as 'A.G.A.', Emily's major Gondal heroine, whose middle initial has been supposed to stand for Geraldine, e.g. by Fannie Ratchford in *Gondal's Queen*.[12] In a second poem of 17 October 1838, Julius writes of Geraldine,

> I can forget black eyes and brows
> And lips of rosey charm
> If you forget the sacred vows
> Those faithless lips could form – [.]

The 'sacred vows' were perhaps those taken at her marriage to Alfred, Lord of Aspin. Faithlessness is certainly a characteristic of Catherine Earnshaw, but the above passage cannot be interpreted with total certainty. Are the 'black eyes and rosey lips' those of another lover of Julius, or are they Geraldine's?

In Chapter 7 of *Wuthering Heights* the now well- established Nelly Dean says to Heathcliff,

> ' – tell me whether you don't think you're rather handsome? I'll tell you, I do. You're fit for a prince in disguise. Who knows but your father was Emperor of China, and your mother an Indian queen...?'

The Emperor Julius did not rule China, but this looks like another of Emily Brontë's 'in-jokes', like the remark about Jabes Branderham's relationship to Heathcliff. As Derek Roper observes, the courtly opening of this poem implies 'a different world from that of Catherine and Heathcliff', but there are several hints, intended to mystify the reader, that Heathcliff could have been of noble origin, as indeed he was, *outside* the novel.[13] Just as the discovery of Nelly Dean solved an enormous credibility problem, so the bringing of Gondal-inspired characters back home to Yorkshire was a quantum leap in realism.

There is support for Fannie Ratchford's reconstruction in poem No. 104 where A.G.A. admits to wronging the clear-souled Alfred, and at their parting says, 'I – who had the heart to sin / Will find a heart to bear – [.]' A.G.A. here insists on the wrong she has done to her mild lover. It is hard to discern with total confidence the sequence of events in her life, but it seems sure that she alternates between a calm and a stormy love very much in the manner of Catherine. If it is argued that there is no proof that A.G.A. and Geraldine are the same, this must be agreed. No Gondal reconstruction has succeeded in producing total agreement between critics. In a sense this does not matter, as clearly Geraldine and A.G.A. are very similar women, and indeed it may be futile to look for consistency in the Gondal story, in which characters appear and disappear like dreams.

It is quite hard to penetrate the way in which Emily Brontë chose Catherine's name. It does not seem to be a name with which she had grown up. Of the 53 girls who overlapped with Emily at Cowan Bridge none was called Catherine.[14] It is harder to obtain a list of pupils at Law Hill, but of the 20 girls listed in the Law Hill census of 1841, some of whom were certainly known to Emily, none is called Catherine.[15] None of the pupils at Roe Head whose name we know was called Catherine.[16] Unlike the relatively common Isabella, Catherine does not seem to occur in the many names on Glascar Presbyterian Church register during the time of Patrick Brontë's association with the church. Shelley's friend Catherine Nugent might be a possible source, and there are other literary Catherines. There is a place not far from Halifax called Catherine Slack, and Emily could conceivably have heard of this. Anagrammatically, Catherine shares six of the nine letters in her name with Heathcliff, so in part she actually *is* Heathcliff, but this is perhaps a trivialisation.

A.G.A. had been killed in a long poem of 1843 which we have already mentioned. She returned in a milder form as 'A.G. Rochelle', as later Catherine was to return in a milder form as the second Catherine. It can be said that Emily Brontë's Gondal characters, so far as we can see, are discarded and recreated: they never give up their last potential. They echo and re-echo down the years as though in a hall of mirrors or the scene in *Wuthering Heights* where Catherine, in delirium, seems to travel in time and space.

The choice of a name for the hero of the novel may have been initially hard to solve. As we have seen, Jabes Branderham and Heathcliff seem to be related in different ways to Julius Brenzaida, but Heathcliff's name is pure inspiration and owes nothing to Gondal. It is explained in the book as a name which had once been given to one of the Earnshaw children who had subsequently died.[17] But Heathcliff himself uses his name as surname as much as forename. It is quite impossible to guess at which point in the development of the story Heathcliff acquired his name, though when we come to consider an early layer of the book in Brontë family history, we shall see that the parallel name 'Welsh' was applied to a supposed orphan in eighteenth-century Ireland.

Julius Brenzaida took Gondal by conquest.[18] He had no right to it, and it is fair to see him as a usurper, especially when he betrays Gerald, 'His false hand clasped in Gerald's hand' and in an uncopied poem we see Gerald imprisoned and facing a captive's tomb.[19] As we have already noted, it was Gerald who supplied the name of Edgar, even though Alfred, the early mild lover of A.G.A., also merges his character in that of Edgar. Gerald is Julius' 'kinsman'; we may suppose him related to Geraldine (A.G.A.) and this is one example of the stifling family closeness of Gondal heroes and heroines which is transferred to *Wuthering Heights*. After his overthrow and betrayal Gerald is imprisoned; this element returns in *Wuthering Heights* in the imprisonment of Nelly and of Linton Heathcliff. Thoughts of prison were always near to Emily's mind.

Elements of their formation may have been the parsonage cellars, where it is possible to suppose (though there is no clear evidence) that the children played at an early age, and Wesleyan hymns where the image of a prison is often found, e.g. in the well known 'And can it be...?'[20]

The character of Edgar represents one of the enigmas of *Wuthering Heights*. He has the power to attract Catherine, and this power is not as some commentators seem to think purely that of status or wealth. In Chapter 10 Nelly reports Catherine as being 'almost over-fond' of him, and it is more significant than some critics notice that in the famous speech in Chapter 9 analysing her feelings for Edgar and Heathcliff she does not deny that she loves Edgar and even gives an account which may be understood as a normal, natural form of love. Edgar appeals to part of Catherine's character just as Alfred appeals to part of A.G.A.'s. The evidence for relations between A.G.A. and Alfred in Gondal is chiefly to be found in poems 76 and 92, though there are other minor references. In 76 A.G.A. addresses a musing, gentle speech to 'A.S.', whom it would be perverse not to identify with Alfred. This poem was begun on 6 May 1840, precisely 15 years after the death of Maria Brontë. It was completed more than three years later, in July 1843; it is impossible to say where the first part ends and the second part begins. In the poem A.G.A. recognises a quasi-religious feeling that

> I know our souls are all devine
> I know that when we die
> What seems the vilest, even like thine
> A part of God himself shall shine
> In perfect purity.

The link with Maria seems clear.

In stanza 7 A.G.A. compares Alfred to her 'golden June/All mist and tempest free'. Edgar is not quite free of all tempest, showing some petulance and impatience towards Catherine's love for Heathcliff, but often he is mild and understanding. As we have seen, after their marriage Catherine flourishes. A.G.A. says of Alfred that like the June sun 'So heaven's sun shines in thee'. These summer references are carried over to the speech of Catherine in *Wuthering Heights* already referred to when she says that Linton evokes love which is 'like the foliage in the woods. Time will change it as winter changes the trees.'

Poem No. 92 is set in Aspin Castle, where the theme of continuity into a second generation is addressed in the form of portraits on the castle wall. If we make the assumption that 'Sidonia's deity' is A.G.A., then she was 'Lord Alfred's idol queen,/So loved, so worshipped long ago'. In the poem Alfred has died and become a ghost, which haunts the castle 'With spirit eyes of dreamy blue'. His daughter, conversely, has a 'large dark eye', as is shown by the portrait. This she apparently inherited from A.G.A. Alfred 'Wanders unsheltered, shut from heaven', but in *Wuthering Heights* this attribute seems to have been transferred to Heathcliff (Chapter 34).

It is not enough to see Heathcliff as an exile from Gondal, an intruder who has developed from Julius Brenzaida. The strange and important thing about him is that he combines Emily's Gondal invention, the Liverpool and Irish heritage stirred by Branwell's visit, and various usurper tales, which may well have formed the basis of Julius' character and behaviour and seem to have affected Emily's mind very deeply. Heathcliff's story is

a cuckoo's, sir – I know all about it; except where he was born, and who were his parents, and how he got his money, at first...

in a passage in Chapter 4 which I shall suggest was written during the expansion process of 1846, and using the kind of punctuation which, in its similarity with that of the poem manuscripts, makes one think Newby followed Emily's own. There is some irony in her remarks: she knows all about Heathcliff except some of the very points we are most anxious to hear about.

Patrick Brunty, son of an Irish (and probably Irish-speaking) corn-roaster, who himself had a strange wandering history, was born in 1777 and left his homeland in 1802, emigrating forever (though he probably paid one or more visits to his home country) and rejecting his Irish origins to such a degree that the young Brontës fell in love with Scotland rather than Ireland. An alien in Yorkshire, he adopted a new surname and became more Tory than the Tories. Like Heathcliff he was an emotional person, bereft of a lover for most of his life; he often ate alone, but his vivid narrative style equalled Heathcliff's as the young boy tells Nelly in Chapter 6 about his escapade with Catherine and the Lintons. Mr Brontë could be considerate and charming, but sometimes showed himself otherwise. For example, he cut up a dress belonging to his wife:

Charlotte herself used to relate the story of the mutilated dress, as a strong proof of her Father's iron will and determination...he would...take no cognisance of his own hard and inflexible *will*, which ran itself into tyranny and cruelty.[21]

The authenticity of this incident has often been doubted, but here is Charlotte's own testimony to her father's strong and unbending mind. This inflexible will was Emily Brontë's genetic and environmental inheritance.

There is much more mystery about the origin of Heathcliff which needs to be explored. As we have seen, some readers consider Earnshaw's story of the waif found 'starving, and houseless, and as good as dumb in the streets of Liverpool' must be a cover. They cannot see why Earnshaw needs to travel to Liverpool at all, and wonder how far this mystery is meant by Emily Brontë as a hint that Heathcliff is Earnshaw's illegitimate child, and so Catherine's half-brother. If this is so, it casts a strange glow over the relationship between the two children, whose love, for example as shown in Catherine's tentative signature as 'Catherine Heathcliff' in the book studied by Lockwood, would be incestuous.

It is not until the next page that Catherine is shown becoming 'very thick' with Heathcliff. Her first reaction is to spit at him. But if Emily Brontë already saw a major element of the book as the affinity between these two, it does not follow that she yet knew what kind of affinity it would be. The incest theme does run through the book, though it is never explicit and modern readers will not always feel comfortable at acknowledging it. Whatever his genetic origin, Heathcliff is brought up as a brother to Catherine, being given 'the name of a son who died in childhood'. But Nelly does seem to hint at more, as she describes Earnshaw's fury when he finds Hindley persecuting the 'poor, fatherless child, *as he called him*' (my italics). Surely in this sentence Nelly is hinting that Earnshaw knew Heathcliff's real parentage. Indeed, though Heathcliff's alien appearance is emphasised in Chapter 1, which we have seen was probably written in early 1845, he is so 'naturalised' as the book proceeds that Lord David Cecil has no difficulty in assigning him to the 'children of storm' with Catherine and the other Earnshaws.[22]

Perhaps Heathcliff's father was Emperor of China. What more can we know of 'the mother's side'? Returning from Liverpool, Mr Earnshaw collapses into a chair and announces that 'he would not have another such walk *for the three kingdoms'* (my italics). He means England, Ireland and Scotland. He next suggests that the waif is 'as dark almost as if it came from the devil'. Nelly and the others crowd round to look at this dirty, ragged child, and though it could talk, 'it only stared round, and repeated over and over again some gibberish that nobody could understand'. This child, found on the Liverpool streets, did not speak English. While it is possible that Emily is hinting at a non-European origin, or even a Gondal origin (though we don't know much about the language of Gondal), the language spoken might well have been her grandfather's tongue, of which her father must certainly have known something. Heathcliff is alien yet at home, a stranger, yet closely linked, just as the Irish have been in England, and still are. The reference to 'the three kingdoms' seems to emphasise the underlying thought.

Another example of the disturbing alien in Brontë work is Bertha Mason, who is given a West Indian origin to explain her strangeness. It should not perhaps be forgotten that as well as the centre for Irish immigration, Liverpool was the northern focus for the slave trade and indeed Mellany and Charlotte Hayne were fellow but much older pupils at Cowan Bridge, and they are said to be Creoles.[23] This may be confirmed by Mellany's Christian name. If Heathcliff's outcast character is not wholly attributable to an Irish origin, it may derive in part from Emily's thought about the position of ex-slaves or half-castes.

As Geraldine, Catherine's first name, the first initial of 'A.G.A.' was Augusta. Augusta had been the name of Lord Byron's half-sister, Augusta Leigh, who was widely believed to have had an incestuous relationship with him, the product of which was a girl called Medora, perhaps one of the sources of Anne's and Emily's place name, Zedora. Lord Byron was dark, deformed and romantic. Many commentators have seen a link between him and Heathcliff, who has been called a 'Byronic hero'. In Emily's imagination Augusta and Lord Byron contributed to Catherine and Heathcliff dark romance and an aura of incest.[24]

The notion of the romantic wandering outcast was commonplace in the writings of the generation before the Brontës, but there appear to be several real-life examples of cuckoo-in-the-nest stories which may have caught her fancy. To begin with, it seems most likely that the family were brought up on the Irish legend of 'Welsh', supposed to be a foundling discovered on a cross-channel boat, but perhaps actually an illegitimate son of an Anglo-Irish squireen.[25] The Brontës continually showed interest in orphans; it seems likely that they saw themselves as orphans descended from an orphan, and all tales of orphans seemed interesting and appropriate because of this. The story of 'Welsh' has been examined at length in various places.[26] Another similarity between him and Heathcliff is the surname used as a Christian name, a phenomenon that, as we have seen, seems to have fascinated Emily Brontë since she invokes it again in naming Hindley. Welsh (or Walsh) was a name used twice in Brontë ancestry, for a Walsh Brontë was a brother of Patrick's to whom Emily would certainly have heard reference made on occasions. But the legendary Welsh, with his cuckoo-like story, and his name perhaps reflecting this, is certain to have attracted Emily's passionate interest. It was not only Welsh's origin that became one of the underlying facets of Heathcliff, but his alleged manner of acting, denying the true heirs and enforcing a bitter regime on his dependants. Of course, it can be argued that the legend of Welsh as we have it has been read back by nineteenth-century commentators such as William Wright into late eighteenth-century Ireland from the *Wuthering Heights* plot by then published. Although to some extent this may have happened, as I showed in *The Brontës' Irish Background*, Wright's evidential base cannot be dismissed.[27] It seems most probable that a family story tracing the Brontës' troubles and strange isolation to a set of circumstances in which this usurper features was told by Mr Brontë at parsonage breakfasts when Emily was very young, and that she was thrilled by such tales. Emily's obsessions were not lightly to be evaded.

As a child, Emily must several times have felt herself robbed. First she was supplanted in the love of her young mother by the arrival of Anne, then her mother died. Her affections were transferred to Maria, but she lost Maria when the older girl was sent to school at Crofton. Maria returned, ill. She had not yet recovered when her education was renewed by sending her to Cowan Bridge. We know what Charlotte's imagination made of Cowan Bridge and we know that Emily hated schools. All these external forces colluded to give Emily the feeling that a power (and perhaps a masculine power, since her father arranged some of these events and stood darkly as a mysterious cause behind others) was usurping her birthright. Even without the legend of Welsh, it is not improbable that a malevolent masculine entity would have formed imaginatively in Emily's psyche.

It is quite well known that there are three other 'orphan/usurper' stories which Emily Brontë is likely to have encountered and which seem to have played a part in her obsessive interest in the Heathcliff figure both in Gondal and *Wuthering Heights*. The first two of these are located at Ponden and concern the Heaton family. One had taken place many years ago when a certain Robert Heaton had to buy back the house after it had been usurped by a rogue relative, Henry Casson. The second concerned Elizabeth Heaton, daughter of the Robert who had rebuilt Ponden in 1801, who had married a Leeds grocer, John Bakes or Bates and been ill-treated by him, dying three years after her marriage. Both these stories, almost certainly told to Emily by one of the Heatons in her childhood, seem to be buried in the structure of *Wuthering Heights*.[28]

Yet another story, unearthed by Winifred Gerin at Halifax, seems likely to have been well-known at Law Hill during Emily's time there. It concerns the activities of Jack Sharp, a nephew of the local landowner John Walker.[29] This man was adopted by Walker, became possessed of his house, and when forced out of it tore it to pieces. He then built Law Hill itself, and took his revenge on the family by employing and systematically degrading a cousin of Walker's, Sam Stead, just as Heathcliff is in the process of degrading Hareton. Since Emily must have first heard this story in 1838 or possibly early 1839, while at Law Hill, it is easy to see how it could contribute to the early layers of *Wuthering Heights*. The common feature of these stories is ingratitude, a trait much in Emily's mind, and one of which she much suspected herself.

Law Hill itself was thought to be a possible origin of Wuthering Heights at one time. There is very little in the building of Law Hill which might encourage such a view, but it does seem probable that the close proximity of farm animals and the day-to-day business of life on a working farm may have been learned at Law Hill, where the farm was an integral part of the house as it was in so many cases at that time.

The one poem contemporary with this stage of writing the novel is the undistinguished 'I know that tonight the wind is sighing' (122), dated August 1845 and confirming its date by the internal reference to the 'soft August wind' in line 2. Possibly it comments on the enclosed feeling Catherine and Heathcliff experience in the wash-house, from which they break out to see how the Lintons are spending their Sunday. At the heart of the poem is the treachery so often on Emily's mind. The captive's friends have perhaps forgotten him: 'Their brows are unshadowed, undimmed by woe.'

During the first part of this second period of writing the novel, Emily's mind is working on the theme of treachery. It will be Catherine's treachery to her friend, however justified by her rationalising about the economic means to help him rise, which precipitates the tragedy of their downfall (in so far as the book can be seen as tragedy). First the friendship has to be established, then it has to be decisively set aside; all this begins as Catherine and Heathcliff burst out from their imprisoning wash-house.

9

Autumn and Winter: After the Poem Revision

Through much of 1845 Emily Brontë's spirits were higher than we see at any other point in her life. There may be many reasons for this, and we may reasonably assume that *Wuthering Heights* was one. The great confidence shown in the series of major poems written between February and June of this year transfers to the novel at the time of the apples and pears, and then work is temporarily laid aside for the selection and revision of poems ready for submission to Aylott and Jones. If Charlotte's discovery was of 'Silent is the house', this interruption took place in October, and was much resented. The state of *Wuthering Heights* does seem to confirm the interruption, with Chapters 4 and 5 being speedy, breathless narrative (outside the direct apostrophes to Lockwood, to which we shall return). This is consistent with excited work in September and early October, leading to a rushed ending as Charlotte insists on the priority of poetry.

As we know, Emily Brontë frequently returned to her store of poems to re-read them and revise them. This autumn, there were more and even brighter poems to return to, for in the course of selecting, she would see the seven very strong poems of early 1845, five of which were selected for the 1846 edition. Such reminders could not help but increase her literary confidence. The fruits were to be seen in the next sections of *Wuthering Heights*.

Chapter 6 of the novel deals with a day in November 1777, probably the 17th, though I do not suggest that Emily Brontë yet knew this. It can be dated by reference back from the subsequent chapter, but the wetness of Heathcliff's clothes, the lights burning in the Lintons' living room and the 'shivering in corners' mentioned by Heathcliff all suggest that the author had a late autumn scene in mind even as she wrote it. Chapter 7 is a long setpiece dealing with Christmas Eve and Christmas Day 1777. By this time Emily Brontë has discovered the technique she is to use for the next section of the book, which would proceed in long, detailed, play-like scenes, each one carefully observed, with links in between that seem scanty. In this context it needs to be remembered that the Brontës' first love had been drama: their toy soldiers actually played dramatic parts. Chapter 6 (pp. 87–92) describes the events of the Sunday when Catherine and Heathcliff escape for 'a ramble at liberty'. New names are readily invented, without much allusion, for this exciting chapter: 'Jenny', 'Robert', 'Skulker', though they will generally not be used again (Skulker returns on p. 181). Isabella and Edgar's names are first used, Edgar already showing signs of compassion as he notes Catherine's bleeding foot. Heathcliff several times shortens Catherine's name to Cathy in this scene. The detail in the chapter is fairly expansive, with events at Thrushcross Grange moving in uninterrupted sequence: it is all narrated by Heathcliff, coming like a messenger in Greek tragedy with his eye-witness account. We may recall Horace's discussion in *Ars Poetica* balancing the impact of events witnessed by the spectator against the longer lasting effect of those narrated.[1]

The next five weeks pass in half a sentence, which leaves us at the raising of the curtain on Christmas 1777 (Chapter 7); then there is a continuous narrative, chronologically, until p. 101. This second 'set piece' chapter is observed by Nelly and is again detailed, even mentioning the carols and the precise method by which Catherine reached Heathcliff by climbing across the roof of the house. The 'Gimmerton band' has adapted the original place name of Gimmerden (p. 64), which may echo Shibden. 'Gimmerden' is never used again. (It might be possible to suggest that the two places are distinct but adjacent, but it seems most likely that the original name had been made up sufficiently far away in time for Emily Brontë to have forgotten it. In general, her memory for generalities seems excellent, but for the precise words, not so.) Christmas 1845 seems a likely composition date for this section.

We have one other piece of writing by Emily Brontë from this time: 'No coward soul is mine', often compared to *Wuthering Heights* because of its transcendentalism. This bears a date, 2 January 1846, and therefore, if our chronology is correct, precedes the writing of the comparable passages in *Wuthering Heights*, Chapter 12, by some weeks. The poem text is as follows:

No coward soul is mine
No trembler in the world's storm troubled sphere

I see Heaven's glories shine
And Faith shines equal arming me from Fear

O God within my breast
Almighty ever-present Deity
Life, that in me hast rest
As I, – Undying Life, have power in thee

Vain are the thousand creeds
That move men's hearts, unutterably vain,
Worthless as withered weeds
Or idlest froth amid the boundless main

To waken doubt in one
Holding so fast by thy infinity
So surely anchored on
The steadfast rock of Immortality

With wide-embracing love
Thy Spirit animates eternal years
Pervades and broods above,
Changes, sustains, dissolves, creates and rears

Though Earth and moon were gone
And suns and universes ceased to be
And Thou wert left alone
Every Exsistance would exsist in thee

There is not room for Death
Nor atom that his might could render void
Since Thou art being and Breath
And what thou art may never be destroyed[.][2]

In Chapter 9 of the novel, after saying she would be degraded to marry Heathcliff (at which point he slips from behind the settle where he has escaped notice) Catherine twice moves into sublime poetry, first when she says that her soul and Heathcliff's are the same, while 'Linton's is as different as a moonbeam from lightning or frost from fire', and second in one of the best-known passages from the novel, which argues that 'every body' has a notion of an existence beyond themselves. 'What were the use of my creation if I were entirely contained here?', she continues. 'My great miseries in this world have been Heathcliff's miseries...' She then modulates to the metaphysical, using words very similar to the poem:

> If all else perished and *he* remained, I should still continue to be; and, if all else remained, and he were annihilated, the Universe would turn to a mighty stranger. I should not seem a part of it.

At a later stage, she is capable of quarrelling with Heathcliff, and her thoughts do not sustain this mystic unity with him. But at this point the tone echoes the poem, and they may well be linked chronologically.

This third set piece begins in Chapter 8, at p. 108, and consecutively deals with Catherine's attempts to see Edgar while getting rid of Heathcliff and Heathcliff's consequent chagrin; Nelly's determination to chaperone Linton and Catherine; Catherine's display of temper; the return of Hindley; Heathcliff's intervention to save Hareton from being killed; Heathcliff's apparent departure for the barn (but he does not go); Catherine's confession to Nelly that she will marry Edgar, but that she loves Heathcliff with a different kind of love; and the passage mentioned above where she talks about the unity of her soul and that of Heathcliff (which Heathcliff does not hear); the discovery that Heathcliff has left and the thunderstorm at night when the east chimney falls. The whole section is dramatic and taut; we may well feel here with Charlotte that 'Emily never lingered over her work' as we read this, the most memorable passage, just as the poem quoted is perhaps the most memorable poem.

The autumnal nature of the scene, said to be in summer (as the then chronology demanded), is expressed in the midnight collapse of a tall tree, damaging the chimney and in turn the kitchen fireplace. It is clear that this is a reference again to High Sunderland, whose east chimney was over the kitchen. The tree's fall is sharply described: 'a huge bough fell across the roof, and knocked down a portion of the east chimney-stack, sending a clatter of stone and soot into the kitchen fire'. Emily and Charlotte both show interest in split trees, as is shown in Emily's drawing from Belgium and Charlotte's symbolic chestnut tree in *Jane Eyre* (borrowed from the present passage). To complete the trio, Anne uses a similar image in 'Self-communion', her long autobiographical poem, written after *Wildfell Hall*.[3]

This single day, from the afternoon until the middle of the night, occupies from p. 108 to the first part of p. 126 in the Penguin edition, and 20 pages in the Oxford Classics. It turns out towards the end of the passage that this is a summer scene, but Emily apologises for the darkness of the night. Even before the storm the weather is wild and it is raining, the fire is lit in the kitchen and it becomes dark well before bedtime. When Joseph goes to look for Heathcliff he describes the night as 'black as t' chimbley!' Nelly adds, as narrator,

> It *was* a very dark evening for summer: the clouds appeared inclined to thunder, and I said we had better all sit down; the approaching rain would be certain to bring him home without further trouble.

But it had certainly been raining earlier at 'an hour past dinner time' (p. 109).[4] Precise weather details may have been added, but the original conception seems to envisage wet, wintry weather. I should certainly not wish to insist on this point, but it seems likely that Emily Brontë wrote this passage as part of the sustained effort following the composition of 'No coward soul' in the first part of 1846, then realised later that it would have to take place in summer.

The manner in which the omission of the early part of 1778 is handled is interesting, and we shall have cause to return to it. Towards the end of the Christmas narrative Catherine has climbed across the roof of the house and lets Heathcliff out of his imprisonment in 'the garret' then comes down to talk with Nelly. The exuberance of the scene is noteworthy but now Nelly breaks off with, 'But, Mr Lockwood, I forget these tales cannot divert you.' There follows the discussion with Lockwood in which Nelly proposes to omit not just some months but three years. Lockwood will not allow this and presses her to 'continue minutely'. In reply she says she will ' be content to pass to the next summer – the summer of 1778, that is, nearly twenty-three years ago.' I shall suggest later that this passage is part of the rewriting.

The transition to 1778 turns out to be a short passage, and Nelly does achieve her intention of passing to 1780 quite soon. The hesitation has proved to be beneficial to the story, and that part of it which occurs at the start of Chapter 8 could not have been left out, as it explains who the young Hareton was and briefly shows the deterioration in Hindley's character, which is necessary to exacerbate the friction between him and Heathcliff. How far we can ascribe Hindley's character to that of Branwell is unsure. After his dismissal from Thorp Green Branwell seems to have wasted his time round the parsonage, lamenting his life and perhaps exaggerating the closeness he claimed with Mrs Robinson. That this situation had an effect on *Wuthering Heights* seems most likely, without however providing Emily Brontë with any precise model.

At this stage the dramatic tension peters out. Catherine is feverish and distraught at Heathcliff's departure and is finally taken to Thrushcross Grange. The old Lintons catch the fever and die as a result:

> ... the poor dame had reason to repent of her kindness; she and her husband both took the fever, and died within a few days of each other.

The abruptness of these deaths is dismissive in the extreme. The old Lintons have played their part like Gondal lay figures, and they can be dispensed with. Their creator simply has no emotional energy left for them. Edgar's marriage to Catherine follows after three years which are completely blank. No attempt is made to deal with them, and we see once again an approach to novel-writing which reminds us of a play; Greek tragedy or Shakespeare appears to underlie this technique.

The next set piece is dated September 'on a mellow evening'. Heathcliff returns to confront Catherine and Edgar in a scene to which Gondal elements still cling: Gondal characters often seem to wander overseas and then return home changed. The heroine is blithe and seems to have benefited from her marriage to Edgar. The Gondal theme of treachery without remorse seems to be invoked. Still, her delight in the return of Heathcliff knows no bounds: she seems quite light-headed and ends the scene, after a long evening lasting from p. 132 to p. 139 in the Penguin and an equivalent nine pages in the Oxford Classics, with the startling remark, 'I'm an angel!' The mellowness of the evening may take something from a March evening, as this is the likely month of composition. Candles are lit in the chamber when Heathcliff proposes to stay 'an hour or two'. As in other places in the novel, we have an almost three-dimensional feeling and the final 'angel' speech is acutely realised.

Next day Catherine takes Isabella over to Wuthering Heights in the afternoon and it is at this point that Isabella begins to be curiously attracted to Heathcliff, an irrational, Gondal-like manifestation.

Emily Brontë describes accurately the symptoms of unrequited love:

> ...Miss Linton fretted and pined over something. She grew cross and wearisome; snapping at and teasing Catherine continually, at the imminent risk of exhausting her limited patience. We excused her to a certain extent, on the plea of ill-health – she was dwindling and fading before our eyes.[5]

Before Emily's eyes was Branwell, pining in vain for Mrs Robinson of Thorp Green from whom he had parted the previous summer, and of whom news may have been hard to secure. Branwell certainly pined, and Emily uses this ever-present sight, changing the gender of the lorn lover.

Within the next few pages cruel, even sadistic elements are developed in Heathcliff's make-up. He would wrench Isabella's finger nails 'off her fingers, if they ever menaced me', and says that the most ordinary thing Catherine would hear of if he lived with Isabella would be painting on her 'mawkish, waxen' face the 'colours of the rainbow, and turning the blue eyes black, every day or two'. It must have been such passages as this which shocked Charlotte and Anne as they heard them read out that year.[6] We recall the dissension felt throughout the household as recorded in Anne's poem 'Domestic Peace'.[7]

The tension is a little relaxed at the beginning of Chapter 11, while Nelly takes the opportunity to anchor the story in the past once more. The result is an intensely topographical page, chronologically in early winter 1784 and perhaps actually written in February–March 1846. Bearing in mind the identification of Thrushcross with Shibden and Wuthering Heights with High Sunderland, let us watch Nelly leaving the Grange on a journey to Gimmerton. In the first paragraph she calls Wuthering Heights 'the farm', almost suggesting a relationship between it and Thrushcross similar to that of a home farm with its overseeing mansion. If this suggestion is admitted, the distance between the two houses may seem to have lessened, though this is only a fleeting change, for the houses are as far apart as ever later in the novel.[8]

'One time, I passed the old gate, going out of my way, on a journey to Gimmerton.' Thus Nelly begins the second paragraph.

We have not heard of 'the old gate' before; it suggests that Emily has very clear topography in her mind. And why does she tell us that Nelly was going out of her way at that point? There can be no reason within the logic of the novel, but it seems as though Emily Brontë wants Nelly to leave by the old gate, yet knows this is not the usual way to Gimmerton. As readers, we have been given no information about what the normal way would be, but to the author this is a rational concern and she excuses Nelly. During the occupation of Shibden Hall by Anne Lister, which coincided with Emily's stay at Law Hill, alterations were carried out there which included a new carriage drive to the east replacing a previous exit to the north, clearly visible on the 1835 map where Old Godley Lane borders the mansion.[9] We can visualise Nelly walking out of the estate into Old Godley Lane and turning right, aiming for a village somewhere in the vicinity of Northowram.

The next short paragraph reads,

> I came to a stone where the highway branches off on to the moor at your left hand; a rough sand-pillar, with the letters W. H. cut on its north side, on the east, G., and on the south-west, T.G. It serves as a guide post to the Grange, and Heights, and village.

In subsequent paragraphs the sun shines 'yellow on its grey head' and it is described as a 'weather-worn block'. This guide post, its position and its orientation, are very vividly before the writer's eyes. Its orientation and the directions exactly correspond to a location at Stump Cross, substituting High Sunderland for W.H., Northowram for G. and Shibden Hall for T.G.

Nineteenth-century maps have the letters G.P. (for 'guide post') by the side of the junction at Stump Cross, where Old Godley Lane meets the Leeds Road. Amazingly, an inspection of the site in August 1996 found the stone still extant, precariously standing on the narrow division between the Leeds Road and the road to Northowram. Its orientation is as Emily Brontë describes it, one side facing south-west and still prominently displaying the letter H (not T.G.), deeply cut into the stone. Presumably H stands for Halifax. However, there are no other letters, the north-west and south-east sides having marks that appear to relate to a fixing, perhaps to an iron fence. It is possible that directions on these sides could have been erased, but it does not seem probable. We may think it likely that Emily Brontë would see this pillar on a school walk from the south-west angle, note the letter H and assume similar markings on the other sides.

It is important to note that this similarity between an existing guide post and the description given in *Wuthering Heights* cannot be coincidence. The firmness with which Emily orientates this stone towards the south-west, just as the case in reality, confirms that this junction is the junction Nelly now stands at in *Wuthering Heights* and sets the seal on the accuracy of Emily Brontë's imaginative recall of the area round Stump Cross. The visitor to the scene today must think away the traffic, the later nineteenth-century buildings and the urban environment. Maps from the mid-1830s show this junction as a rural meeting point of lanes, which were little more than cart tracks despite turnpike status.

Having established that Emily Brontë had not forgotten the origin of her location in the land between High Sunderland and Shibden, we can conveniently look at two or three confirmatory passages which also deal minutely with a clearly visualised geography. To do so we must first return to Chapter 10, in which Heathcliff returns to Gimmerton on 'a mellow evening in September' (the year turns out to be 1783). It is clear that in these two or three pages Emily Brontë has to see Thrushcross Grange sharply in her mind's eye. We need to see what she saw in the light of the directions given on the guidepost we have already examined. Nelly tells us,

> On a mellow evening in September, I was coming from the garden with a heavy basket of apples which I had been gathering. It had got dusk, and the moon looked over the high wall of the court, causing undefined shadows to lurk in the corners of the numerous projecting portions of the building. I set my burden on the house steps by the kitchen door, and lingered to rest, and drew in a few more breaths of the soft, sweet air; my eyes were on the moon, and my back to the entrance, when I heard a voice behind me...[10]

In this short description, Heathcliff is already at the kitchen door, in the 'porch', as appears a few lines later. He is not seen by Nelly, partly because he is in total shadow, partly because she is looking at the moon, in the east. The 'court' is the area behind the back of the house, presumably paved. We are at the rear, non-ceremonial side of the mansion, which faces north. The 'high wall' of the court seems to be the back wall of the eastern part of the house. A little later, Heathcliff glances up at the house where the moon is reflected in the leaded, mullioned windows and appears as 'a score of glittering moons'. This window, over the court, faces east to reflect the moon.

Heathcliff importunately demands that a message be taken to Catherine to say he is waiting. Nelly reluctantly takes it, interrupting the married couple in the room above. There is a detailed description of the location:

> They sat together in a window whose lattice lay back against the wall, and displayed, beyond the garden trees and the wild green park, the valley of Gimmerton, with a long line of mist winding nearly to its top (for very soon after you pass the chapel, as you may have noticed, the sough that runs from the marshes joins a beck which follows the bend of the glen), Wuthering Heights rose above this silvery vapour – but our old house was invisible – it rather dips down on the other side.

As we know from the guide post, Wuthering Heights is not strictly in the same direction as Gimmerton, but we are to think of the heights as a range of hills stretching from Gimmerton in the north-east towards the old house in the north-west.

A page later, Edgar gets up from his seat and crosses the room to another, which looks over the court, but this window is not meant to be *opposite*, but on a wall that is at right-angles to the first window. (Incidentally, if Edgar and Catherine had been sitting at this window, the one where the moon was reflected, they would have heard Nelly and Heathcliff talking at the beginning of the scene: besides, we have been told that the window where they sat was fastened back.) The room where Edgar and Catherine are sitting seems to be equivalent to the room called 'the Oak Room' at Shibden.

Six months later, in Chapter 15, it seems to be the same room that Catherine occupies, though it is called 'her' room. She is found 'in the recess of the open window, as usual'. Nelly looks out of the window and sees 'a large dog, lying on the sunny grass beneath', presumably on the garden lawn. It is Sunday afternoon, and Edgar is at service in Gimmerton chapel. Nelly watches the conversation between Heathcliff and Catherine, but she is not at ease, and finally she can 'distinguish, by the shine of the westering sun up the valley, a concourse thickening outside Gimmerton chapel porch'.[11]

The sun has now moved to the West and is shining on the range of hills where Wuthering Heights is in the west also, and Gimmerton in the east. We know from the previous passage that just beyond the chapel the glen bends round and a 'sough' joins it, which presumably gave its name to the chapel when it first appeared and was called the chapel of 'Gimmerden Sough'. Now Nelly sees the congregation emerging from the chapel and worries that Edgar will be home soon and find Heathcliff in the house. This topographical diversion has taken us away from the main theme, and it is time to go back to chronology.

A major climax of the novel has been reached, after one year's intermittent but intense work. It is again deep winter and Catherine once again tormented, this time in life and not as a child ghost. Chapter 12 constitutes another expansively treated scene, its centrepiece again a bed. The curtain rises as Catherine, who 'believed she was dying' unbars the door of her room whence she has been driven by the quarrelling of Edgar and Heathcliff. Careful attention to the dramatic chronology (based on Sanger) needs to be given, though I am still inclined to think that Emily Brontë has not yet realised the need for iron control on it. Indeed, it may be the problems she encountered in relating this scene to Chapter 3 that eventually caused her to adopt a rigid scale; though even this could not solve the anomaly in Catherine's age which now emerges.

Sanger, modified by Inga-Stina Ewbank, considers that 9 January 1784 is the date when Heathcliff comes and embraces Isabella, and the row and Catherine's sulk follow.[12] 9 January 1784 is said to be a Monday (though that is not actually the case with the real 9 January 1784). It is therefore in the middle of the night of Thursday/Friday 11–12 January that Catherine unbars the door and begins her bizarre delirious conversation with Nelly. The core of it is childhood reminiscence, as Catherine picks feathers from the pillow and is reminded of her early rambles across the moors with Heathcliff, and how she tried to intervene to save the life of young lapwings in a nest. She expects to find blood on the feathers, but Nelly tells her to 'Give over with that baby-work!' as the feathers begin to fly like snow. By this time Emily is writing with careful consciousness of the snow scene in Lockwood's dream, from Chapter 3.

Lockwood saw 'obscurely a child's face looking through the window'. Now, later, yet years earlier, Catherine sees the same face, 'gazing earnestly at the mirror'. Nelly tries to convince her it is her own. In trying to solve the anomaly presented by the fact that the face in Chapter 3 is that of a girl ghost, while Catherine lived to be a woman, Emily produces here an incredibly telling and intense scene, all her intuitive and subconscious artistry projected on this tormented figure in the bed at Thrushcross Grange, almost willing herself physically to Wuthering Heights. 'Nelly, the room is haunted!' she says, 'I'm afraid of being alone!'

It will be remembered that one strand of the origin of *Wuthering Heights* seemed to be the demand by the southern stranger for an explanation of the events in the oak closet, the wild dream and the child ghost. In Chapter 12, the climax, he is about to receive this. If that were all the novel had remained, simply an explanation of the ghost, a Gothic ghost story, this passage would provide the dénouement. But by this time the dimensions of the book had enlarged far beyond finding a rational explanation for a ghost. Nevertheless, the outline of the things said in this delirium scene may well have originated in an intention to provide the answer to the questions posed in Chapter 3.

The clock strikes 12, and the day becomes 12 January. Catherine's long speech returns us to the child she was at the age of 12. It forces us, and perhaps the author, to look carefully at chronology:

> I pondered, and worried myself...most strangely, the whole last seven years of my life grew a blank! I did not recall that they had been at all. I was a child; my father was just buried, and my misery arose from the separation that Hindley had just ordered between me, and Heathcliff...
>
> ...supposing at twelve years old, I had been wrenched from the Heights, and every early association, and my all in all, as Heathcliff was at that time, and been converted, at a stroke, into Mrs Linton, the lady of Thrushcross Grange, and the wife of a stranger...

The child ghost, then, is not the ghost of a dead person, but that of a girl jerked out of childhood into adulthood, someone dead to childhood, but not physically dead. The author seems to imply that Lockwood's vision was caused not by death, but by trauma, and was somehow an echo of the psychic ferment Catherine was now undergoing at Thrushcross, as she projects her image across the moor to Wuthering Heights.

We never know whether Lockwood understands this and indeed our feeling about him may be that he is too crass to do so. Other readers may, however, be convinced, but the chronology is still intractable, and Emily Brontë cannot solve it, whether it is at this point that she invokes her almanack or later. The arithmetic simply does not add up. The dramatic date is 12 January 1784, and the event Catherine recalls took place seven years ago when she was 12. She is now 19, and the separation from Heathcliff must have taken place following the death in October 1776 of her father. Lockwood's arrival at Wuthering Heights is (later?) dated 1801, and the scene in the oak closet is apparently in late November 1801, i.e. a further 17, almost 18, years from the date of the delirium, and therefore 24, probably 25 years from the date of Catherine's separation from Heathcliff.[13]

However, in Chapter 3 the ghost claimed to have been 'a waif' for 20 years. Before basing any discussion on this figure, it will be well to remind ourselves that it is not an adjustable figure, but one deeply embedded in Emily Brontë's consciousness as she allows Lockwood to write it, for she repeats the figure four times on the same page, three times in context and once randomly.

'It's twenty years,' mourned the voice, 'twenty years, I've been a waif for twenty years!'

We have already been prepared for this figure by Lockwood's aside, 'why did I think of *Linton*? I had read Earnshaw twenty times for Linton.' The number is so insistently repeated that we have to see it as fundamental, and I have already proposed a tight subconscious connection with Emily's own trauma at the death of Maria.[14] Yet, of course, it is at odds with the generally careful chronology of the novel. Catherine has been exiled from childhood about 25 years by 1801 and the two dates simply will not harmonise. This, it seems to me, is because the child ghost's 'twenty years' is an absolutely fundamental keystone of the book, and even when it turns out to be inaccurate, it is not changed.

Catherine's delirium continues beneath the moonless sky at Thrushcross. Once again she returns to the worry about her room at Wuthering Heights, imagining she can see Joseph sitting up late to lock the gate after she has returned. She goes on, 'they may bury me twelve feet deep, and throw the church down over me; but I won't rest till you are with me . . . I never will!' This final reiteration of the number 12 concludes Catherine's current concern with it, but it has been stamped on our minds as firmly as the number 20 in Chapter 3.

There is now added to the chronological problem a topographical one. In the course of her delirium, after she has had a vision of Joseph sitting up late, Catherine says,

> It's a rough journey, and a sad heart to travel it; and we must pass by Gimmerton Kirk, to go that journey!

Our recent visit to the direction post has not prepared us to expect Gimmerton or its kirk to be located between Thrushcross Grange and Wuthering Heights, and in all the descriptions of the route there are no others which suggest this. For example, when Lockwood tries to leave Wuthering Heights for home on the snowy day before the dream of the child Catherine, the difficulty of the journey is stressed but no one says 'a major landmark on your way is Gimmerton Kirk'. Catherine's remark is meant to have a double meaning. She wants to say she must be buried before she can return to Wuthering Heights, to haunt it. Topographically, she is in error, and perhaps the author hopes we shall not notice the problem posed by this *double entendre* which is not actually double.

At the end of the same chapter Isabella elopes with Heathcliff so that the two protagonists are now both married to the wrong partners. Heathcliff's embrace has encouraged Isabella, and it is possible that initially Emily Brontë saw this elopement as forming the major part of Heathcliff's revenge. She was now in a position to believe that she would complete her book no later than her sisters would complete theirs, though they may well have been expressing serious doubts as she read it out to them. At this stage, I have suggested, she did not envisage the second generation as completing the story by palinode, and she had only to ensure that the frustrated Heathcliff of the ghost scene would be united with the spirit of his eternal love. Even at this stage in the writing she must have realised that this would require both Catherine and Heathcliff to die.

10

The Development of the First Version

It was in February that the poem edition was finally sent to Aylott and Jones, thus freeing the three Brontë sisters for an unhampered assault on their three 'tales'. Catherine symbolically expects 'the birth of an heir' in Chapter 13 (p. 172) in what will turn out to be February 1784. The overlap between Catherine and Emily Brontë should never be ignored, and this may be an indication that the birth of her novel, *Wuthering Heights*, was now in prospect. The dramatic date of the next four chapters, 13–16, is February–March 1784, mirroring the possible composition date of March 1846. That precise dates were tidied at the final revision a year later, we must allow, and there seems to be a slip back to chronological muddle when Heathcliff is asked by Catherine,

> Will you forget me – will you be happy when I am in the earth? Will you say twenty years hence, 'That's the grave of Catherine Earnshaw ...?'[1]

Whether this is a second inconclusive attempt to account for the child ghost's cry is uncertain; it almost looks like a smokescreen designed to suggest to the reader that Lockwood's vision did take place 20 years after Catherine's death (she is speaking on 19 March 1784 and will die next day). It appears to be based on an uncertain time-scale which has not yet been forced under the control of the almanack.

There is no doubt that these chapters reach a peak of confidence in Emily Brontë's art. They excel all but the most outstanding poems and seem to build on the literary and philosophical insights of those poems. We can readily suppose that the final effort to fair-copy these poems, which may be dated no later than early 1846, has brought them clearly before Emily's mind, and shown her a coherence within them, and between them and the earlier tracts of the novel, which she had hardly realised. Deeply self-doubting as the Brontës were, this clear visual evidence that she could write and had both a message and medium must have invigorated her for the task of completing the book, and to that end she now worked (so far as we can see) consistently from March to early May, leaving late May and early June for the copying process.

We might now return to 'No coward soul' and compare it with Catherine's Platonic speech to Heathcliff on the eve of her death, Chapter 15, pp. 196–7. This will, perhaps, have been composed some ten weeks or so after the poem, which was not, of course, included in the 1846 poem edition. It is possible that a closer link between the copying date of the poem and the novel chapter could be provided if we knew when precisely the poem was copied into the A manuscript as A 31. Clearly both form part of a nexus of thought and feeling which can securely be located to late winter 1845–6.

Catherine tells Nelly that the frustrating Heathcliff who now glowers at the wall over the fireplace is

> ...not my Heathcliff. I shall love mine yet; and take him with me – he's in my soul. And,' added she musingly, 'the thing that irks me most is this shattered prison, after all. I'm tired, tired of being enclosed here. I'm wearying to escape into that glorious world, and to be always there; not seeing it dimly through tears, and yearning for it through the walls of an aching heart; but really with it, and in it... very soon... I shall be incomparably beyond and above you all.'

'Heathcliff' here in some sense 'exists in' Catherine, as in 'No coward soul' Emily writes of her God

> Though Earth and moon were gone
> And suns and universes ceased to be
> And thou wert left alone
> Every Exsistance would exsist in thee

There is apparently no need for physical bodies to remain since Catherine can subsume Heathcliff just as God can subsume every 'Exsistance'. This is 'Undying Life' of the kind Catherine will experience when she is 'incomparably beyond and above you all'.

It is with 'love' that God's spirit 'animates eternal years', and Catherine will preserve Heathcliff through love ('I shall love mine yet'). Both passages summarise a view which has been put forward in the novel and the poems before, rejecting the bodily prison in favour of a transcendental life in 'that glorious world' outside.

This, the final scene in which Catherine and Heathcliff meet on earth, is full of the foreboding attached to an adulterous liaison when the spouse may return at any moment. Of course, there has been ambiguity throughout about whether Catherine's relationship with Heathcliff was adulterous; we have seen that their intimacy dates from childhood and goes deeper than the romantic relationship Catherine has with Edgar. But as the sun begins to sink in the west and Nelly sees the 'concourse thickening outside Gimmerton chapel porch' that Sunday afternoon, Heathcliff is determined to leave quickly, like a lover about to be caught by a wrathful husband. Yet he has had no difficulties about overcoming any violence Edgar can offer.

It seems certain that at this point Emily Brontë does feel that Heathcliff's passion is adulterous, and surely Branwell's current situation was responsible for this. Though no one knows whether in reality there was any adulterous relationship between his ex-employer, Mrs Robinson, and him, Branwell seems to have had no doubt himself that they were involved together. From the day he was dismissed from Thorp Green until his death, Branwell was continually lamenting the separation he had to suffer, so that his perpetual heartbreak – no less real for the probability that it was based on illusion – was borne in on the other members of the family daily. Heathcliff's anguish now reflects this.[2]

Chapter 16 is a short one, dealing with the birth of the child, the death of Catherine and the funeral. Heathcliff bursts into impassioned prayer:

...I pray one prayer – I repeat it till my tongue stiffens – Catherine Earnshaw, may you not rest, as long as I am living! You said I killed you – haunt me then! The murdered *do* haunt their murderers. I believe – I know that ghosts *have* wandered on earth. Be with me always – take any form – drive me mad! only *do* not leave me in this abyss, where I cannot find you! Oh God! it is unutterable! I *cannot* live without my life! I *cannot* live without my soul.[3]

He asks Catherine *Earnshaw* to haunt him, and of course in the child at the window scene it is the girl Catherine who does this. Once again we have a return to the implications of the delirium scene, when Catherine saw herself effectively making the transition from her state as a girl, 'half savage, and hardy, and free...' at the age of 12 directly to becoming Mrs Linton, 'the lady of Thrushcross Grange'. The power with which these feelings of deprivation are expressed surely underlines Emily Brontë's terrible yearning for the 1820s and her childhood, the date of the almanack she would turn to for the chronology of her story.

With Catherine dead, she now required only to show how the haunting of Heathcliff eventually led him to his own satisfying death, and thus answer the questions posed at the start of the book about the identity of the ghost and the reasons for Lockwood's host's anguish. The book was approaching a necessary length to fill the one volume allocated to it. In April Charlotte was able to write a letter stating that the Bells were 'preparing' a work of fiction, with its carefully balanced elements, three 'tales' of equal proportion. A child had been born, perhaps, but nothing was to come of this child. Heathcliff has married Isabella for revenge. There will be no need to follow her story, and indeed even in the final version Emily Brontë has no particular interest in Isabella except as the agency through which Linton Heathcliff is born. The chief matter remaining is to show how Heathcliff is haunted by the ghost to the point where he dies and is reunited with her. Thus it seems sure that Chapter 17, narrated by Isabella, which deals with Heathcliff's violence towards and victory over Hindley, Isabella's humiliation and Heathcliff's final success in usurping the ownership of Wuthering Heights, all formed part of the first version, but did not conclude it, though Chapter 18 (Volume II, Chapter 4) is clearly the beginning of the second part.

There is one other small piece of evidence which locates Isabella's speech in Part I, the first version, and suggests a time lapse before the second generation story is tackled, causing a memory lapse. In Chapter 13, Isabella returns from her runaway marriage to Heathcliff, perhaps suggested by the runaway marriage of Anne's pupil Lydia Robinson. She asks Joseph, on her arrival at Wuthering Heights, ' "Have you no place you call a parlour?" ' His reply is firm: ' "*Parlour!*" he echoed,... "Nay, we've noa *parlours.*" ' Just possibly he is lying, but though uncooperative Joseph does not usually lie. Yet in Chapter 21 (Volume II, Chapter 7) we find that

Linton 'spent his evenings in a small apartment they called the parlour...' according to Nelly. It recurs twice, and is described as 'the little parlour' when Nelly transfers to Wuthering Heights after Lockwood returns south. It seems best to suppose that in the earlier version Emily had not envisaged a parlour, but it became necessary when Linton Heathcliff had to live there.

At the start of Chapter 18 (Volume II, Chapter 4) Nelly skips over 12 years before turning to contemplate the later childhood of the second Catherine, who seems to repeat the experience of her mother in having a happy childish existence for 12 years, then beginning disorientation consequent on entering the adult world. Even in the first version there must have been some mechanism for Lockwood to allow a lapse of time before hearing the details of Heathcliff's death.

I have suggested that in this first 1845–6 writing Emily Brontë was largely led on by the forces liberated when her Gondal characters became reincarnated in Yorkshire. Her original plan was to answer the fairly conventional question, why is this ghost haunting this room in this old house? By the end of 17 chapters (as we now have them) she has given a satisfactory tale-teller's account and has poured on to paper much passion-charged narrative, thus amazingly fulfilling needs she has not realised. We see her in April or May 1846 wondering how to complete her story in an artistically satisfying way; as Charlotte said later, 'she did not know what she had done'.[4] It seems likely that she would have become so involved in the traumatic separation of Catherine and Heathcliff that she would not rest until she had reunited them. Lockwood's tenancy of Thrushcross Grange is for a year. There is no intrinsic reason why he should not remain there, to hear of Heathcliff's death which happens during his year of tenancy, and is reported to him immediately by Nelly. Possibly in the first version this is how things were arranged; we can never know.

The intensity of the writing of most of the final two chapters in the published version seems akin to the work examined so far. Heathcliff's death is a climax which surely had to take place in the first version, and I therefore suggest that these chapters were written in Spring 1846. Only after it became necessary to prolong the book and Emily Brontë found this task congenial, did she begin to think of the device of having Lockwood go away and return later, so that Nelly could still be his interpreter, narrating not only the death of Heathcliff, but the details of the life and development of the younger Catherine. It is at the end that Heathcliff begins to use the bedroom in which Lockwood first encountered Catherine's ghost ('that with the panelled bed to get through', as Nelly puts it). Nelly discovers his body after noting an open window. Heathcliff had died, not in the room where the story logically began, but where it began psychologically.

In May 1846 Anne Brontë wrote a poem (subsequently entitled 'Domestic Peace' by Charlotte) in which she laments the destruction of peace in the Haworth household. As I have suggested in various contexts, it is not sufficient to interpret this as Anne's lament on Branwell's disintegration.[5] Anne insists on the plural pronoun in laying the blame for the strife that has broken out: '*We* rudely drove thee from our hearth'.[6] The 'we' here can only be the three sisters, either with or without the addition of Branwell. The poem edition had caused dissension, but *Wuthering Heights* added to it. As Charlotte says in the 'Preface to Wuthering Heights' (1850), 'If the auditor of her work, when read in manuscript, shuddered under the grinding influence of natures so relentless and implacable... Ellis Bell would wonder what was meant, and suspect the complainant of affectation.' There were certainly two auditors, Charlotte and Anne; their complaints fuelled the dissension.

The timing of this stage of the dissension among the Brontë sisters must relate to 'Domestic Peace' and must therefore be connected with the Winter and Spring work on *Wuthering Heights* in preparing it for publication. The relentlessness and implacability of Heathcliff, Hindley and Catherine develop in the long set piece scenes we have just examined, hence the necessity of placing their composition at this date. We may reasonably consider May and June 1846 as times of revision and copying, and it may well have been at this time that the books as a whole were first read aloud. Isabella's elopement with Heathcliff may relate to the elopement of Anne's ex-pupil, Lydia Robinson, in Autumn 1845, while some summer touches to Chapter 8 may have been added in this May to June revision in 1846. By 4 July, the novel texts were ready to be sent away. Charlotte's closing date on *The Master* is 27 June 1846, and the letter requesting the submission of the three novels is dated 4 July. It is impossible to see how Charlotte could have copied the whole of her novel in the seven days or so indicated, and we must presumably take the 27 June as an 'end of copying' date. Emily must also have been copying and revising (none too carefully) during May and June, writing out her book in conventional script as she had with the earlier 'C' poem manuscript. It is not at all sure that she would have been satisfied with her book as she finished copying: but Charlotte, the leader, wanted it done, and so it was done. The books were enclosed in the brown paper parcel for the first time and perhaps posted at some date not much later than the letter, which was received by Colburn and on which Colburn scribbled a note to his clerk asking him to 'state the nature of the stories'.

11

Rejection and its Consequences: Return to Fictional Poetry

Charlotte's letter to Henry Colburn is extant, but his reply is not.[1] It is a fair assumption that the three novels followed the letter to his publishing house, though we cannot be quite sure of this: it must be a bare possibility that on reading the plots, he turned the books down out of hand. Whether this was the case or not, he turned them down eventually. The next fact we know is that the three 'tales' were returned, presumably from a second publisher, 'on the very day' that Mr Brontë had his eye operation in Manchester, i.e. 25 August 1846.

We need now to think what that publisher said, and note what consequences followed. This will require a little imaginative deduction, but the possibilities seem to be limited. As a consequence of whatever was said, Emily and Anne returned to writing Gondal poetry, which we shall soon examine. There was also a discussion, possibly a heated disagreement, between the sisters, as a result of which Charlotte decided to extract her novel and allow it to travel separately. In fact, she temporarily discarded *The Master* and started to write *Jane Eyre*.[2] Anne did not discard *Agnes Grey* and it went on to be resubmitted, perhaps without change or with little change, for she now started on her second novel. Emily, if our thesis is right, added to *Wuthering Heights*, increasing its length greatly.

What kind of reply from the publisher can have produced such reactions?[3] Surely he broadly accepted *Agnes Grey*, totally rejected *The Master* and made comments regarding *Wuthering Heights* which were not completely negative, but suggested it ought to be toned down, balanced in such a way as to seem less harsh. If his reply about *Wuthering Heights* had been very encouraging, Emily would not have returned to Gondal in September, but would have been spurred on to perfect the novel; if his reply had been completely damning, she would have abandoned it. If he had condemned *Agnes Grey* Anne would not have resubmitted it in (probably) the same form. She too returned to Gondal, but that had happened before when she wanted to help Emily.

On further consideration we might think it possible that this publisher actually was Newby. If *Agnes Grey* had been accepted by any publisher, the sisters would surely have returned to that publisher. There is also the matter of Charlotte's very harsh view of Newby, and the fact that she says nothing whatever of the meeting with him in 1848 when she and Anne rushed to London to try to clear up the muddle caused by his advertising techniques.[4] Further, Charlotte was very jealous in later years of her youngest sister, as has been many times noted.[5] If Anne's novel were the first to have been accepted, and Charlotte's turned down on that occasion, this would account for this exacerbation of Charlotte's contempt for her sister. There is no proof whatever that it was Newby who replied to the three sisters in August 1846, and sent back their novels, but it is an attractive possibility.

What kind of objections would a publisher have expressed to 'Ellis Bell' at this stage? It is quite likely that Charlotte's subsequent 'Biographical Notice' (1850) answers some of these, as well as those printed in reviews after the whole book was published. If we have been correct about the content of this earlier version, it was even more 'rude and strange' than the final version. Heathcliff gains his revenge through Isabella and the brutalising of Hindley, and goes to Catherine at his death. Then they perhaps range the moors together as ghosts. It was not a cheerful tale, told as it had been by 'a spirit more sombre than sunny'; when she had created Heathcliff, Catherine and the rest, 'she did not know what she had done'. Charlotte says she has re-read *Wuthering Heights* prior to writing this introductory notice; indeed she has, as part of a process of civilising the book, making many editorial alterations by way of smoothing Emily's way with the Victorian reader. But this procedure was not done through envy, since Emily had had to wait even longer than Charlotte for her work to be approved by a publisher and printed. *Wildfell Hall*, on the other hand, Charlotte wished to suppress.

Agnes Grey, however, was not at issue. Charlotte reprinted it now without the extensive alteration she imposed on Emily's book. There are sombre pages in *Agnes Grey*, concealed to some extent by the apparently conventional overall plot. In however low-key a way, Agnes is finally happy and fulfilled as she marries Weston. The book does not jar the sensibility so overtly, and we can imagine Newby, or whoever the publisher was, reading it quickly and seeing the clear prose and the romantic outcome as satisfactory and publishable. If he had been disinclined to publish it, rejecting both it and *Wuthering Heights*, as well as Charlotte's novel, possibly the Brontë sisters might have given up novel writing completely. It appears to me almost inescapable to conclude that it was Anne Brontë who blazed the trail in the publication of fiction, just as she was the only one of the three sisters to publish a poem outside the edition of 1846, though of course Branwell had published poetry to his credit.[6]

We need now to return to the literary productions we do have from the period immediately after the rejection of *Wuthering Heights*. Both sisters began Gondal poems on Monday, 14 September 1846; both were poems of some significance, showing development from the poems written before the novels were in hand. Both are narrative poems, dealing with children, and they share a common theme in rebellion and alienation. Anne's is a wonderful evocation of boyish companionship and betrayal, owing a little to the Heathcliff/Catherine childhood relationship. Comment on this most interesting poem must be reserved for another occasion. Emily's we may examine now, to see how she was thinking in the pause between her first work on the novel and her return to it at the end of September or beginning of October 1846. Perhaps we should also note the moment of cooperation between the two 'twins', as Ellen Nussey once called them, whose literary and possibly personal twinship was under threat.

We have already glanced at Emily's poem, beginning 'Why ask to know the date – the clime?' and continuing for 148 lines in copied form before degenerating visually into a chaos of fresh narration composed apparently straight on to this page of the manuscript, which had up to then been largely reserved for revised and fair-copied work. Anne's poem was of 150 lines; perhaps Emily's copied 148 lines correspond in time to them. Anne wrote a second poem in October, and possibly some of the chaotic narration following line 149 in Emily's poem date from the beginning of that month, but by then it seems as if the two sisters had made a decision to return to novel writing: the transition from *narrative* poetry would not have been hard. We need to examine the poem now, concentrating first on the processes revealed by authorial alterations, then examining the implications of the story-line.

Very brief mention was made of 'Why ask to know the date?' in the early part of this book. It is a narrative poem, differing from earlier narratives in several ways. Two major points are that it is not clearly finished, and it is not clearly a Gondal poem. The task of an editor with this poem is an impossible one, and Derek Roper rightly treats the text with great caution. He gives us all the variants and substitutions which are legible, and presents a version which does not attempt to complete Emily Brontë's incomplete thought processes. There is no clear indication of precise time-scale in the writing, though the work is headed by a date, 14 September 1846. The poem occurs in the Gondal booklet, B, but does not use a single Gondal name or date. It is revised and fair-copied up to line 148, but thereafter there are many changes on the page and it appears to be a draft worked out directly on to the sheets of what had always been regarded as a fair-copy book.

Chronologically, the poem is interspersed with *Wuthering Heights*, being abandoned, taken up again, further abandoned and once again taken up – or so it seems from the state of the manuscript. Attention was given to this poem right up to May 1848, and possibly beyond. During this time *Wuthering Heights* was finished and a new novel begun, but the poem remained in the background. The material of this poem must have been thought fascinating, and it is the last literary work with which we can be sure Emily Brontë was concerned. In dealing with it, we need to have one eye on *Wuthering Heights* and another on the following novel, with which we shall be concerned later.

The date at the heading coincides with that of Anne's new poem and need not be challenged. Even in this first section, lines 1–148, there are more than 40 verbal alterations, though it had been revised before copying, and we can envisage an earlier draft sheet or sheets. 14 September will be the original composition date, and copying into the copy-book may have been about the end of the month. The next work on the poem could be as late as mid-1847, when the novel had reached completion. What is clear is that it was written with the experience of writing the first version of *Wuthering Heights* behind the author and that it had an initial psychological function of providing her with an outlet for energy left over when the novel seemed to have failed. Some elements of it seem to be grappling with moral considerations raised in response to the novel's content.

Emily begins, 'Why seek to know the date – the clime?' and on revising changes 'seek' to 'ask'. She goes on,

More than mere words they cannot be:
Men knelt to God and worshipped crime,
And trampled worms like thee and me[.]

This fourth line gave her a lot of trouble; in revision she seems to have envisaged 'crushed the weak like thee and me', and possibly a word something like 'ruthless', before settling on her final choice, 'And crushed the helpless even as we[.]'

'Seek' is perhaps more poetic, less natural than 'ask'. The 'crush' and 'worms' of line 4 reappear from *Wuthering Heights*, Chapter 14, where Heathcliff declares: 'The more the worms writhe, the more I yearn to crush out their entrails.' Enigmatic in its context, this statement appears to have been dissolved in the poem for clarification. The grammatical problem with 'thee and me' is that one cannot be sure whether the words are the object of 'crushed' (perhaps unlikely) or in the object case after 'like'. Emily Brontë must have seen the ambiguity and decided to remove it. What she wants to say is that the 'I' of the poem, and the reader too, are accomplices in the worship of crime.

The remaining verbal changes in the first, scene-setting part of the poem, up to line 26, are the substitution of 'look on' for 'value' in line 7, 'With' for 'At' and 'sympathy' for 'worth than we' in line 8, 'week after week' for 'And week by week' (line 11), 'a' for 'the' (line 13), 'human gore' for 'reeking gore' (line 18). 'And I confess that' for 'And much I tell thee' (line 26) begins a new section in which the soldier narrator explains his reasons for involvement in the war. Perhaps the poet thought 'value' life was too strong, as the soldier was engaged in killing, and 'worth' is part of the same idea. Beginning line 11 without a conjunction strengthens it, though the loss of 'reeking' perhaps has the opposite effect. 'I confess' is clearer than the alternative. All these alterations seem to have the aim of strengthening the poem while making it more intelligible: a result, perhaps, of comments of the rejecting publisher, as well as the distant influence of Horace and others.

In lines 26–34 the soldier explains his position. He gives his reasons for fighting as 'hate of rest' and 'thirst for things abandoned now'. These appear to be Emily Brontë's reasons for writing the poem: she hates rest and yearns for a fictional world like Gondal, though it is important to note that nowhere is the name of the country mentioned, and we have been told in line 1 that it doesn't matter. Even in Gondal, and more so in the A poems, actual feelings of the author are often directly presented.

Continuing to look at the major changes in this first part of the poem, we note in lines 51–4, a four-line stanza between longer ones, Emily Brontë originally wrote:

I've often witnessed wise men fear
To meet with distress which they forsaw; [sic]
And seeming cowards nobly bear
Anguish that thrilled the brave with awe:

In revision she tidies line 52 for the rhythm, thrusts in the theological 'sinning' in line 53 and substitutes 'A doom' for 'Anguish' in line 54. Line 52 ends as 'To meet distress which they forsaw;'. There seem to be some gains and some losses in this revision.

In line 60 'fearful' natures become 'timid' and 'strangely strong' (or 'strung') becomes 'strangely nerved' to avoid the alliteration. Line 61 has a major overhaul, beginning as 'To desperate deeds that shamed the strong', considering whether to change 'the strong' into 'strongest' and ending as 'To deeds from which the desperate swerved –'. In line 61 'These may be told' becomes 'These I may tell', producing a slightly clearer line. We can see that in these changes both euphony and clarity of verbal expression are affected.

These examples of revisions to the first half of the poem will show the kind of tinkering which may well have taken place throughout Emily Brontë's labours. On the whole an improvement results, but occasionally a substitution seems less satisfactory. There is almost an air of desperation in the process at times, as though the revising author has lost confidence in her vision. The uncertainty of the meaning of the first line, possibly implying Gondal, possibly suggesting that Gondal has faded to an insubstantial ghost-world, indicates the uncertainty of the author about her creation.

Her mind is still running on inconstancy. The end of this part of the poem comes with the opening of the captive's locket, in which were found two curls of hair, suggesting a 'tale of doubtful constancy'; this reflects Emily's concern with treachery like that of

Catherine's when she seems to abandon Heathcliff for Edgar. Just possibly Emily had a previously created Gondal character in mind, but it seems more likely that it is the psychological characteristic rather than the person of whom she is thinking. Who now in her life was the traitor – Charlotte who removed her novel from the trilogy, or Emily who was preventing Anne's from being published? Or had she betrayed the Gondal world by using some of her poems for the 1846 edition, removing Gondal references?

Certainly the B manuscript seems to have been no longer sacred to Gondal themes, presented in an organised manner in a defined order. This poem was copied unfinished into the booklet, ending abruptly with this example of inconstancy at line 148. Worse was to come, as the book began to be used as rough paper to compose the rest of this poem directly on. Meanwhile, we can suppose that the diversion had succeeded, and that by the end of the month Emily was ready to follow Anne as she looked through the old almanacks searching for a clear chronological basis for Helen's diary in her newly begun novel *Wildfell Hall*. However, we shall leave this process to continue with our consideration of the narrative poem, even though we cannot fix the date of this further composition.

Bearing in mind the persistence with which Emily Brontë returned to this poem, we need to summarise the story-line to understand her fervent concerns in late 1846 and 1847. We have already suggested that Gondal was ceasing to be a refuge, and this new world is not unequivocally Gondal. Wherever it was, we read that it was somewhere where the inhabitants had learnt 'from length of strife' to laugh at death. Gondal had frequently been involved in civil war, as intermittently had Haworth parsonage, but strength may here have been gained from stories told by Uncle James Brontë from Ballynaskeagh, who visited the parsonage in 1846. Branwell's state was almost incoherent at times, and his sisters certainly saw him as a cause for dissension; and there was friction between the sisters, details of which have to be deduced, as they are certainly not narrated by Ellen Nussey or Mrs Gaskell.

The scene of the poem is set in autumn, the very warm autumn of 1846 when 'September shone as bright as June'; this tropical September appears also in the new parts of *Wuthering Heights*.[7] Crops in the land of the poem were not harvested properly, but

> ...kneaded on the threshing floor
> With mire of tears and human gore.

The narrator goes on,

> And I confess that hate of rest,
> And thirst for things abandoned now,
> Had weaned me from my country's breast
> And brought me to that land of woe.

We are never told who this narrator is, but we recall that Emily has been extending the range of her narrative personae, and this nameless man speaks for her as clearly as Nelly Dean. He talks for the Emily who has set aside Gondal for a rejected novel, thirsting for a return to an abandoned world. He intervenes in the war to free 'One race, beneath two banners fighting', and comments: 'When kindred strive – God help the weak! / A brother's ruth 'tis vain to seek.' In war the narrator becomes hardened but as in 'Julian M. and A. G. Rochelle' there were faces that 'could move / A moment's flash of human love'; and he hints that he could tell many stories of apparent cowards showing 'strange courage'. The story continues with an account of a captive taken by the narrator, who is the leader of the opposing group, spared because he is rich, and despite his wounds he is not to be killed unless he is willing to pay for such a 'privilege'. Once again Emily Brontë is dealing in violence and death.

The prisoner is threatened with a dungeon like that in 'Julian'. But for the meantime the soldiers occupy his mansion, a larger version of Thrushcross Grange. He is lodged in an empty room in his now shattered house with the full moon beaming on his face,

> Through shivered glass, and ruins, made
> Where shell and ball the fiercest played.

Emily Brontë has reverted to a much earlier scene, from a poem written in October 1837 (No. 11) in which a 'sudden chasm of ghastly light' shone on broken walls. Here the light was colder:

> ...wan moonlight smiled
> Where those black ruins smouldering lay...

Once again we see how certain scenes recurred to the poet, so that she was perpetually reworking past efforts.

Both the prisoner and the captor 'yearned for morn' but it was slow in coming. At daybreak, the prisoner is robbed of the locket previously mentioned, and the rival curls are disclosed. At this point the fair-copy ends and later lines are more heavily altered, though an even later section has more changes still. From now on the stanzas seem to be composed straight into the book. The narrator now urges the prisoner to die, speaking in 'contemptuous tone' and reminding us of Heathcliff's words to Hindley, Isabella and others. Soon, however, there comes a change. The narrator repents of his 'Harsh insults o'er a dying bed' and listening to his conscience 'haunting me' and whispering, 'God will repay – God will repay!'

This change of heart is unexpected; the captor now continues his thoughts of God with:

> He does repay and soon and well
> The deeds that turn his earth to hell,
> The wrongs that aim a venomed dart
> Through nature at the Eternal Heart.

Yet his mind is not quite rid of its ruthlessness. He watches as 'A look to melt a demon's soul' crosses the face of the captive, and hears a plea, 'not to me' but 'To mercy's source'. Still he will not relent. Up to this point in the poem, the captor has shown himself much like Heathcliff at his most dogged and unfeeling.

Then, he says, he was 'adamantine stone'. Heathcliff, too was 'stone' both according to Charlotte, who compares her sister to a sculptor, and to Emily herself, who allows him within the text to be described as 'whinstone'.[8] Within the novel, Heathcliff hardly relents; but Emily Brontë finally does.

Somewhere in October, then, Anne and Emily perhaps discussed their novels. The following suggestion is totally conjectural, and it is not possible for too much weight to be put upon it, but there do seem to me to be indications of its likelihood. We must remember that in all probability *Agnes Grey* was accepted. Emily, then, was standing in the way of her sister's work being published so long as she refused to add to *Wuthering Heights* so as to make up the three-volume set. Let us suppose that up to now she had been adamant against any further additions. As she said, 'I wish to be as God made me', so she may have tersely maintained that the book was as she wished and no modification could be contemplated. But this change of heart in the poem suggests that she now exhibited the characteristic that Charlotte claimed of her 'though full of ruth for others...' [9] And perhaps, like the narrator, she did begin to feel that the unrelieved ruthlessness of Heathcliff, except in regard to Catherine, might be as misleading as possibly Anne was suggesting.

I have already suggested in many places that in *Wildfell Hall* Anne is deliberately criticising *Wuthering Heights*. Her criticism focuses on events in the first 17 chapters of the novel; she presumably shared the feeling Charlotte had about the questionable morality of creating such beings as Heathcliff.[10] We may reasonably suppose that as the two sisters discussed, even argued over their future as writers in early October 1846, Anne will first have urged Emily to finish *Wuthering Heights* (though Emily will have maintained that it was finished), and second have told her that she intended to write a new novel herself which should take the major characters in Emily's book and examine them from a very different angle, consistently de-romanticising them. If the captor's change of heart in 'Why ask to know the date?' is an indicator, it indicates that Emily was ready to redress the artistic and moral balance in her novel, remove the obstacle to Anne's work being published, and force herself to engage again in the world of Wuthering Heights and Thrushcross Grange, despite a distaste which she seems to have shown by abandoning the book for two months.

There is a further point. If, as has been many times suggested, the satiric elements in *Wildfell Hall* point to a conscious comment on *Wuthering Heights*, we can suppose that Anne Brontë had before her a text of the points she wished to satirise. The time-scale for writing *Wildfell Hall* suggests a beginning at about the same time Emily Brontë began her continuation and revision of *Wuthering Heights*. Therefore it may be reasonable to expect to find as objects of satire only the parts of *Wuthering Heights* which appeared in the first version.

Points taken over from *Wuthering Heights* and examined in *Wildfell Hall* include an exploration of violence and its results, the long-term consequences of a woman having a relationship with a dark-haired Byronic hero, narrative technique involving a persuasive narrator called Ellen (Anne's version is 'Helen'), drink and its consequences, and a heroine who marries in haste to repent at leisure. The last mentioned is represented in *Wuthering Heights* by

Isabella Linton, who is no more adequately treated by Emily Brontë than Hindley Earnshaw, if we are to look for moral cause and effect. Of course, Emily Brontë was not looking for these, at this level. Anne's focus was different, so that she puzzled over the impatient elopement of Isabella, just as she had wanted to examine the violent behaviour of other members of the community near Gimmerton. Violence is hardly felt in *Wuthering Heights*, hence Anne's most careful writing of the scene in which Frederick Lawrence is attacked irrationally by Gilbert and is dazed, made sick and can hardly get to his feet.[11]

Similarly, a main feature of Anne's book is the unprecedented way in which Helen leaves her husband, Arthur, with whom she had been infatuated. But there *is* a precedent, for Isabella leaves Heathcliff without a qualm. This action must have been of deep significance to Anne, though this may not be the place to consider why. However, since we are engaged in working out a chronology for the development of *Wuthering Heights* the significance should be probed. Surely it would be fair to take this as further indication that Isabella's elopement and Heathcliff's punishment of her were part of the first version of Emily's novel. Pondering over this event, Anne perhaps wondered what had happened to Isabella, and tried to visualise the steps leading up to her decision to defy Heathcliff and leave. This part of Isabella was incorporated in Helen Huntingdon, sought out by her brother as Edgar does not seek Isabella.

It seems possible that Anne Brontë also wished to counter the Romantic incest theme which flows beneath the surface of *Wuthering Heights*. Whether or not Catherine and Heathcliff were related by blood (if it is thought that Mr Earnshaw's story of finding Heathcliff is a cover-up), their childhood relationship is a brother and sister one. Anne takes this and shows us a real brother and sister relationship between Helen and Frederick. Gilbert, the young man who loves Helen but needs regulating by her, brutally attacks Frederick, thinking that he may be Helen's lover and hence a rival. Mockingly, Anne is showing us a corrective to the Heathcliff/ Catherine friendship.

Encouraged by her success with *Agnes Grey*, Anne Brontë intended to make further use of a first person narrative, but she saw the value of a narrative within a narrative, as used by Emily in *Wuthering Heights*. She needed to underpin her story with a very accurate time-scale, suitable for a diary, and so returned to the almanacks for 1822–7, which the two sisters had been using for their systematic Gondal chronology in 1844. Outside these years *Wildfell Hall* uses looser chronology, more like that of *Agnes Grey*. But while the diary is being written, Anne plainly has these almanacks in front of her. As we move into a consideration of the second phase of *Wuthering Heights* we shall see that the close control of time noted by C. P. Sanger derives from this second phase. This can be explained by supposing that the two sisters shared the almanacks as they worked, as they are seen sharing a table in the 1837 diary paper.[13] Even though the years chosen by Anne for her story implied almanacks that were not appropriate for the years Emily had already marked out in her first version of *Wuthering Heights*, they could and did provide a framework.

Wildfell Hall has as its closing date 10 June 1847. This seems likely to be the date when Anne completed the novel. She had twice as much work to do as Emily, who had to adapt rather than start afresh. Though we cannot be quite sure how this *Wildfell Hall* date relates to the new *Wuthering Heights*, perhaps it might be reasonable to see it as approximately coinciding with the date of completion of Emily's book. The above has been a digression, and it is now time to return to the long narrative we have been considering, 'Why ask to know ...?'

The final part of the poem produces a host of verbal variants which is hard to quantify. Whole lines are recast, whole sections crossed through, though they seem integral to the story and clearly Derek Roper is right to print them. For example, lines 149–54 are crossed through, but this leaves lines 155–6, the end of the soldier's speech, without context and incomplete. Lines 172–89 can be omitted more easily; the first four are philosophical, treating the soldier's views on divine retribution. They show only two verbal changes, and it seems Emily Brontë decided they could not be perfected.

After the four philosophical lines, the rest of this discarded passage speculates on whether the captive, over whom the soldier is supposed to be keeping guard, has heard his muttered insults. These were contained in the lines previously jettisoned, and in lines 155–6. Once it had been decided to remove them, there was no point in the thoughts provoked in line 177 ('I know my prisoner had heard me speak'). In these excised lines the soldier watches the prisoner pray 'To mercy's source but not to me –' and feels remorse over his stony-hearted rejection of the unspoken plea.

The remaining narrative is hard to make out. At times one cannot be certain of the order of Emily Brontë's thoughts as she grapples with alternative words, syntax and images. Imagery is blood-charged and the poem is filled with remorse for cruelty. The captive, later described as of 'ancient' name (replacing 'noble' and 'lordly') is left dying, while the soldier goes into the courtyard to refresh himself at a gory fountain and in a cannibalistic touch eats food also 'dyed with crimson'. In the yard he meets a wild girl child, daughter of the captive, who is looking for her father. She has been stabbed four times and is called a 'piteous wretch' but the soldier will not listen to her and spare his captive.

It is not clear what effect the constant changes have in this part of the poem. The child's stabbing is made more personal to the soldier by the allegation 'You stabbed my child and laughed at me', instead of 'They pierced...'; 'every orphan' is described concretely as a 'flower' instead of abstractly as a 'hope'; the captive has a 'choking voice' instead of a 'bursting heart'; the enemy will 'hang up' five victims (as Heathcliff does with animals) rather than 'murder' them. All these seem to be alterations in the direction of concreteness.

The final lines of the poem are blotted and the writing is fierce and impatient. The captive's daughter hates 'like blackest hell', and Emily finishes the narrative abruptly:

> And weary with her savage woe
> One moonless night I let her go[.]

The word 'weary' was substituted for 'wearied' and 'savage' for 'gloomy', the second perhaps a considerable improvement, as the child is shown as wild rather than depressed. Her four stabbings do not seem to have sapped her strength, and we may have here another example of the way in which violence in Emily Brontë does not cause lasting injury or death, just as in Chapter 17 of *Wuthering Heights* Hindley is assaulted by Heathcliff, tries to defend himself with a strange knife and has an artery or 'large vein' cut, is kicked, trampled and has his head dashed repeatedly against the stone flags, but next morning is sitting by the fire 'deadly sick' but not unwilling to talk.

The end of this poem is so swift that we look closely at the words 'weary' and 'let her go', perhaps linking the weariness and its consequence with the author as much as the narrator. Symbolically, this bloodstained child may be Emily's poem and her wearied impatience with it may be indicated in the loss (but not death) of the child. The story is to be dragged to the surface again in May 1848, perhaps as a respite from another novel.

12

The Development of Part Two

It is not too difficult to see where Emily Brontë began writing the second part of the novel, though in the completed text the passage occurs much later than the halfway stage. Chapter 32 begins, 'This September I was invited to devastate the moors of a friend, in the North.' As we have seen, it is likely that Emily Brontë began writing in mid-October, with September 1846 fresh in her mind. In the narrative poem 'September shone as bright as June', and as Lockwood walks down the valley towards the sandstone direction post, past the 'church' – it has changed somewhat from the original dissenting chapel – which now looked 'greyer', he says, 'It was sweet warm weather – too warm for travelling: but the heat did not hinder me from enjoying the delightful scenery...' Very seldom can the word 'heat' be used to describe September weather, but the autumn of 1846 began with a hot September, which makes its appearance both in the poem and in this chapter of *Wuthering Heights*.

Strictly, it is incorrect to say that the chapter begins with the words, 'This September', since before them is printed a date: 1802. It seems to me that the detailed chronology of the novel was constructed in October 1846, with the almanacks in front of Emily and Anne as they worked. '1801', as we have seen, may have come from the date on the front of Ponden Hall, with perhaps a subconscious glance at the date when Mr Brontë arrived in Liverpool. Once this date was settled, the next year had to be 1802. The influence of Patrick Brontë as an oral story-teller is frequently neglected, but this chronology acknowledges the link between his birth and childhood, and the birth of the elder Catherine, the arrival of Heathcliff, etc. I do not suggest this convergence is rationally planned, but it responds to a deeply involved part of Emily's mind.

Lockwood immediately becomes involved in misapprehensions, just as he has been (as we read the book) or will be (as Emily Brontë perhaps wrote it) in some passages in Chapters 1 and 2. The reasons for these misapprehensions is never explored: they add to Lockwood's confusion and discomfiture, but they do not seem structural. It will be recalled that the younger Catherine does not seem integral to the original story, and in fact there is no clear indication that she had been thought of as the original versions of Chapters 1–3 were written. She is indeed very prominent in the second part of the book, and is perhaps the only new character with vital life. She makes her entrance in the completed text not in Chapter 1 (most of which, as we have said, appears to date from the first strand of writing), but in Chapter 2, a great deal of which was perhaps added in Autumn 1846. In this chapter, in her earliest remarks, she is sulky and negative, though later (in Chapter 18) we hear that she 'could be soft and mild as a dove...her love was never fierce; it was deep and tender.'

Just as the mercenary soldier in the narrative poem had repented his hardness, so now Emily Brontë changes her tone. Whatever was said in the rejection note from the publisher, added to the weight of criticism by Charlotte and Anne, caused Emily to review her tactics. Not that she reviewed her essential attitude or wished to withdraw what she needed to say; but the publisher, representing the southern audience, had misunderstood her novel, and worse had been added in that Charlotte and Anne had also lacked understanding. The new sections of the book therefore begin with misunderstanding as a major theme, though this is not crucial to the story. In Chapter 32 Lockwood arrives to settle business, as he tells Nelly, with 'your master', meaning Heathcliff. 'He's gone out at present,' she replies, 'and won't return.' The new master is Hareton, but we take the housekeeper to mean that Heathcliff 'won't return'. Indeed he won't, being dead; but we are not prepared for the shock which follows within three lines, when we are told of the death, 'Three months since'. Lockwood arrives to speak to Heathcliff, is told that he must settle with the younger Catherine, and then this is corrected by Nelly to say that he must settle with herself, all within a third of a page of print. Emily Brontë is unsettling the reader, provoking the misunderstanding she has already received and which she expects to continue.

But a little before we have seen the younger Catherine teaching Hareton to read and arguing over the pronunciation of 'contrary' (a significant word). The whole tenor of what Emily now adds to her book is *contrary*: it is a palinode. Like Heathcliff and Catherine, the younger Catherine and Hareton go out for rambles on the moors, but they will be securely married early in 1803, after the action of the novel is over. A fictional restoration is to take place, leaving Hareton Earnshaw in possession of his heritage, in consonance with the name over the door of Wuthering Heights on page 2 of the original version.

Emily's task now was to write the story of the second generation in such a way that there were no chronological anomalies. She also had to fill out the previous writing in places to provide a sound link. The length of the story as submitted in 1846 needed to be approximately doubled. It consisted of the chapters now numbered 1 (part), possibly a small part of 2, 3–17 and parts of 32 and 33. The expansion was effected both by writing completely new chapters (18–31) and by adding parts to the existing chapters, beginning with the 'mistakes' at the beginning and again at the start of Chapter 32. It may never be possible to work out exactly what was added piecemeal to the 'first part', but it is interesting that chronological data are generally given by Nelly in apostrophes to Lockwood.

For example, the end of Chapter 7 provides us with the only occasion on which a precise year in the 1770s is mentioned. Three pages before the close of the chapter Nelly breaks off from her Christmas description to say, 'But, Mr Lockwood, I forget these tales cannot divert you,' and for a short while Lockwood becomes a character in the novel as he discusses with Nelly his preferences in story-telling styles. Nelly then proposes to 'leap over some three years', interestingly bringing herself to 1780, when Catherine was 15, and just short of the 'twenty years' of the ghost child. Lockwood will not have this: he introduces a digression, allowing Nelly to justify her literacy in the well-known 'I have read more than you would fancy' speech. This looks like a justification in answer to objections made either by the other Brontës or by the publisher. Then, as a final marker, she gives a careful chronological indication: '...I will be content to pass on to the next summer – the summer of 1778, that is, nearly twenty-three years ago.' (She should have said, 'Just over twenty-three years ago.')

It has often been remarked that Emily Brontë makes very few precise references to exact dates in the novel, yet has a perfect control on the chronology. Such dates as there are seem all to be added now, in the rewriting, and it must also be said that the control is not actually perfect. Another accurate date (perhaps the only one combining day and month) is '20 March' – the death of the elder Catherine and the birth of the younger one. This is given in Chapter 21, in the words 'This twentieth of March was a beautiful spring day...', notably well into Part Two of the novel according to the theory we have been developing. *Spring* had already been chosen for Catherine's death, as is shown by the 'ousels' – blackbirds – building their nest after Catherine's death on the second page of Chapter 16, when the buds are also well formed. This precision of dating is part of the new approach to chronology introduced by the use of the almanacks shared with Anne.

The chronology of *Wuthering Heights* has been studied successively by C.P. Sanger, Charles Travis Clay, S.A. Power and A. Stuart Daley, with some minor additions by Inga-Stina Ewbank.[1] They have established a firm framework, but there are some anomalies, and it is part of my purpose in this chapter to show precisely where this dating framework begins. There are some small differences between the various chronologies, and a few unresolved matters outside the major problem of the 'twenty years' in which the ghost child roamed the moors. The first anomaly may result from a printer's error, though an understandable one. In Chapter 22 Nelly appears to give a time clue by saying she is 'hardly forty-five'. This is in the second part of the book, where chronology is very tightly controlled, so we are surprised that it does not tally with two other clues. On p. 220, at the margin of the second part, Dr Kenneth, commenting on Hindley's death, says he was barely 27 and adds to Nelly 'that's your own age; who would have thought you were born in one year?' It can be deduced from this that both Hindley and Nelly were born in 1757, and this agrees with a further clue on p. 118, characteristically given in the text after a dash, where Nelly says to Lockwood, talking of the catechism through which she puts Catherine when she wants to marry Edgar '– for a girl of twenty-two, it was not injudicious.'

Nelly was *not* 45 in 1800, the date of her clue of Chapter 22; she was 43. Examination of Emily Brontës 3s and 5s will show their liability to confusion. There is a further example of this in reverse, when in Chapter 32 she tells Lockwood that Heathcliff has died 'Three months since'. This has been a crux for chronologers, A. Stuart Daley finally agreeing with Sanger, against the intermediate writers, in deciding that Heathcliff died in April, *five* months before her present conversation.[2] To suppose a confusion between the numerals would solve this anomaly as well as the previous one. Towards the end of the novel, Emily Brontë seems determined to give us firm, accurate 'time checks' in a way she does not do in the earlier parts. Some of these concern Linton Heathcliff's age. In March 1800 he is 'wanting some months of sixteen' (p. 249); in February 1801 'it wants four years and more to his being of age' (i.e. 21) (p. 288). Edgar's age is clearly stated on a day in September 1801 to be 'thirty-nine' (p. 313), and in the first sentence of a new chapter (25) Nelly tells Lockwood, 'These things happened last winter, sir' (p. 288). In Chapter 32 we hear that Joseph went to Gimmerton fair on 'Easter Monday', and this turns out to be another clear indication of the way in which Emily Brontë used her almanacks, since it turns out that this day has to be 27 March, though in 1802 Easter Monday was not on that date. This contrasts sharply with part one; there events take place on Christmas Eve, but we are not told what day of the week this was. There is plainly an increased accuracy of dates in part two.

Time and date clues in the first half of the novel seem to be of two kinds, apart from the emotive 'twelve' and 'twenty' we have already discussed.[3] Some appear to be entirely embedded in the text, such as that in Chapter 8, when Nelly says of Catherine, 'At fifteen she was the queen of the countryside; she had no peer: and she did turn out to be a haughty, headstrong creature.' This sentence seems to me to be phrased in a manner quite consistent with the rest of the second phase of writing (late 1845–1846), and the chronological implications of mentioning Catherine's age do not seem strong. A similar integral reference may be the one in Chapter 10 where Isabella's age is given:

> She was at that time a charming young lady of eighteen; infantile in manners, though possessed of keen wit, keen feelings, and a keen temper too, if irritated.[4]

The dramatic date of this remark, calculated by the almanack, is late 1783, and Isabella would thus have been born in late 1764 or 1765. On p. 89 she is said to be one year younger than Catherine, whose year of birth can be calculated in various ways as 1765.[5] The reference to 'eighteen' is therefore an error unlikely to have been perpetrated once a tight chronology had been applied. Such slight anomalies are the mark of time references in the first part of the

book. But there is evidence that as part of the rewriting and extension process Emily went back to the first part to try to tighten time
references where she could. It seems possible that at first Nelly's
long narrative was unpunctuated by Lockwood and was simply
cast in the form of a monologue. In the rewriting this narrative was
broken up to give Lockwood a chance to interpolate small details
about himself, exhibiting misunderstandings characteristic of a
southern audience and perhaps mirroring remarks made by the
rejecting publisher of mid-1846. We have already noted that it is in
one of these 'apostrophes to Lockwood' that Nelly gives one of the
three precise clues about the years of the novel, at the end of
Chapter 7, when she says she will pass on to 1778 'twenty-three
years ago', and this is consistent with the 1801 of the beginning of
Lockwood's story. But these dates, I have suggested, were added
only at the point of rewriting in 1846–7.

Examining this passage closely, we see Nelly coming to the end
of her dramatic narration of the events of Christmas (1777), with
the report of her reproof to Heathcliff as he threatens to pay
Hindley back for his cruelty. This account ends with the words,
'while I'm thinking of that, I don't feel pain.' Nelly then turns to
Lockwood and we have three pages in which the reader is given
what might be called 'justification' for the narrative. During these
pages the difference in attitude between people in the North and
the South is discussed; Nelly explains why she is able to narrate
intelligently, and the time-scale is marked twice. This incident
constitutes one of the clearest examples of the 'apostrophe to Lockwood' episodes, which punctuate Nelly's story in part one of the
novel, but which do not advance the story and appear to be later
interpolations.

When we tried to observe Emily Brontë constructing and writing
her novel as first submitted, we noted that it consisted largely of
dramatic scenes like those in a stage play. Looked at from one
vantage point this is how the first half of the novel we now have
appears. We could divide it differently, however. We could consider the times and dates when Lockwood hears the story. On his
return from his second visit to Wuthering Heights, in late November 1801, he feels in 'low spirits' and asks Nelly to entertain him
with Heathcliff's story. There follow three pages, at the beginning of
Chapter 4, while Nelly clears some of the narrative ground. She then
begins her narrative proper, continuing to near the end of Chapter 7,
when we have the first break, and the date of 1778 is given.

Nelly proposes to leave Lockwood at this point: it is 11 o'clock at night. He tells her he will stay in bed in the morning, and begs her to continue, which she does, launching straight into her tale at the start of Chapter 8. The next two chapters constitute an hour and a half's narration, for when Nelly next looks at the clock it is half-past one. The second break consists of the last paragraph in Chapter 9 and the first page of Chapter 10. Four weeks now elapse, at the end of the third of which Heathcliff sends Lockwood a brace of grouse, '– the last of the season'. Chronologers have calculated that this dates the episode to about 10 December, since under the Game Act of 1831 the season ended then. It must be about 17 December, therefore, when Lockwood persuades Nelly to continue. This section constitutes the third period of narration.

This time there is less pretence of fitting Nelly's narrative into the time available. It lasts from the start of Chapter 10 to nearly the end of Chapter 14, where Nelly breaks off with some perfunctory remarks, and Dr Kenneth is announced in a short, rather flat paragraph. Chapter 15 begins with a similarly prosaic short paragraph, showing Emily not particularly interested in authenticating Lockwood's memory of Nelly's tale. It now proceeds for a chapter and a little more, until Nelly turns to Lockwood and asks him a question about the blessed in heaven (p. 202). He declines to reply and she doesn't press him, though she had said she would 'give a great deal' to know his answer. The narrative then continues across the boundary between first and second halves to the end of Chapter 24, when Nelly stops to discuss the time-scale ('These things happened last winter') and Lockwood's supposed attraction to the younger Catherine. There is no apostrophe to Lockwood at the point of the long jump in time, 12 years, at the start of Chapter 18.

It is the suggestion of this book that Lockwood, with his '1801' and '1802' develops into a character during the rewriting of the novel, partly in response to probable criticism from the rejecting publisher, who may have found the communication gap between northern peasantry and southern readers unbridged in the first version. Hence in part the 'confusions' section in the first two chapters, and the red herring of Lockwood's attraction to Catherine Heathcliff. Let us examine more closely what is added by the apostrophes to Lockwood we have just noted.

The three pages at the start of Chapter 4 produce more chronology: Nelly corrects Lockwood's impression that she has been at Thrushcross Grange for 16 years with the words: 'Eighteen, sir; I came, when the mistress was married . . .' This addition is part of the tight chronology of the second part, underlining the date 1783 as the date of Catherine's marriage. This section of the chapter is made up of dialogue between Nelly and Lockwood, and may strike us as rather flat. There are further mistakes and clarification. How far any such passage existed in the early version it is impossible to say.

We have already examined the next apostrophe, at the end of Chapter 7, in which Nelly explains more about the time-scale, and her own narrative capacity. In the next one, at the beginning of Chapter 10, there is more accurate timing to add to the 'eleven o'clock' and 'half-past one' we have already read. 'It wants twenty minutes, sir, to taking the medicine,' says Nelly. Emily Brontë also takes the opportunity to suggest one or two ways in which Heathcliff might have become a gentleman, perhaps to cover another credibility gap. Within three pages we are back in Nelly's continuous narrative. The final apostrophe, at the close of Chapter 14, coincides with the close of Volume I in the two-volume work. It constitutes a false pause, and may have to do with a decision on where precisely to end Volume I: the writing of this and the following paragraph is perfunctory, as we have seen. It will be noted that the volume division does not coincide with any obvious break, such as the beginning of Chapter 18 might provide; this is surely part of Emily Brontë's effort to conceal the joins in the rewritten work.

It has to be admitted that she succeeds in her effort to blur the division between part one and part two. We can see that there were in general three processes to be carried out in lengthening and softening the book for acceptance. One was begun by Lockwood returning to Thrushcross Grange so that he could be told the end of the story, including Heathcliff's death. In the first version this must have been told without Lockwood going away, perhaps during the continuation of his illness. A second was developing the new generation so that they could modify the rough impression given in Part I, both for the sake of publication and to answer the criticisms of Charlotte and Anne, the latter of whom was writing her answer to *Wuthering Heights*, possibly just across the table from Emily, passing almanacks to and fro during the process. A third was tightening the time-scale consequent upon the decision to place the story in a closely-knit temporal frame.

Evidence of the speed with which Emily finally worked as she neared the end of her project comes from the way in which the place name 'Peniston' developed. In the first volume of Newby's edition, p. 151, it is 'Pennistow Crag', becoming 'Peniston Crag' on p. 276. On the same page it becomes 'Penistone Crag' and in Volume II 'Penistone Craggs' on pp. 79, 80, 85 and 135, but 'Crags' on pp. 97 and 379. 'Pennistow' seems to be the earliest form. The two West Riding villages with this name are both 'Penistone' and this seems a likelier form. The spelling on p. 151 may perhaps be Newby's misreading of the manuscript. It does seem that neither Emily Brontë nor Newby bothered to proof-read this name, and the variance between singular and plural 'Crag' and the one or two gs looks very careless. Charlotte grumbled about Newby's typesetting, but this may have been because she wished to grumble at something, and we should probably see in these anomalies further evidence of Emily Brontë's lack of interest in spelling. There is a little more congruity in the forms of the word used in the second part of the book, and we must take these differences as a further indication of the lapse of time between first and second phases of composition.

A few words need to be said about the characters developed in the second part of the novel. The second Catherine is the most important. She echoes the behaviour and attitudes of her mother, but in a more acceptable way. It is through her that the fortunes of the Earnshaws will be retrieved and the clashing values reconciled. Her moodiness in the opening pages (especially Chapter 2) is not sustained as we find out more about her in the second part of the book. This may suggest that a moody young woman was sketched in to the original design, but on the whole even in this section Catherine seems to be part of the new writing, introduced to assist the confusion process.

The element of parody is strong in part two. Catherine's love for Linton is a whimpering ghost of her mother's love for his father. Her love for Hareton takes on the playful sincerity of her mother's love for Edgar. Linton himself is a totally new creation of part two, and despite his debased imaging of Heathcliff is perhaps nearer to one of the stupid children of *Agnes Grey*. Doubtless Emily Brontë would learn at first hand from Anne her stories of the Blake Hall children on whom the Bloomfields are modelled, but as *Agnes Grey* had been read aloud, as we may reasonably presume it had been, Emily could study the weak and frustrated violence of such children, taught by their father to despise kindliness and wreak vengeance on birds and animals. The influence of the young

Bloomfields is a further argument for the priority of *Agnes Grey* over the second part of *Wuthering Heights*, but it is also part of Emily Brontë's sly riposte to incorporate their characteristics in the young Linton Heathcliff and make them a plot instrument.

Heathcliff himself becomes grimmer than ever during the second part. Even those who have felt an understanding for his appalling behaviour in the earlier chapters may lose patience with him now, as his transcendental love is replaced by materialist vengeance. To effect his aims he enforces marriage on Catherine and his son, this 'whey-faced whining wretch'. Perhaps a key passage glances at a theme from *Wildfell Hall* as Catherine says, '...people hate their wives sometimes, but not their sisters and brothers...' The conversation continues with a discussion on whether Isabella actually left Heathcliff or not: a topic close to the major theme of Anne's novel.

13

The Three Housekeepers of *Wuthering Heights*

As we have seen, Nelly Dean has to explain why she is such a literate narrator. It would have been possible to integrate an explanation within the text: she could have been shown as a child reading books or discussing them with the Earnshaws or Lintons. Her explanation looks like a justification in answer to an objection. Psychologically, Nelly seems to take on quite an affinity to her creator, and enables Emily Brontë to tell her story subtly, guiding our reactions. Nevertheless, Nelly does not seem to have been part of the original plan, though a housekeeper was necessary from the start. In the end, Emily Brontë requires no fewer than three housekeepers at Wuthering Heights to tell the story fully. This requirement is undoubtedly cumbersome, though not very prominently so, but it does add weight to the suggestions we have been exploring.

A housekeeper is needed as early as the beginning of Chapter 3 to lead the Waverley-like visitor, Lockwood, to his bedroom, the ghost room. It is essential that she does not know the story of the room, and that Heathcliff does not know where she is putting the guest for the night. She therefore explains to Lockwood that her master has 'an odd notion about the chamber' and Lockwood asks why. Almost incredibly, the housekeeper does not know. This is because she has 'only lived there a year or two'. At this point any housekeeper will do for the task of putting Lockwood in the ghost room. Since I have suggested that much of Chapter 2 is from a later stratum than Chapter 3, it is not necessary to suppose that Emily Brontë had decided that the housekeeper would be called Zillah, who plays no part in Chapter 1. Nelly herself had been the housekeeper at Wuthering Heights in the past, as became clear to Emily as she wrote the next stage of the novel, beginning at Chapter 4. She is able to tell Lockwood the tale that the other housekeeper cannot.

It is not until Emily becomes deeply involved with part two of the novel that she realises that it will not do for the housekeeper to have been employed long at Wuthering Heights, since if she had been she would have known why Heathcliff did not wish the oak chamber to be used. Yet Heathcliff would have needed a housekeeper. Let us see how Emily Brontë approaches her creation, a few pages into Chapter 18 and just at the beginning of the part of the book she must have added in 1846–7. Catherine the younger has escaped from Nelly's care and Nelly has had to follow her across the moors until she comes to Wuthering Heights. She knocks 'vehemently' for admittance.

> A woman whom I knew, and who formerly lived at Gimmerton, answered – she had been servant there since the death of Mr Earnshaw.[1]

It will be necessary for Nelly to talk to this housekeeper and hear details of the events at the Heights, but it is not strictly necessary for her to have known the woman beforehand. It seems that Emily adds this detail by way of additional local colour.

This unnamed housekeeper makes a further appearance in Chapter 21, during Nelly's 'business visit' to Gimmerton. What more natural than that they gossip about events at Wuthering Heights? The woman is on her home territory, Gimmerton, and proves expansive with detail. At this point, though we cannot allege this firmly, it seems possible that Emily has forgotten that Zillah (if she has yet acquired the name) will need to be a stranger. She quickly gets rid of the earlier housekeeper in the following hasty words:

> That housekeeper left, if I recollect rightly, two years after he [Linton Heathcliff] came; and another, whom I did not know, was her successor: she lives there still.[2]

This is a slightly cagey way of introducing Zillah, whose name Nelly subsequently uses freely. It seems possible that at this point it had not been decided that this second housekeeper would need a character, unless it is this passage which is the interpolation. That this new housekeeper would have to be the one who led Lockwood to the ghost room must have gradually became apparent to the writer.

The next reference to Zillah is at the start of Chapter 23, during the first page of which Joseph is twice mentioned by name, and then we have

> The housekeeper and Hareton were invisible; one gone on an errand, and the other at his work, probably.[3]

On the next page Zillah's name is introduced without explanation as Linton cries 'I wonder where Zillah is!' A little later he adds, 'Zillah is constantly gadding off to Gimmerton since papa went.' This is quite interesting, since it was the earlier housekeeper who had connections at Gimmerton, rather than Zillah. In Chapter 24 Catherine is telling Nelly she has visited Wuthering Heights, and specifically says Zillah is the name of the housekeeper there; we already know, and so does Nelly, but possibly this was in reality he first time the name had been used. After this Zillah is mentioned again, and indeed narrates almost the whole of Chapter 30.

Zillah is a character firmly associated with part two of the book. The white heat of writing seen in part one is somewhat diluted in this second part and Zillah's tentative introduction seems to be managed haltingly. The speedy departure of the first housekeeper, with her Gimmerton associations, only to be replaced by someone Nelly does not know, but who is also tempted to gad off to Gimmerton, seems suspicious. Of course, Nelly must not know Zillah too well, since if she does she will tell her about Heathcliff's strange obsession. Later the country people say (as a matter of local gossip) that Heathcliff 'walks', and it is indeed surprising that Zillah knows nothing of this aspect of his strange behaviour. Nelly characterises her at the beginning of Chapter 30 as 'narrow-minded' and 'selfish', presumably to explain her lack of interest in the family she serves. It will not quite do; we come to the conclusion that Zillah began as a plot necessity and only later grew into a person. It will have been part of the rewriting stage that Zillah grows slightly in Chapter 2, and takes the blame for Heathcliff's disturbed night in the second part of Chapter 3.

Incidentally, it is to Zillah we look for a partial explanation of religious life in Gimmerton. It was in Lockwood's dream that we first encountered 'the Chapel of Gimmerden Sough'.[4] Lockwood, awake, describes its situation for us:

We came to the chapel – I have passed it really in my walks, twice or thrice: it lies in a hollow, between two hills – an elevated hollow – near a swamp, whose peaty moisture is said to answer all the purposes of embalming on the few corpses deposited there. The roof has been kept whole hitherto, but, as the clergyman's stipend is only twenty pounds per annum, and a house with two rooms ...[5]

It is surely clear that he is describing the building which is called 'the kirk' on the final page, where Lockwood seeks the three headstones of Edgar, Catherine and Heathcliff, and the 'grey church' at the beginning of Chapter 32. Edgar attends this building in Chapter 15 where it is called 'Gimmerton chapel' and Nelly can see the crowd outside it by the light of the westering sun. Although we get from Chapter 3 an impression of a dissenting chapel, it is impossible to draw distinctions between the 'Chapel of Gimmerden Sough' where the moss embalms the few corpses in the graveyard, 'the church' Lockwood passes on his way down the valley, the 'kirk' where he seeks the headstones, and the 'chapel' lit by the evening sun up the valley.

Yet Emily Brontë feels uneasy about all this and calls upon Zillah to help (or confuse) us. 'Joseph and I generally go to chapel on Sundays,' she says in Chapter 30.[6] During Lockwood's first visit, the Chapel of Gimmerden Sough is soon to lose its roof; by the time of the last visit slates are jutting off here and there. Nelly follows Zillah to explain that 'the Kirk has no minister now.... they call the Methodists' or Baptists' place, I can't say which it is, at Gimmerton, a chapel.' It is not clear whether this passage is to throw dust in our eyes so that we may think the Chapel of Gimmerden Sough is dissenting (as we might have expected from Joseph) and is not the same as the kirk, or whether Nelly's explanation has had to be interpolated on a final reading when the jutting slates of the kirk are found to imply that no services could be held there.

It will be recalled that according to the thesis of this book, Emily Brontë began her novel, after detailing the arrival of a young man at a carefully described castle-like residence, with his experiences in a room with a ghost. He was to have two dreams, the second requiring an explanation from a local inhabitant about the identity of the ghost, the first about a preacher, Jabes Branderham, whose initials correspond with a major Gondal hero and who subsequently disappears entirely from the book, leaving only the feeling that one object of it has been to attack or ridicule lengthy sermons of a dissenting type. The chapel, however, remains an important element and in its decayed state is still with us on the last page. It would be possible to complain that Emily Brontë has left us confused, or to explain that the Chapel of Gimmerden Sough is only a dream chapel (though in the passage quoted Lockwood has denied this). However, the chapel and its vicissitudes clearly come from Emily's subconscious, and though her intellect apparently recognised that there was an anomaly, she was unwilling to remove the dissenting element of the chapel from her story on revision. Hence the misleading remarks made by Zillah.

Housekeepers in *Wuthering Heights*, apart from Nelly, are lowly, expendable creatures. As quickly as Zillah was conjured from dust she is abolished: 'And how are you transplanted here, Mrs Dean? tell me that', asks Lockwood in Chapter 32, finding her at Wuthering Heights. 'Zillah left, and Mr Heathcliff wished me to come, soon after you went to London, and stay till you returned,' replies Nelly.[7]

This removal makes necessary the arrival of yet a fourth housekeeper (though she never goes to Wuthering Heights) who is as taciturn and incompetent as the others. It is she that Lockwood encounters smoking a meditative pipe on the horse-steps at the Grange when he returns in 1802. She cannot know anything about the goings-on in the Heathcliff, Earnshaw or Linton households either, or she might tell Lockwood before Nelly can do so. She serves a brief purpose and vanishes from the plot.

14

Sculpting the Statue: A Chronology of the Process of Writing *Wuthering Heights*

The aim of the second part of his book has been to delve into the processes by which *Wuthering Heights* emerged from the rock through the work of the 'statuary's' tools. We are now in a much better position to express this process chronologically, as proposed at the beginning of the search. It must be stressed that there can be no complete certainty in this chronology: the reader is asked to test these theories by reference to the arguments which have been built up in the body of this section and which I shall not now present again. This chapter will therefore consist of a patchwork of provable facts, theories generally accepted by Brontë scholars, and conjecture based on my previous arguments. At this stage, these will no longer be differentiated, and it will be necessary to refer to footnotes or earlier pages to evaluate various parts of the account. It is necessary at this point to make it quite clear that the statements below vary considerably in their degree of evidential support.

December 1844

All three Brontë sisters are at home for Christmas. It had become obvious by about October that the school scheme which Charlotte had been pursuing for some years was not feasible. Emily and Anne, possibly with Charlotte, began to consider whether their stories could be turned into saleable commodities. The evidence of Anne's poem 'Call me away' written on her return to Thorp Green in January suggests that the two younger sisters had been involved in Gondal, but this is also the last occasion on which they could have met to discuss writing fiction, and we have sufficient basis for an opinion that Anne was writing *Agnes Grey* during the middle of the year.[1] Though *Agnes Grey* and *Wuthering Heights* appear so different, they both begin with scenes related to the emergence of the two sisters into the world of teaching, Anne at Blake Hall in 1839, and Emily at Law Hill in 1838.

An agreement to adopt this as a starting point meant for Emily a willingness to abandon Gondal or at least to alter it in such a way that any public which could be coaxed to read their books would recognise an English scenario. It should not be supposed that she was necessarily unwilling to do this, since she herself had favoured realistic settings on earlier occasions.

January 1845

Once Anne had returned to Thorp Green, it is likely that Emily began work on recreating the scene at High Sunderland, which she had evidently visited during the winter of 1838–9. There are no poems recorded for January 1845, and it is into this gap that the first and parts of the second chapter of *Wuthering Heights* can be fitted.

February 1845

The poem 'Enough of Thought, Philosopher' is dated 3 February 1845. A complex poem of 56 lines, it is likely to have taken several days to complete. It is likely to have provided a diversion from the novel, still in its early stages.

March 1845

During a period of snowy weather the poem 'Cold in the earth' was written and dated 3 March. The pervasive snow made a strong appearance in this first part of *Wuthering Heights*, especially Chapter 3, where Lockwood is lodged in the chamber with the strange closet for a bed. Here he dreams of a figure (Jabes Branderham) naturalised from Gondal, and of Catherine Earnshaw, a recreation at this stage of one of Emily's lost sisters, but merging with elements of Gondal and Law Hill. She does not know how to explain this ghost child, and no clear solution is forthcoming. At this point, then, it seems likely that the novel is allowed to lapse. It is possible to speculate on letters from Anne at Thorp Green, though there is no trace of such letters. Emily seems unaccountably buoyed up this spring, possibly in contrast to what she hears about Anne and Branwell.

April–June 1845

This is an amazingly fruitful period in Emily Brontë's poetry, leading to the production of over 200 lines of poetry of highest quality: 'Death' (10 April); 'Stars' (14 April); 'A thousand sounds of happiness' (22 April); 'Heavy hangs the raindrop' (28 May) with its counterpart 'Child of Delight! with sunbright hair'; and 'Anticipation' (2 June). The poems suggest much increased confidence, but they may be seen as another interlude in the composition of *Wuthering Heights*, which at this stage must have consisted of the bulk of present Chapters 1 and 3 with some of Chapter 2 and possibly other material not present in the finished version.

June and July 1845

Brontë biography shows a summer of turmoil, with Anne finally leaving Thorp Green, Branwell losing his post there, Charlotte going on holiday with Ellen Nussey, and Emily and Anne going on a 'journey' which should have taken them to Scarborough but which ended in York. The diary papers written by the two youngest sisters do not mention the novels, though 'Passages in the Life of an Individual' is often thought to be *Agnes Grey*. Emily is writing the story of the Emperor Julius, whose characteristics become merged with those of Heathcliff. On the journey to York the pair act out parts of the Gondal story, but Anne (according to her diary paper) is much less involved in the saga than Emily.[2]

August 1845

Emily wrote a rather uninspired poem about a Gondal prison on an unknown date this month. But for some reason the novel began to take hold of her again. It seems likely that it was now that she discovered the voice of Nelly Dean (Emily Jane) and began the story of Heathcliff's arrival from the beginning. This 'very beginning' was the 'very beginning' of Emily Brontë or Prunty, an outcast's story in Liverpool. This part of the story is located in time by the promise to bring apples and pears home. The first of a series of theatrical scenes shows the arrival of Heathcliff. This part of the novel will proceed in a sustained series of such scenes, made up with one eye on the distant precepts of Horace about events on stage and events reported. Novel writing will not be uninterrupted, however.

September 1845

Emily's imagination returns to the topography of Shibden and High Sunderland. She begins to see the contrast between the windy heights and the rich lowland as integral to her story. Always acutely interested in contrasts and dialectic, she develops Lockwood's position as a tenant of the wooded park in the valley and finds that her Gondal character Gerald can be turned into Edgar L., the prosperous squire's son. Several Gondal characters are turned into Yorkshire people. The girl ghost of the winter begins to subsume traits from Geraldine.

As Catherine and Heathcliff escape from their washhouse prison, prisons and their constraints are strongly in Emily's mind, and she assembles fragments for a poem, 'Silent is the house' which she copies into her Gondal notebook early next month.

October 1845

It is not clear why Charlotte is searching for poetry to edit and form the basis of an attempt at publication, but this is evidently the case. If she knew of the fiction being produced by the two younger sisters it is not easy to see why she decided to interrupt the flow of writing. It is clear that her discovery of Emily's poetry, generally agreed to be the B (Gondal) notebook, has to do with the school failure and the need to earn money by writing, but it is surprising that Charlotte did not prefer fiction. One possible explanation is that her own attempts to draft the book which eventually became *The Professor* were proving difficult. The evidence is that having discovered the poetry, possibly with 'Silent is the House' the final poem copied into the booklet, she tried to interest Emily in editing it and met with reluctance.[3] It is generally thought that this reluctance was because of the personal nature of the poetry, but an additional point may be that Emily was by now very involved in her novel and was unwilling to be drawn away from it.

There is still dispute about the degree to which Emily collaborated in the editing of her poems, but Derek Roper has shown that she did at least play some part in the process, presumably laying aside her work on *Wuthering Heights*.[4]

November and December 1845

Assuming the poetry editing to be perfunctory or speedy, Emily Brontë was ready to resume consistent work on the novel by some time in November. She took the story from the Sunday on which the two children escaped to watch their neighbours at Thrushcross Grange on to Christmas. Edgar's rivalry with Heathcliff was recapitulating Gondal episodes but the tone and locale of the novel was releasing a new power and intensity in Emily which may have been accentuated by the increased confidence aroused by re-reading and editing her strongest poems.

January–April 1846

Emily's strong poem 'No coward soul' was written on 2 January. The tone of this poem accords with the next section of *Wuthering Heights*. The weather at Boston, Lincs, a county adjacent to Yorkshire, was warmer than usual for the time of year (January an average of 5°F above normal, February an average of 4°F above normal, March a little above normal). There was no snow in January. Thus Emily Brontë was able to write summer scenes in weather that was 'unusually fine' (February). There was a patch of snow from 9–13 February and a little snow on 19 March. The thunder on 26 March may have influenced the storm scene in Chapter 9, though this seems a little late for this chapter to be under construction.

It must be remembered that there is no poetry being written in these confident months, and that is surely because *Wuthering Heights* is currently an obsession. The white heat of this section of the novel is very noticeable, and it seems likely that it gave rise to such remarks of Charlotte's concerning her sister as that 'she never lingered' over a task.

It is on 20 March that Catherine the younger is born, and a possibility that the date is chosen to reflect the actual date; however, this does not accord with the date of the storm mentioned above. The tense and inspired writing begins at this point to calm and it may be that Emily was discussing with Charlotte and Anne how near they were to offering their tales to the public.

April–May 1846

6 April 1846 is the date of Charlotte's letter announcing the preparation of the three novels. Emily Brontë now had to complete the story of Heathcliff's love for Catherine and his revenge. She did this in Chapter 16 and parts of 17, and perhaps early versions of parts of Chapters 32 and 33, with a substantial part of Chapter 34, relating Heathcliff's death.

June–July 1846

The completed first version was copied and perhaps somewhat revised ready for despatch to Henry Colburn.

4 July 1846

This is the date of Charlotte's letter requesting permission to send the three 'tales' to Henry Colburn. A note suggests that Colburn asked to know the nature of the tales, and it is assumed but not proved that the three novels were then sent to him. We do not have any letter in which he rejected the novels and we have no idea why he did so. Such decisions were made quickly in the mid-nineteenth century, and we can be fairly certain this process could have taken place by the end of July.

July and August 1846

It is an open question whether there were two more rejections during late July and August or only one. I have argued above that the August rejection was perhaps by Newby himself.

24/25 August 1846

Emily and Anne, at Haworth, received the rejected novels back from this publisher. It can perhaps be inferred from what happened later that *Agnes Grey* was substantially accepted, while Charlotte's book, then called *The Master*, was rejected outright. *Wuthering Heights* was neither praised nor damned. It is likely that the changes introduced by Emily were intended to answer the objections raised, and there are probably further echoes of these objections in Charlotte's later comments on the book and perhaps also her editing of 1850. The two sisters at Haworth sent on *The Master* to Manchester, where Charlotte was attending their father while his eyes were operated on. Mrs Gaskell records the return of the novel.[5]

August and September 1846

We can reasonably infer a discussion between the three sisters when Charlotte returned from Manchester. At the end of it, Charlotte withdrew completely from the consortium and began work on *Jane Eyre*.[6] This left the three-volume set short of a volume. Initially, as we can see from what happened in September, it was not clear what could be done to save the situation, and it must have seemed as though Anne's contribution to the set, which must have been approved, would have to be abandoned.

14 September 1846

Both Anne and Emily wrote narrative poems with Gondal or part-Gondal reference. It is notable that Anne's poem is a gain in strength from her earlier Gondal work, reflecting the acceptance of her novel and the growing confidence that brought, while Emily's casts about for some time, beginning with a question and indicating changes of mind and attitude. In the first part of 'Why ask to know...?' we see Emily writing to distract herself and in a context which reflected the civil war in the Brontë household.

September 1846

On the evidence of *Wildfell Hall* we can suppose that Anne disliked the tone of *Wuthering Heights* in its first version. This is amply supported by Charlotte's later remarks.[7] Anne's objections were now underlined by the qualified rejection by publishers. She took exception to the way in which violence and drunkenness were portrayed in *Wuthering Heights,* and the way in which Emily had allowed events to occur without probing the psychological and moral consequences. The way in which Isabella ran away from Heathcliff may have been a major point.

If Anne's novel had been accepted and *Wuthering Heights* criti-
cised as unsuitable but not irremediable, so long as Emily refused
to remedy it she was standing in Anne's light. Anne must have
announced her intention to write a new novel which would comment on *Wuthering Heights* and take over some of the situations.
However, Emily finally agreed to change and expand the rejected
book so that it could fill two volumes and still be issued with *Agnes
Grey*. These changes would have the effect of tempering the harshness of the book, showing Emily relenting as her mercenary would
relent in the contemporary narrative poem. Anne was wishing to
expand her diary style which had been at the edge of the method in
Agnes Grey. The two sisters agreed to use almanacks from the
1820s. This focused Emily's mind on the precise time-scale of
Wuthering Heights. If one objection of the publisher had been the
confusing narrative approach, tightening the time-scale would give
sound indicators to the public. Hence we have tighter time control
introduced in part one and a flood of time references in part two.

September and October 1846

Emily wrote the chapter now known as 32 and in previous editions
as Volume II, Chapter 18. This includes September weather based
on that of September 1846, and mirrored in the weather of the
narrative poem contemporary with this part of *Wuthering Heights*.
It may be that Lockwood's second visit was originally to have been
located at the centre of the book and was later transferred to its
present position. The dates 1801 and 1802 also seem to be provided
at this point, matching Anne's attention to dates in the 1820s. The
construction of Emily's time-scale would be more difficult than
Anne's and it must surely have been produced on a chart at this
stage. A few anomalies escaped Emily during the imposition of the
time-scale, but the original ghost girl's cry did not, causing some
fluffing in what is now Chapter 12.

November 1846–about June 1847

During this period Emily Brontë added her new chapters and
revised the rest of the book, giving Lockwood and Nelly more to
say by way of explanation, inserting the 'apostrophes' we have
noted, and tightening the time-scale. Nevertheless, there is evidence of haste in the final preparation, such as the speedy writing

which allowed numbers 3 and 5 to be confused, and the careless accumulation of housekeepers. Two reasons for this could be pressure from Charlotte and Anne as they finished *Jane Eyre* and *Wildfell Hall* and Emily's self-doubt or impatience. Spellings of Peniston and the transformation of Gimmerden into Gimmerton were not even noticed by her as she sped to complete the book. Nor did she pick these points up later at proof stage.

August 1847

Proofs arrive at Haworth. There are some manuscript corrections in a copy of *Agnes Grey* but nothing corresponding to this is known for *Wuthering Heights*, and we do not know the precise status of Anne's corrections. It is not a proof copy.

December 1847

The three-volume set is published in the early part of the month. A review in *The Spectator* is dated 18 December.

15
Objections and Implications

The reader may well have reached this point in a state of general assent to what has been written in these pages, yet at the end feel with a sense of shock that their effect has been to undermine the value of Emily Brontë's extraordinary book. It will be as well therefore to take stock and consider the implications of the theory which has been advanced and the strength of the evidence produced.

First, it may be noted that the idea that *Wuthering Heights* is not a seamless whole is not a new one. E.F. Benson's comments on the structure of the book go beyond what we have already noted.[1] He considers it strange that Lockwood's interest in the younger Catherine is not developed, and sees this as an element of the initial planning of the novel which was later abandoned. His comments may seem harsh and to lack perception, as he goes on to say,

> No single author could have planned a book in so topsy-turvy a fashion...Nellie [sic] Dean must recount [the previous history of Heathcliff] to [Lockwood], and it takes so long that he must needs fall ill so that his convalescence may be beguiled with it. Nobody planning a story from the first could have begun with an episode so misplaced that such an awkward device must be resorted to.

As a novelist himself, Benson knew about planning, and is surely correct within his limits to note that the planning of *Wuthering Heights* is confused. Of course, this matter is ultimately of little weight in judging the value of the book, but it is none the less a perfectly fair point to make.

Benson is not alone in considering that Emily Brontë was not the sole author of the book. There has been a persistent strain of criticism which seeks to involve Branwell, at least in parts of the book. This legend may stem from Branwell himself, as he is reported to have claimed to have been involved in the early chapters by a friend, William Dearden.[2] An early commentator, Alice Law, developed this in her book, *Patrick Branwell Brontë* (Alan Philpott, undated). Stylistic arguments were used by Irene Cooper Willis to refute the thesis, who asserted that

> The author of *Wuthering Heights* was first and foremost a spectator of events, an observer of drama from the outside.[3]

It is just this 'spectating' side of Emily, content to watch and allow events to unfold, which renders it apparently unnecessary for her to plan the book from the outset. Though Ms Willis points to minor variations in style, she shows a homogeneity of approach throughout the narrative which surely removes Branwell from the account. Anne, as we shall see, may not be able to be removed so easily.

Another commentator, already mentioned, who has pointed out anomalies in *Wuthering Heights* is Q.D. Leavis. Publishing in 1969, she deplores attempts to gloss over the problems in the design of the book: 'Desperate attempts to report a flawless work of art lead to dishonest ignoring of recalcitrant elements or an interpretation which is sophistical.' She goes on to suggest that *Wuthering Heights* 'has all the signs of having been written at different times...' She sees the origin of the novel as Heathcliff's status as an illegitimate son of Earnshaw and the half-brother of Catherine. The Romantic theme of incest was to have been the nub of the story. I find this interpretation of Heathcliff's birth and arrival at Wuthering Heights convincing. The book does seem to deal with an identity that hovers over the boundary between brother/sister love and sexual unity. Even if we doubt that Heathcliff is Earnshaw's son, he is Catherine's adopted brother. The incest theme must haunt the story. However, I have suggested that this was not the very first beginning of Emily Brontë's 'tale', which is congruent with Anne's contemporary story of 'when we first began to teach'.

Q.D. Leavis considers that Emily Brontë, as a first novelist, tries to do too much, and hence includes various large themes which cannot be reconciled. As well as the *King Lear* theme previously mentioned, she sees a Romantic child theme, and a social comment novel contrasting Wuthering Heights with Thrushcross Grange. There are some persuasive arguments to support these points.[4] Unlike some commentators, Q.D. Leavis sees the second part of the book as relevant to its interpretation. She does not use many examples from this part, but does note the continuity between the experience of the class-based taunting of Hareton in both parts.

How do most commentators avoid discussing the anomalies in *Wuthering Heights*? Remarkably large numbers seem to do so by annihilating what we have called part two, the section composed, according to our theory, between October 1846 and June 1847. Of the ten articles in the *New Casebook* on *Wuthering Heights*, edited by Patsy Stoneman, only one, by Lyn Pykett, meets the point directly.[5] Overwhelmingly quotations and examples come from the Catherine/Heathcliff story, and though many purport to discuss the structure of the novel, and in fact do so to some effect, they do not regard the palinodic character as worth much, or any, space. Yet we are still confronted by the stark point made by an unfashionable critic, Romer Wilson, many years ago. Wilson is often dismissed as one of the 'purple heather' school of writers, but she addresses elementary matters which are left untouched by later writers. Considering the book from a biographical standpoint, she interprets the central Catherine/Heathcliff theme as a personal attempt by Emily Brontë to get to grips with her own divided psyche. And when Catherine is dead, says Romer Wilson, 'Emily did a curious thing, she rewrote the story as it might have been without Heathcliff as hero.' And surely this is how the two halves of the book strike us. The second part does seem like a palinode, in which the younger Catherine and Hareton replace with their human relationship the supernatural relationship of Heathcliff and the elder Catherine. This, I suggest, is because in some respects it *is* a palinode.

Much of Lyn Pykett's description of *Wuthering Heights* seems to me to comprehend the issues facing Emily Brontë and to accord, from a very different viewpoint, with the step-by-step account I have tried to draw of the way in which the book was developed by a writer whose experience was built on her poetry some of which needed to expand into narrative verse in order to fit in with a Gondal concept. It will perhaps be in order to follow Ms Pykett through some of her chapter.

Acknowledging the objections made to the retelling of the story in part two made by Leo Bersani, Rosemary Jackson and others, she notes that they have felt a loss of power, quoting Bersani who calls it 'a rather boring second half', and Jackson, who charges it with 'inauthenticity'.[6] She notes that Sandra Gilbert and Susan Gubar, also represented in the *Casebook*, have suggested that at the end patriarchal history has been 'redefined, renovated, restored' and 'the nineteenth century can begin'. Against this, Lyn Pykett wishes to place a concept of the rise of 'feminine authority' in this novel. Using the traditional terms 'Gothic' and 'Domestic Romance', Pykett points to supporting theory which sees the book taking its place in a movement towards centralising women's position in literature and outside politics.

I have suggested that the chapters and other material added to *Wuthering Heights* between late 1846 and early 1847 were motivated by two things, rejection by a publisher (possibly Newby) and dialogues with Anne Brontë which may have allowed Emily to reconsider what she wished the effect of the novel to be. It seems likely that Anne remained dissatisfied with *Wuthering Heights* even as she saw its modification, but for practical as well as artistic and moral reasons Emily was willing to add to what she had written. As in the case of the poems, she may well have been reluctant; so much is suggested by the gap in production during which she returns to Gondal poetry. But the poem she writes works on the need for revaluation and revision of attitude and at the end of this internal process she is ready to share with her sister a common approach to fiction; though this common approach is not thorough-going and will not bring *Wuthering Heights* so far into the realm of morality as to win Anne's whole approval.

But it is more feminised. The second Catherine, from a position of power, cajoles Hareton back towards a civilisation which is responsible, and not weak. The fierceness of Heathcliff is diminished; he doesn't care whether his vengeful plans are fulfilled or not; Lockwood, distant and less effective cousin to Gilbert Markham and Fergus, leaves the North and closes his account, with the breezy northern femininity of Catherine and the practical organising skills of Nelly in possession of Hareton. It is certainly a return to the Domestic; the elemental tumult at the Heights is over. Lyn Pykett makes the point that the civilising effect of literature is more usually introduced by a male character teaching a female. Here, the roles are reversed.

Ms Pykett goes a little further. She suggests that *Wuthering Heights* participates in, investigates and explores, the feminisation of literature. In particular, she refers to the novel form, and it is clear that as Emily Brontë writes her first novel in 1845 and early 1846, she is thinking deeply about the nature of her art form. After the summer of 1845 Charlotte and Anne would have been discussing the current progress each had made on their respective 'tales' and there is plenty to suggest that Charlotte had access to a wide range of novels to underpin her theory. On the evidence of her character, Emily Brontë would be likely to reject any kind of formulaic approach to fiction writing: she looks at the task of preparing a narrative as one parallel to writing for the stage. Whether we see *Wuthering Heights* as a five-act play as does Melvin R. Watson, or draw analogies with Greek tragedy, as suggested by Emily's interest in Horace, it is dramatic and poetic values which emerge most strongly in most of the novel.[7] But rejection gives Emily time to think, not only about the content of her book, but also about the form. Her control of the book as civilising influence then mirrors that of the younger Catherine.

It will be seen from this brief excursus into twentieth-century criticism that there are a number of writers who have looked carefully at the lack of overall homogeneity in *Wuthering Heights* and have not necessarily found this a problem in according the book very high status. As I have suggested, many critics disregard part two and still find they can discuss the book on an extemely elevated plain. The purpose of my chronological investigation has been to show how Emily Brontë may have arrived at the finished text, which at the end she published, just as she published versions of poems which some may see as unjustifiably modified from her earlier versions. It is hard to see precisely what the effect of the book as submitted to a publisher in 1846 would be. Nelly's narrative may have been uninterrupted: this would remove the very desirable mediation between reader and incredible characters that Nelly's apostrophes to Lockwood provide. The time indicators may have been much less systematised, though Emily Brontë's method of referring backwards and forwards in time was already prominent, transferred from the Gondal saga's dreamlike timelessness. We can see that this could prove a serious stumbling-block to readers, as to the writer in removing contradictions. The firm almanack-based time-scale is surely a great improvement.

It is harder to pinpoint ways in which the addition of the second generation improved Emily's work. There is certainly need for critics to look in detail at the crucial chapters, Nos 18–33, and to affirm their value. Lyn Pykett's work is one such genuine approach. The point made by Q.D. Leavis cannot be sidelined: it is all too possible to produce readings of *Wuthering Heights* which do not take account of the finished novel. Honest, perceptive and careful readers will know instinctively that these later chapters complete and do not undermine the book. It is for literary critics to show why this is so.

I should like to complete this part of the book by anticipating objections to the way in which I have sought to show how Emily Brontë worked towards her finished masterpieces both poetic and fictional. To begin with, we may discuss objections from those who feel that the Halifax topography suggested as a basis for the book simply isn't represented in readers' perceptions of the moorland scenes, the remoteness of the two houses, etc.

There are two ways of looking at this point, one considering positive reasons for assigning a Halifax location, the second considering how the novel came to be associated with the landscape of Haworth. It is of course perfectly true that the outdoor habits of the Brontës, leading to their thinking of Haworth moor as an extension to their own parsonage house, are well documented. As Charlotte said, Emily really did 'love the moors'.[8] Considerable parts of the ambience of Haworth moor do penetrate *Wuthering Heights*. The large distances between Thrushcross Grange and Wuthering Heights, and from these houses to Gimmerton, reflect Haworth as much as or more than Halifax. There are lapwings and heather, stone walls, thorn trees, larks and high rocks equally near Haworth and near Halifax.

But those who adhere to Top Withens as an influence on *Wuthering Heights* need to consider how it entered the legend. After the death of Charlotte, biographical and topographical questions began to be pursued with energy and enthusiasm. Ellen Nussey, Charlotte's life-long friend, was the major primary source for investigators. She knew Haworth, having walked the moors with the family as teenagers and as adults. She knew little of Halifax. She could not guide enquirers to High Sunderland, nor Shibden, and Law Hill may have been an uncomfortable blur in her mind. Miss Patchett, under whom Emily had worked at Law Hill, refused to give details on account of Charlotte's negative reporting of the Law Hill experience.

It is certainly true that the town of Halifax itself is abolished entirely from the topography of *Wuthering Heights*, but once that is allowed, and allowance made also for the expanded distances in Emily's novel, there can be much more conviction that High Sunderland and Shibden are very much in her consciousness as she plans her work. The natural scenery at the North of Halifax is every bit as dramatic as that of Haworth. Approaching the valley from Dewsbury and Hipperholme (which interestingly has the rhythm of Gimmerton), the hill behind High Sunderland rears up in front of the traveller.

The green fields and woods on the left, with a stone house set in parkland, seem to mirror Thrushcross Grange. The sightseer has reached Stump Cross, and is looking over the site of Shibden Grange to the hall. He or she should park the car near the sand-stone pillar and walk to High Sunderland, using one of several winding routes. It will be surprising if the wind does not increase on the walk. There is nothing now to be seen of the old house, but the elements are still raw; the site is exactly as Emily Brontë describes.

There is much research to be done to discover more about Emily Brontë's important experiences at Law Hill. Miss Patchett's silence is most regrettable, though quite easy to understand. She would certainly recognise the close links Emily's work had with Halifax and Southowram. The owner of Shibden, Anne Lister, whose life and work are now being explored by dedicated researchers, was a controversial figure in her own lifetime, and has since emerged as a Tory lesbian, whose immense diary deals with her commercial interests but also with her love affairs. She was certainly on visiting terms with Miss Patchett and it is in-conceivable that Emily heard nothing about her.[9] But when well-meaning biographers tried to discover what Emily's experience of the school was, Miss Patchett's silence could have been variously motivated.

As for the careful chronological framework I have proposed, based partly on a study of Emily Brontë's earlier working methods, Charlotte's two passages of comment, the 'Biographical Notice' and the 'editor's Preface' to the 1850 edition do give substantial external evidence to counter the notion of prescient forward plan-ning. Among the points made in the two passages we note, 'Neither Emily nor Anne was learned... they always wrote from the impulse of nature...' (Biographical Notice); 'Having formed these beings, she did not know what she had done.' (Preface); '...the creative gift...sets to work on statue hewing...' (Preface); '"Wuthering Heights" was hewn in a wild workshop, with simple tools, out of homely materials. The statuary found a granite block on a solitary moor:... He wrought with a rude chisel, and from no model but the vision of his meditations. With time and labour, the crag took shape...' (Preface). These extracts forbid us to think that the novel was written speedily and without angst. Earlier biographies of the Brontë sisters were often unclear on precise chronology. This has had to be built up cautiously over the years, and a great deal has been added in the last 20 years. This is the first exploration of the development of *Wuthering Heights* which is able to take into account these new understandings of Brontë chronology. The Brontës are the most reticent of nineteenth-century authors and the use of circumstantial evidence about their lives is inevitable. Having made that quite clear, I should like to discuss objections other than topographical ones to matters I have discussed, and try to answer these objections.

First, the question of the form of the novel as submitted in 1846. There may be objectors who wish to argue that we have no precise knowledge of what that submission was like, and it could have been the novel as we now know it. In answer to this, I have tried to lay out exact details of the numbers of pages involved in the final three-volume presentation of *Agnes Grey* and *Wuthering Heights*. The question has to be asked how three novels, *The Master*, *Agnes Grey* and *Wuthering Heights*, in which one was almost as long as the others put together, would have been acceptable either to a publisher or to the Brontës, having regard to Charlotte's careful balancing of length in the published poem edition. Her letter to Colburn is very specific: '...three tales, each occupying a volume...'[10] If the novel of 1847 was the same as that submitted in 1846, how is it that it occupied two volumes when finally issued?

In proposing this piecemeal planning of the novel, it may seem that I have set the clock back to before Sanger's discoveries of 1926 about the tight chronology of *Wuthering Heights*. This aspect of the book is rightly pointed out as evidence of Emily Brontë's intellectual control of the material. In reply, I should agree that Sanger is quite right to discern this chronological underpinning, but note that almost all the chronological clues are given in the parts of the book I see as added in October 1846 to June 1847. Much chronology is found in Chapters 18–33 and the apostrophes to Lockwood by Nelly Dean which interrupt her story. I do not deny that chronology is very important in the novel, and that the shifts and references back and forth across a period of time are crucial, and were inherent even in the first version, but this whole element was accentuated and systematised in the revision.

The third objection might be the radical one that by throwing doubt on Emily Brontë's forward planning of the novel, I am undermining its status. As I have suggested, much of this status derives according to critics from its compactness, its intensity, its drama, its poetry, its daring, its depth of treatment, its range in raising issues both social and psychological. Critics mainly concentrate on part one. Those who go on to part two see different virtues in the book, interpreting it as a dialogue, an attempt to domesticate the wild, a logical extension and meditation on issues raised in part one. Sanger's evidence of chronological control has possibly misled some commentators to see more order in the structure than is actually present, and an emphasis placed on Emily Brontë's pre-planning which overvalues this element of the novel. Sanger's discovery is quite valid, the chronological control adds to the book, and the second version is better than the first would have been, but that does not mean we have to argue against the implication in much critical work that the first part is more essential than much of part two.

Emily Brontë has been compared to Beethoven: both stormy geniuses whose work has great resonance in a Romantic mode. The knowledge that Beethoven worked furiously at his compositions, revising and changing his plans, does not diminish him. If it is accepted that Emily Brontë's work was revised and altered out of recognition as a result of rejection by a publisher, leading to a dialogue with her sister Anne (and probably also Charlotte) and a change of mind concerning the main aims of the book, this does not diminish or invalidate in any way our respect for the composition and production of this unique book.

Part III
Postscript

16

Emily Brontë's Second Novel

The evidence that Emily Brontë was writing a second novel during her last year of life begins to accumulate from Charles Simpson's *Emily Brontë* of 1929. Simpson was the first to present details of the contents of Emily's writing desk, which included the reviews of *Wuthering Heights* and a letter and envelope which are the subject of the first part of this chapter. In more recent time the letter, from T. C. Newby, Emily's publisher, has been discussed in Winifred Gerin's *Emily Brontë* (Oxford, 1971), in *A Life of Emily Brontë* (Blackwell, 1987), The Brontë Society's *Sixty Treasures* (written by the then librarian, Juliet Barker, 1988), and by Juliet Barker in her own name in *The Brontës* (1994). An accurate transcription is given by Dr Barker in *Sixty Treasures* and there is a good photograph of the letter and its envelope. In *The Brontës* she makes deductions from the available evidence and suggests that Charlotte destroyed the novel.[1]

Evidence of this second novel excites the popular papers to headlines, and it is undoubtedly an awesome thought that *Wuthering Heights* once had a sister. It is nevertheless sometimes suggested that the evidence for such a novel is not strong enough for us to be sure, and my object in these pages is to support the assertions made by the above commentaries and show that there is really no room for doubt about this second book. A combination of the aspects of the evidence put forward in *A Life of Emily Brontë* with that of *Sixty Treasures* will show this. Juliet Barker rightly emphasises the point in *Sixty Treasures* as follows:

> The envelope is of the same paper as the letter which has been folded four times to make it fit exactly into the envelope. There can be no doubt, therefore, that the two belong together and that Emily was preparing a second novel.

Her photograph shows both letter and envelope, but is too small for these assertions to be checked.

With help from the Brontë library staff, I checked the letter carefully in spring 1995. The letter is on one folded sheet of paper $7\frac{4}{10}'' \times 9\frac{3}{10}''$. It has indeed been folded four times, and the recto of the letter has been darkened through time, showing that it has spent most of its time outside the envelope, which is similarly darkened. The verso of the letter is not so darkened, showing that it was not exposed in the same way. The envelope has been sealed with red sealing wax, as Dr Barker rightly says, and it measures $2\frac{7}{16}'' \times 3\frac{15}{16}''$. As the reader will calculate, the letter when folded easily fits in the envelope. There is also a darkened line of wear on the top of the rear of the envelope, showing how far the letter extended when folded inside, and also perhaps suggesting that despite the evidence of the darkened recto and envelope, the letter was kept inside for some time.

The text of the letter is as follows:

Dear Sir,

I am much obliged/ by your kind note & shall / have great pleasure/ in making arrangements/ for your next novel I/ would not hurry its/ completion, for I think/ you are quite right / not to let it go before/ the world until well / satisfied with it, for much / depends on your next work / if it be an improvement on / your first you will have

established yourself as a / first rate novelist, but / if it fall short the Critics / will be too apt to/say that you have expended / your talent in your / first novel. I shall / therefore, have pleasure / in accepting it upon the / understanding that its com-/ pletion be at your own/ time.

[the following words seem perhaps hastier]

Believe me,
my dear Sir,
Yrs sincerely
TC [ill-formed] Newby
Feb. 15. 1848

The envelope reads only 'Ellis Bell, Esq[.]', and in the top right corner, where a stamp might be, '$\frac{1}{2}$', (half the dispatch? half a penny?). It is therefore not the envelope in which this letter was delivered to the parsonage, which would have to have had an address on it. It is hardly a rash speculation to suppose that this envelope was inside one with 'Acton's' name on it, and that Newby had written to Anne about *The Tenant of Wildfell Hall* at the same time, and enclosed a letter to 'Ellis' with that for Acton. *Wildfell Hall* was published in June 1848.

This letter does not give a great deal to go on, but it is absolutely clear that it proves that Emily Brontë was in the process of considering and/or writing this second work. Here it is necessary to examine Newby's text in a bit more detail and ask a few questions. First, what could have been 'kind' about the note Emily had sent to him? Obviously Emily had praised either Newby himself, his way of publishing, printing or advertising *Wuthering Heights*, an encouraging note he had previously sent, or other matters concerned with his publishing. She may have adverted to the reviews of *Wuthering Heights*, but these were early days and it is more likely that she is merely reacting positively to the actual publication.

It seems fair to assume that she had briefly mentioned the second novel (her communication is a 'note' not a 'letter'), and the word 'completion' seems to imply that she had suggested some progress on it. She had also pointed out, it is evident, that she would not rush into print. Newby concurs. It is only a short step beyond the evidence to suppose that the novel is more than just an idea in her head and has some physical existence on paper, though she is far from satisfied with it as yet. This is about as far as we can proceed by reasonable deduction from the text.

There are two large issues about which we can only speculate, relating them if possible to what we have discovered about Emily's working methods so far. One is the matter of the subject of the novel, and the second is what happened to it. On these points commentators so far have been able to produce little positive. Juliet Barker thinks that possibly the novel was near completion, and that Charlotte destroyed it. As she says, if Newby had received it, he would have published it, and it is therefore clear that it was not sent to him. But she may be assuming a bit too much about its state, since in context the word 'completion' may not imply that it was near this point. Dr Barker assigns ill-health as the reason why the book was never actually finished and delivered.

We might usefully recall Emily's habit of beginning work and abandoning it when she felt dissatisfied with it. Despite the high point of 'No coward soul' (January 1846) and the final outcome of *Wuthering Heights*, the history of the long poem 'Why ask to know the date?' shows what might happen. This poem was left incomplete at the end of the second spirt of composition, just as it had been put aside to recast *Wuthering Heights* in autumn 1846. In May 1848, Emily returned to it, suggesting that within three months of Newby's letter she had encountered insoluble problems with the second novel. But she did not work on this new version of the poem for long, completing only 25 lines before again giving up, this time, to judge by the state of the manuscript, in an emotional flurry, whether of anger or despair. By 13 May, she had acknowledged that she could write no more.

There is a paradox about Emily Brontë's methods of composition which has emerged during the course of this book. On the one hand, when gripped by passionate inspiration, she will write page after page speedily and illegibly, as in the *Ars Poetica* translation. On the other, when struggling, she will work in a flurry of uncertainty, crossing out and revising slowly. Frustrated, as at the end of 'Why ask to know the date?' she will break off, possibly in anger. This may well have happened to the second novel.

Returning to the point made by Juliet Barker, ('If...as seems almost certain, Emily did begin a second novel...'), we can emphasise that there is enough evidence to conclude that Emily certainly did begin a second novel, but what is uncertain is the stage it had reached. Talk of 'completion' sounds encouraging, but Newby's use of this word in context does not indicate how near completion could have been. It should not be hurried, and that is all we know.

My next section will consist of little more than speculation, for we have nothing but circumstantial evidence to work by in considering what this novel could have been like. With *Jane Eyre*, *Wuthering Heights* and *Agnes Grey* all successfully in print, it is unlikely that the Brontë sisters would not have reviewed the future together during December 1847. *Wildfell Hall* was not yet published, and Anne may not have been ready to join any such conference, but it is inconceivable that Charlotte and Emily would not have talked together at his time about their plans. Thematic links between the sisters' novels so far had been evident, and it seems likely that this feature would continue. We shall therefore look at

Charlotte's preparations for her next work, but before doing so, we shall try to perceive ways in which Emily's thought had been moving.

For example, politically minded commentators have thought they could discern an element of class-consciousness about *Wuthering Heights*. Years ago, Arnold Kettle pointed to what he considered through Marxist eyes to be a radical side to the book, and such a line is interestingly pursued by Stevie Davies in *Emily Brontë: Heretic*. She sees a possibility that Emily might have been on the verge of becoming 'a war poet and a poet of the class war'.[2] It needs to be remembered that in their childhood the Brontës were acutely interested in political matters and enthusiastically partisan. Mr Brontë himself was a firm Tory, who nevertheless expressed himself very forcibly in letters to various authorities on matters concerned with public welfare. The admittedly unreliable William Wright deals in considerable detail with some political propositions alleged to have been outlined by Hugh Prunty, Emily's grandfather.[3] Their authenticity must be regarded with scepticism, but if their origin was not through Hugh, it has not yet been discovered who was their author. We know for certain that Emily's uncle, William Brontë, was a member of the United Irishmen during the 1798 rebellion.[4] We also know that another uncle, James, visited Haworth, and though we cannot be quite sure when the visit took place, a date in 1846 seems the best guess.[5] The Irish background of the Brontës has been consistently misunderstood and downgraded, as Charlotte hoped it would be, but it needs to be remembered that Anne, at any rate, went so far as to say she would like to return 'home' with her uncle. It seems probable that Emily shared this loyalty at times, and the famine topic of 'Why ask to know the date?' may well have links with it.

It may well be that Emily's interest in lonely rebellious figures owes a good deal to the Romantic, Byron-based image which had become a stereotype. But she took this image over and made it her own, and in Heathcliff developed it in a way which chimed with her own personal intuitions about herself and her family. Heathcliff is an exile because Emily Brontë felt herself an exile. This is no less true in the second half of *Wuthering Heights* despite Emily Brontë's efforts at reconciliation. Throughout her poetry, she has given prominence to 'rebels' and outsiders. It is hard to see how any new work of fiction would fail to include such a character at its heart.

'Why ask to know the date?', like other poems before it, deals
with civil war and rebellion. If this is a Gondal poem, Gondal has
advanced a long way, involving now psychological and emotional
responses to war which are far from prominent in the early days.
Perceptions of the flaws in human society go deeper, the language
more strident. 'Our own humanity' in the 1848 recasting of the
poem are 'Feet-kissers of triumphant crime'. They crush down
justice and honour Wrong. The hint of corruption in the soft Lintons, overcome when they merge by Catherine's marriage to Hareton with the solid Earnshaw stock, may have been explored in the
new novel.

A feminist miscroscope has searched the Brontës for attitudes
to the validation of female autonomy which was fermenting in
the mid-nineteenth century. In *Wildfell Hall* we can feel this is
being addressed consciously, and Charlotte once again tackles
the question in *Shirley*. It is not clearly an issue in *Wuthering
Heights*, and we have no evidence on Emily's ways of thinking
about all this, despite the fact that she was often associated in
people's thoughts with a 'masculine' image: her nickname, 'The
major', M. Héger's comment about her masculine cast of thought,
Charlotte's own 'stronger than a man, simpler than a child'.[6]
Yet it is possible that Emily tackled these questions in the
new novel, whether overtly or not. Juliet Barker, who thinks
Charlotte may have destroyed the book because of its unconven-
tional theme, may have some of these possible characteristics in
mind.

What we can do is to look at Charlotte's next book. This is likely
to have been discussed with Emily at least, if not also Anne. There
was certainly a cause of disagreement between the two sisters,
which would further surface in July when Charlotte and Anne
left Emily at home, by her own firm wish, when they went to
London to talk to their respective publishers in order to demon-
strate that they were separate individuals.[7] Charlotte disliked
Newby intensely, but Emily and Anne continued to trust him.
This situation must have been discussed forcefully during December 1847 and January 1848. As we know from his letter, Newby was
expecting to publish Emily's next book. Charlotte's advice must
have been strongly against this. Despite this point, it is likely that
there would be some overlap between the theme of *Shirley* and
Emily's next work. This is the case with all Brontë work up to this
point.

By 12 January 1848 Charlotte was still writing in conditionals, 'If I ever do write another book...'[8] By 15 February, the date of Newby's letter to Emily, she talks of a book beginning to exist; 'It makes slow progress thus far...but I shall be industrious when the humour comes.' After Emily's death Charlotte found composition hard, feeling 'keenly the loss of Emily's encouragement and advice'.[9] One may suppose that the sharing of ideas had continued into 1848, and that there would have been significant discussion by February of the themes that each sister would be developing. We know that Charlotte was concerned at writing a book whose theme was wholly industrial. She worries in a letter of 28 January 1848 that she might deal with situations she cannot know for herself, and might make a mess of the matter.[10] We can see behind this a suggestion that she might write an industrial novel. A similar suggestion may well have been made to Emily. Returning to a theme which could include the industrial revolution, Charlotte decided to send away to Leeds for copies of the *Leeds Mercury* dealing with the Luddite disturbances in the West Riding.[11]

Characteristics of Emily's second book are only to be guessed at, but we have now reached a point where the guess can be an informed one. In Heathcliff, a Gondal hero became an exile in Yorkshire; the new hero may have been in an industrial area, perhaps Halifax. Haworth, too, would have been a reasonable setting for him. Emily's topographical realism would have required clarity of location, though we cannot know if she had solved this problem by February 1848. Or possibly she based her novel on a strong female character, the shreds of whom survive into *Shirley*. I am not sure that I can agree totally with Stevie Davies' guess about the class war; Emily Brontë's work seems so individual in tone that it is more likely that the novel pitted one individual against various aspects of society rather than group against group. There is a good deal of individual violence in *Wuthering Heights*, but it is not necessarily well described, and it is its lack of reality that Anne satirises in *Wildfell Hall*. If Emily's plans included riots, she will have needed to think a great deal about the method of portraying them.

Emily's poetic themes include the relation between Nature and humanity; ways in which the soul might survive after death; personal betrayal and injustice; the imagination; separation and loss. Such themes must have been in her mind as she thought about the new novel. In *Wuthering Heights* she had learned the value of tight chronological control; it seems likely that this time she would want to begin with a plan, but this might prove delusory, since it is actually in the writing that Emily discovers her narrative. It is generally thought that a fragment of Charlotte's called 'John Henry' dates from about the beginning of 1848. This is executed in pencil and has no clue bearing on the story-line as it is intended to progress.[12] Charlotte seems to hope to write herself into the new book. It would not be surprising if a similar fragment once existed in Emily Brontë's hand, perhaps also in pencil and quite probably in Brontë small script. It is quite impossible to guess how much of the story was actually produced.

In these pages I have tried to show that Emily Brontë achieved her artistic success through a combination of inspiration and hard work: this is not a startling conclusion, but it needs to be clearly stated since Charlotte, at least in part, wanted to represent her sister as an impractical 'natural', whose genius required no labour to flourish (she herself counteracts this view with the image of Emily as sculptor). I should like to emphasise the following points about Emily Brontë's attitude to artistic composition:

1. She was sometimes genuinely inspired, in the sense that words came to her unconscious mind which beautifully expressed a feeling, intuition or emotional experience. These short pieces are preserved today as part-poems, never completed.
2. She sometimes took these inspired fragments and wove more words to fit, rationally selecting and harmonising them with the original pieces.
3. She would keep her poems on manuscript slips, recopying them, sometimes on several occasions, and changing them to fit new circumstances in Gondal, or new narratives.
4. She hardly ever seems to have had a plan before she began. The actual writing created the narrative plan.
5. Applying this to *Wuthering Heights* we see that the novel was not pre-planned, but 'grew' along the way, and that a great service was performed by the publisher who rejected it in 1846, so that it had to be expanded, reorganised, and brought under tight chronological control.
6. Probably the second novel was growing from similar 'seeds', and we are unlikely ever to find a plot outline, though it is not impossible that fragments of writing may one day be found.

Notes

Full details of articles and books occasionally cited are found in the notes below. Short titles of books more frequently cited or influential in other ways are expanded in the Selected Bibliography.

ABBREVIATIONS USED IN THE NOTES

AB = Anne Brontë, BB = Patrick Branwell Brontë, CB = Charlotte Brontë, EB = Emily Jane Brontë; EN = Ellen Nussey, WSW = W. S. Williams, Gaskell = E.C. Gaskell, *The Life of Charlotte Brontë*. Barker = Barker (J), *The Brontës*, Bentley = Bentley, P., *The Brontës and their World* (London, 1969), Chadwick = Chadwick, E.A., *In the Footsteps of the Brontës*; EC = Edward Chitham; Roper = Roper (D), *The Poems of Emily Brontë*, Smith = Smith, M., *The Letters of Charlotte Brontë*, WG = Winifred Gerin, 'BST' stands for Brontë Society Transactions.

Charlotte Brontë wrote three published comments on her sisters and their work. They are:

Untitled preface to *Selections from Poems by Ellis Bell* and (separately paged) *Selections from Poems by Acton Bell*.
Biographical Notice of Ellis and Acton Bell, by Currer Bell.
Preface to *Wuthering Heights*, by Currer Bell.

References to these titles have been appropriately shortened. All these pieces appeared in 1850.

INTRODUCTION

1. Ratchford, *Gondal's Queen*, especially p. 31, argues for the all-inclusiveness of Gondal as a key to Emily Brontë's poetry.
2. CB-WSW, 15 February 1848.

1 PHYSICAL CONDITIONS OF WORK

1. Barker, p. 272. However, I re-examined these additions in 1995 and can confirm their proximity in style to Anne's writing rather than Emily's. The entry for Zedora is perhaps the easiest to see (Goldsmith,

p. 188). The e in Zedora has the typical rightward extension of Anne's script letter e.

2. WGEB, p. 38, quotes an extract from Byron's journal as given by Moore in his *Life of Byron*. The influence of this work on Brontë art is amply demonstrated by Alexander and Sellars.

3. EB, 1837 diary paper, reproduced e.g. in Wilks, *The Brontës*, p. 55 (enlarged).

4. Emily Brontë's last-used blotting paper is found in her writing desk and is part of the collection at BPM. There is some reversed blotted writing on it, but this may be by Charlotte, who appears to have used it after Emily's death.

5. Private letter from Stevie Davies.

6. ECEB, Plate 14, facing p. 161.

7. Alexander and Sellars, *The Art of the Brontës*, p. 383.

8. Ibid.

9. Ibid., p. 392.

10. Chadwick, p. 311.

11. Gaskell, Chapter 15.

12. Roper, p. 19.

13. The degree to which all three sisters cooperated in production of the 1846 poem edition has been disputed. The latest word at the time of writing is in Roper, pp. 22–3.

14. I argue for the proposition that *Agnes Grey* and *Wuthering Heights* have a commonly discussed thread in ECEB, p. 197. *The Professor* may also share the agreed background topic of 'early teaching experiences'.

15. Smith and Rosengarten, *The Professor*, pp. xxixff.

2 LEARNING'S GOLDEN MINE

1. Roper, No. 200, p. 221.

2. Patrick studied Latin at Cambridge, and occasionally uses it in writing annotations in his books; Branwell produced a translation of Horace's *Odes*; Anne's Latin Delectus, apparently used at Thorp Green, is in the collection at BPM.

3. Detailed research on this matter led to my conclusions in *The Brontës' Irish Background*, pp. 19, 42, 69, 79, 83.

4. Barker, pp. 319–20.

5. Alexander and Sellars, p. 384.

6. Horace, *Ars Poetica*, lines 1–5, my translation.

7. Irene Tayler, *Holy Ghosts: The Male Muses of Emily and Charlotte Brontë* (Columbia, 1990), discusses the idea that Emily had a 'male muse' (esp. pp. 22–6), relating this to the ideas of Romanticism in general.

8. Horace, *Ars Poetica*, lines 99–107, my translation.

3 INSPIRATION AND LABOUR IN EMILY BRONTË'S POETRY

1. Roper, pp. 18–19.
2. Gondal references were removed from the 1846 poems in the most simple of the various revision processes which seem to have taken place. See Roper, pp. 22–3.
3. Barker, p. 483.
4. Roper, p. 32.
5. Academic caution compels the word 'appears', but the photographs at BPM leave little room for doubt.
6. There seem to be two causes for this. One is the early Brontë enthusiasm for Scott, which has many times been explored, most recently by F. B. Pinion in 'Scott and *Wuthering Heights*', BST, Vol. 21, Part 7, 1996, pp. 313ff. The other is the Scots identification which Patrick Brontë seems to have substituted for his Irish background, on the basis of the mixed ancestry of the inhabitants of Co. Down, See *The Brontës' Irish Background*, e.g. pp. 26, 42, 56, 72, 78.
7. This comment revises my erroneous reading of 'Regive' given in *Brontë Facts and Brontë Problems*, p. 38.
8. This appears to be Derek Roper's view, e.g. in 'Emily Brontë's Lover', BST, Vol. 21, Parts 1 and 2, 1993, pp. 25ff, where on p. 28 he explains that the subject of some A poems 'may lie in Gondal, or in private fictions that Emily did not share with Anne'. The thrust of Roper's comment, and his understanding of the subject of Emily's A poetry, is that it is 'close criticism' that is needed to interpret Emily's poems, not biographical links.
9. Chitham and Winnifrith, *Brontë Facts and Brontë Problems*, Chapter 4.
10. Ibid.
11. M. Peeck-O'Toole, *Aspects of Lyric in the Poetry of Emily Brontë*, pp. 104–21.
12. Ibid.
13. Ibid.
14. See Chapter 5.
15. It is important to note how both Charlotte's Angria and Emily's Gondal grow from incident and character, not narrative design. Early writings are extensively mapped by Fannie Ratchford in *The Brontës' Web of Childhood* and by Christine Alexander in *The Early Writings of Charlotte Brontë*. This may be how many novelists work, but others seem to begin with a comprehensive grip on what they wish to say overall.
16. Ewbank, I.-S., *Their Proper Sphere* (London, 1966), p. 107.

4 DRAFTING, CORRECTION AND FAIR COPY: EMILY BRONTË IN BRUSSELS

1. Smith, *Letters*, p. 268.
2. Ibid.

3. Duthie, E.L., *The Foreign Vision of Charlotte Brontë* (London, 1975), Chapter 2.
4. Barker, p. 388; Davies, *Emily Brontë, Heretic*, p. 47.
5. July 1894, pp. 279ff.
6. Gaskell, Chapter 11.
7. Macdonald, *The Secret of Charlotte Brontë* (London, 1914), p. 283.
8. Ibid., pp. 220–1.
9. Roper, No. 9, p. 41.
10. CB, Preface.
11. Gaskell, Chapter 11.
12. Hugo, pp. 227–8.
13. The story of the Brontës' childhood is well documented in secondary accounts, the clearest recent one being Barker, pp. 150ff. Lonely men appear in the Gondal poetry, e.g. in Roper Nos. 8, 37, 56, 72.
14. *Wuthering Heights*, Chapter 9.
15. CB–EN, May 1842, Smith, *Letters*, p. 285.

5 ORGANISATIONAL SKILL: THE POEMS FROM 1844 TO 1846

1. Roper, pp. 14–15.
2. Facsimile in Wilks, *The Brontës*, p. 73.
3. Roper, pp. 15–16.
4. BST, Vol. 14, No. 2, Part 72, pp. 24–6.
5. Roper, D., 'The Revision of Emily Brontë's Poems of 1846', in *The Library*, sixth series, No. 6 (1984), pp. 153ff.

6 WUTHERING HEIGHTS

1. In the 'Preface' to *Wuthering Heights* (1850), and also in the 'Biographical Notice'. Her reissue of the poems was also prefaced by a short notice. There are thus three places in which Charlotte publicly comments on her sister's work.
2. C. P. Sanger, 'The Structure of *Wuthering Heights*', a paper read to the Heretics, Cambridge, and subsequently published by Hogarth Press, London, 1926. This has been revised and added to, most recently by A. Stuart Daley in BST, Vol. 21, Part 5, 1995, pp. 169–73.
3. E. F. Benson, *Charlotte Brontë* (London, 1932), pp. 174–6.
4. An early expression of this view is in Law, A., *Patrick Branwell Brontë* (Alan Philpott, nd), but it is possible that Branwell himself claimed to have written part of it, according to a letter to the *Halifax Guardian* by Branwell's friend William Dearden, 15 June 1867. This is generally discounted by biographers.
5. Chitham and Winnifrith, *Brontë Facts and Brontë Problems*, Chapter 8.
6. An example of this is the way in which Yorkshire houses and scenes were taken as models for early illustrations. The search is still on,

and up to a point has validity, but can be followed much too incautiously.

7. See Spark, M., *The Brontë Letters* (London, 1966) and Spark M., and Stanford, D., *Emily Brontë* (London, nd).

8. There seem to be three extant letters by Emily Brontë, all short. One or two empty envelopes also seem to imply further letters, and there is at least one record in a letter of Charlotte of her receiving a letter from Emily. This scanty harvest goes some way towards confirming the remark in one of the above that writing a proper letter is 'a feat I have never performed'. Smith, *Letters*, p. 319.

9. See e.g. WGEB, p. 14.

10. CB–EN 14 November 1844, Smith, *Letters*, p. 374.

11. Emily's two transcript books date from February 1844 and Anne also began a new systematised book in early 1844. See Chitham, *The Poems of Anne Brontë*, p. 200.

12. Chitham, *The Poems of Anne Brontë*, No. 36, 24 January 1845.

13. Smith, *Letters*, p. 461.

14. Ibid., p. 481.

15. CB–EN, 26 August 1846, ibid., pp. 494–5.

16. Smith, *Letters*, p. 534.

17. Shakespeare Head, *Lives and Letters*, Vol. III, pp. 206–7.

18. Smith, *Letters*, p. 482.

19. Gaskell, Chapter 15, see above.

20. Smith, *Letters*, p. 561.

21. Ibid.

22. See Chapter 16, 'Postscript' for a discussion of this letter.

23. G. Larken, 'The Shuffling Scamp', in *BST*, Vol. 15, No. 5 (1970), pp. 400–7.

24. CB–WSW, 14 December 1847, Smith, *Letters*, p. 574.

25. Ibid., p. 576 suggests some points which may run contrary to the suggestion that the first edition of *Wuthering Heights* represents EB's punctuation quite considerably. Nevertheless, the manuscripts do not suggest that Emily Brontë understood the rules of punctuation.

26. Chitham and Winnifrith, *Brontë Facts and Brontë Problems*, p. 85.

27. The whole of the Introduction to the Clarendon edition of *The Professor* is worth reading for an idea of how the Brontës viewed the matter of the presentation of their novels.

7 WUTHERING HEIGHTS: THE FIRST PHASE

1. For Emily Brontë's use of the same almanack as Anne, see Marsden (H) and Jack (I), *Wuthering Heights* (Oxford, Clarendon, 1976), Introduction, etc.

2. Stories of Ponden Hall have been explored by Winifred Gerin (WGEB, Chapter 3). It appears in some maps and documents as Ponden House. A particularly useful account of the history of the Heaton family is Mary Butterfield's *The Heatons of Ponden Hall* (Stanbury, 1976).

3. *Wuthering Heights*, Oxford World's Classics (1981), pp. vii–xii.
4. In general it has been left to residents of the Halifax area to realise how closely *Wuthering Heights* mirrors the geography of the north end of Halifax. Among the pioneers in these matters are T.W. Hanson, for long a member of the Halifax Antiquarian Society, and Hilda Marsden. Some of this material is summarised in *A Life of Emily Brontë* and elsewhere, since I consider the period which Emily Brontë spent at Law Hill vital.
5. e.g. in Raymond, *In the Footsteps of the Brontës*, facing p. 209.
6. Ibid., facing p. 96.
7. There are some stunted thorns near Law Hill, but the layout of Emily's school is most unlike Wuthering Heights. Other suggestions for the origin of Wuthering Heights have included Emmott Hall, Colne. (Wilson, *All Alone*, facing p. 252.)
8. Photo by G. Bernard Wood, Bentley, op. cit., p. 90.
9. Copies at BPM, e.g. No. SB 4115.
10. Robert Heaton was a churchwarden at Haworth. He also seems to have been responsible for sheltering the Brontë family on the day of the alarming 'bog burst' (2 September 1824). It is alleged that he planted a pear tree for Emily at Ponden. (Butterfield, *The Heatons of Ponden Hall*, p. 19.)
11. BST, Vol. 57 (1967).
12. Melvin R. Watson in *Nineteenth Century Fiction* (1949), 'more ironic than comic'; David Cecil in *Early Victorian Novelists* (1935), 'drawn in the flat rather than in the round, made individual by a few strongly marked, personal idiosyncrasies' (of Nelly Dean also); 'a source of burlesque', Stevie Davies in *Emily Brontë: Heretic* (1994), p. 187, are other viewpoints.

8   THE FIRST VERSION: ADAPTING GONDAL

1. See ECAB, pp. 124, 125, 127.
2. Visick, *The Genesis of Wuthering Heights*, pp. 30, 62.
3. See ECEB, p. 35.
4. Q.D. Leavis, *Lectures in America* (London, 1969), but also E. Solomon in *Nineteenth Century Fiction*, Vol. XIV, No. 1, pp. 80–3 (1959).
5. 'Gondal Chronicles' seem to have begun being systematised in 1841, long after the beginning of the saga. See ECAB, p. 88.
6. Richard Chase, in the *Kenyon Review*, (Autumn 1947), pp. 487–506.
7. See Roper, Appendix 6 and Appendix 7 for occurrences of the name Alfred in the poems, and for reconstructions of the Gondal story as hinted at in the poems.
8. See ECEB, p. 198.
9. CB, 'Biographical Notice'.
10. Quoted thus in Barker, p. 454, this is likely to be the correct spelling and punctuation.
11. EB, diary paper 1845, location unknown, copies at BPM.

12. Ratchford, *Gondal's Queen*, p. 20; I am inclined to agree with her view.
13. The Gondal actors are all noble, following in the tradition of the ballads and Scott.
14. Registers and other documents at Cumbria County Record Office, Kendal.
15. Law Hill census, 1841, see ECEB, p. 273.
16. There has been no recent attempt to construct a list of Roe Head pupils, and I rely on WGAB, WGCB, WGEB.
17. *Wuthering Heights*, Chapter 4.
18. Roper, pp. 305–7, summarising Gondal reconstructions.
19. Ibid.
20. No. 201 in *A Collection of Hymns for the Use of the People called Methodists*, and still in modern hymnbooks. The stanza I have in mind runs:

> Thine eye diffused a quickening ray,
> I woke, the dungeon flamed with light.
> My chains fell off, my heart was free,
> I rose, went forth and followed thee.

But the image is typical of Wesley.
21. Smith, *Letters*, p. 608.
22. Cecil, *Early Victorian Novelists*, Chapter 5.
23. e.g. WGCB, pp. 9, 333.
24. The name 'Augusta' seems most likely to derive from Byron's associate. See also F.B. Pinion, 'Byron and Wuthering Heights' in *BST*, Vol. 21, Part 5, 1995.
25. See Chitham, *The Brontës' Irish Background*, p. 51. In the *Durham University Journal*, July 1995, pp. 279ff, Christopher Heywood, whose research was largely done in the early 1980s, suggests that accounts of the 'Welsh Brontë' story may have been influenced by *Wuthering Heights*.
26. Chitham, *The Brontës' Irish Background*, Chapters 5 and 6.
27. Ibid., Chapters 1–4.
28. See Butterfield, *The Heatons of Ponden Hall*.
29. WGEB, pp. 76–80.

9 AUTUMN AND WINTER: AFTER THE POEM REVISION

1. Horace, *Ars Poetica*, lines 185ff.
2. Roper, No. 125, p. 183.
3. Chitham, *The Poems of Anne Brontë*, pp. 152ff.
4. Page references here are from the Penguin edition unless otherwise stated.
5. *Wuthering Heights*, Chapter 10, p. 140.
6. CB, 'Preface'.

7. Chitham, *The Poems of Anne Brontë*, p. 128. 'Domestic Peace' is CB's title; the MS has 'Monday night May 11th 1846'.
8. The whole page is worth reading very carefully; *Wuthering Heights*, Chapter 11, p. 147.
9. Shibden Hall records suggest these alterations took place in 1836. Map evidence comes from 'Map of the Parish of Halifax, made in 1834 and 1835 by J.F. Myers' in the Skett collection at Birmingham Reference Library and reproduced in Chitham *A Life of Emily Brontë*, but unfortunately with inadequate reference.
10. *Wuthering Heights*, Chapter 10.
11. Chapter 15, p. 198.
12. The latest formulation of this chronology is that of A. Stuart Daley in BST, Vol. 21, Part 5, 1995, p. 170.
13. Ibid.
14. Chapter 7, above.

10 THE DEVELOPMENT OF THE FIRST VERSION

1. *Wuthering Heights*, Chapter 15, Penguin, p. 195.
2. Barker, p. 494, says, 'There can now be little doubt that there was a relationship between [Branwell and Mrs Robinson]'. However, she offers no new evidence for this assertion. In the same chapter (p. 503) she dismisses speedily the thesis I am currently arguing about the way in which *Wuthering Heights* came to be written. Though I disagree with her assertions and her methodology in both these cases, this does not affect my overall view of the high value of her book.
3. *Wuthering Heights*, Chapter 16, Penguin p. 204.
4. CB, 'Preface'.
5. e.g. in *Brontë Facts and Brontë Problems*, Chapter 9, pp. 97–8.
6. Ibid., and Chitham *The Poems of Anne Brontë*, p. 190.

11 REJECTION AND ITS CONSEQUENCES: RETURN TO FICTIONAL POETRY

1. Smith, Letters, p. 48.
2. Gaskell, Chapter 15, deals with the beginning of *Jane Eyre* and assumes that *The Professor* was still being submitted. The Clarendon introduction to *The Professor* discusses its revisions.
3. It is important to note that there is absolutely no external evidence for this reply.
4. In *The Life of Anne Brontë*, Chapter 10, I give reasons for thinking that this occurred during the Monday of their visit. It seems that Anne was convinced by Charlotte to transfer her allegiance to Smith, Elder and we can suppose that the interview with Newby was unsatisfactory.

5. Her wish to suppress *Wildfell Hall* is explained in CB, 'Biographical Notice'.
6. Especially in the *Halifax Guardian*.
7. *Wuthering Heights*, Chapter 32.
8. *Wuthering Heights*, Chapter 10. Her phrase is 'an arid wilderness of furze and whinstone'.
9. CB, 'Biographical Notice'.
10. CB, 'Preface'.
11. See Chitham and Winnifrith, *Brontë Facts and Brontë Problems*, Chapter 9.
12. See the reproduction in e.g. Wilks, op. cit.

12 THE DEVELOPMENT OF PART TWO

1. The process was begun in the famous article by C.P. Sanger reproducing his lecture to the Cambridge 'Heretics' (Hogarth, London, 1926). A revised version checked by Inga-Stina Ewbank occurs in the Clarendon *Wuthering Heights* (ed. Marsden and Jack), and the most recent update, as already mentioned, is a revision by A. Stuart Daley, in *BST*, Vol. 21, Part 5, 1995, pp. 169–73.
2. In answer to Lockwood's question, 'How long ago?' [did Heathcliff die], Nelly answers, 'Three months since.' (*Wuthering Heights*, Chapter 32). In Chapter 34 Nelly, leading up to a description of his death, says, 'We were in April then.' Since the date of the conversation has been given as September, Heathcliff has been dead *five* months.
3. Chapters 8, 9 and 10 above.
4. Chapter 10, Penguin, p. 139.

13 THE THREE HOUSEKEEPERS OF WUTHERING HEIGHTS

1. Chapter 18, Penguin, p. 228.
2. Chapter 21, Penguin, p. 246.
3. Chapter 23, Penguin, p. 269.
4. Chapter 3, Penguin, p. 64.
5. Chapter 3, Penguin, p. 65.
6. Chapter 30, Penguin, p. 326.
7. Chapter 32, Penguin, p. 339.

14 SCULPTING THE STATUE: A CHRONOLOGY OF THE PROCESS OF WRITING *WUTHERING HEIGHTS*

1. Based on the view that 'Passages from the Life of an Individual', mentioned in the 1845 diary paper, is *Agnes Grey* or an early version of it.

2.	The discrepancy in tone between Emily's diary paper and Anne's has frequently been noticed. Perhaps the first writer to comment was Muriel Spark, in Spark and Stanford, p. 71, where she writes, 'Anne betrays some weariness with Gondal; she seems to have had enough of it, and may have hinted as much to Emily.' The most recent prominent place where the diary paper is partly reproduced (from a new transcription) is Barker, pp. 454–5.
3.	Writing of her discovery of Emily's poems she says, 'it took hours to recocile her to the discovery I had made, and days to persuade her that such poems merited publication' (CB, 'Biographical Notice').
4.	Roper, pp. 22ff.
5.	Gaskell, Chapter 15.
6.	Ibid.
7.	CB. 'Preface'.

## 15	OBJECTIONS AND IMPLICATIONS

1.	See Chapter 6, above.
2.	*Halifax Guardian*, 15 June 1867.
3.	*The Authorship of Wuthering Heights* (Hogarth Press, London, 1936), p. 29.
4.	Q.D. Leavis, *Collected Essays* (1983).
5.	ed. P. Stoneman, *Wuthering Heights* (Macmillan, New Casebooks, London, 1993). See bibliography for full details.
6.	Lyn Pykett in the above, pp. 86–99.
7.	Melvin R. Watson, 'Tempest in the Soul: The Theme and Structure of *Wuthering Heights'* in *Nineteenth Century Fiction*, Vol. IV (1949) pp. 87ff.
8.	CB, 'Introduction to "Selections from Poems by Ellis Bell" '.
9.	Recent works on Anne Lister include two selections from her letters, *I Know My Own Heart* and *No Priest but Love*, ed. Helena Whitbread (Otley, 1992), from Calderdale Archives SH:7/ML/E/1–26.
10.	Chapter 6, above.

## 16	EMILY BRONTË'S SECOND NOVEL

1.	Barker, p. 579.
2.	Stevie Davies, *Emily Brontë: Heretic* (1994), 'Conclusion', pp. 235ff.
3.	Wright, *The Brontës in Ireland* (1893), Chapter 16. Hugh Prunty's alleged propositions have never been fully explained or traced to their source. I have an open mind as to whether they actually represent his thought or not; it would certainly be useful if their source could be tracked down.
4.	Chitham, *The Brontës' Irish Background*, p. 27.
5.	Ibid., pp. 107–9.
6.	CB, 'Biographical Notice'.

7. The most recent secondary account is Barker, pp. 557 ff.
8. CB–G.H. Lewes, 12 January 1848.
9. CB–WSW, 15 February 1848.
10. Quoted with comment in the Introduction to *Shirley* (Clarendon, Oxford, 1979, p. xvi).
11. Ibid.
12. Ibid., Appendix D, pp. 805ff.

Selected Bibliography

Alexander, C., *The Early Writings of Charlotte Brontë*, Oxford, 1983.
—— and Sellars, J., *The Art of the Brontës*, Cambridge, 1995.
Allott, M., *The Brontes: The Critical Heritage*, London, 1974.
Barker, J., *Sixty Treasures: The Brontë Parsonage Museum*, Haworth, 1988.
—— *The Brontës*, London, 1994.
ed. Brink, C.O., *Horace on Poetry*, Cambridge, 1971.
Butterfield, M.A., *The Heatons of Ponden Hall*, Stanbury, 1976.
Cecil, D., *Early Victorian Novelists*, London, 1934.
Chadwick, E.A., *In the Footsteps of the Brontës*, London, 1913.
Chitham, E., *A Life of Anne Brontë*, London, 1991.
—— *A Life of Emily Brontë*, London, 1987.
—— *The Brontës' Irish Background*, London, 1986.
—— (ed.) *The Poems of Anne Brontë*, London, 1979.
—— and Winnifrith, T.J., *Brontë Facts and Brontë Problems*, London, 1983.
Craik, W., *The Brontë Novels*, London, 1968.
Davies, S., *Emily Brontë*, Hemel Hempstead, 1988.
—— *Emily Brontë: Heretic*, London, 1994.
—— *Emily Brontë: The Artist as a Free Woman*, London, 1983.
Dingle, H., *The Mind of Emily Brontë*, London, 1974.
Frank, K., *Emily Brontë: A Chainless Soul*, London, 1990.
Gaskell, E.C., *The Life of Charlotte Brontë*, London, 1857.
Gerin, W., *Anne Brontë*, London, 1959.
—— *Branwell Brontë*, London, 1961.
—— *Charlotte Brontë*, London, 1967.
—— *Emily Brontë*, London, 1971.
Gezari, J., *Emily Jane Brontë: The Complete Poems*, Harmondsworth, 1992.
Hewish, J., *Emily Brontë*, London, 1969.
Hugo, V., 'Mirabeau', in *Etudes sur Littérature et Philosophie Mêlées*, Paris, 1834.
Lock, J. and Dixon, W.T., *A Man of Sorrow*, London, 1965.
Peeck-O'Toole, M., *Aspects of Lyric in the Poetry of Emily Brontë*, Amsterdam, 1988.
Ratchford, F., *Gondal's Queen*, Austin, Texas, 1955.
Robinson, A.M.F., *Emily Brontë*, London, 1883.
Roper, D, (with Chitham, E.), *The Poems of Emily Brontë*, Oxford, 1995.
Shakespeare Head (pub.), *The Brontës, their Lives, Friendships and Correspondence*, Oxford, 1932, reissued 1980.
Shorter, C., *Charlotte Brontë and her Circle*, London, 1896.
Simpson, C., *Emily Brontë*, London, 1929.
Smith, M. (ed.), *The Letters of Charlotte Brontë*, Vol. I Oxford, 1995.
Spark, M. and Stanford, D., *Emily Brontë, her Life and Work*, London, n.d.
Stoneman, P. (ed.), *Wuthering Heights*, Macmillan New Casebooks, London, 1993.
Turner, J. Horsfall, *Haworth, Past and Present*, Brighouse, 1879.

Turner, Whiteley, *A Spring-time Saunter: Round and about Brontëland*, Halifax, *c.* 1905.

Visick, M., *The Genesis of Wuthering Heights*, Hong Kong, 1958.

Wilks, B., *The Brontës*, London, 1975.

Winnifrith, T.J., *The Brontës and their Background: Romance and Reality*, London, 1973.

Wilson, R., *All Alone*, London, 1928.

Wright, W., *The Brontës in Ireland*, London, 1893.

Brontë Society Transactions, especially the parts and numbers cited in the notes.

Index